THE CHILDREN'S CHRONICLE

THE JACOBITE FUGITIVE (*see page* 196)

[*Frontispiece*

THE
CHILDREN'S
CHRONICLE

By
DOROTHY MARGARET
STUART

With six Full-page Plates by H. M. BROCK
and other illustrations

UNIVERSITY OF LONDON PRESS LTD.
WARWICK SQUARE, LONDON, E.C.4

FIRST PRINTED 1944
REPRINTED 1945, 1947

AGENTS OVERSEAS

AUSTRALIA AND NEW ZEALAND
AND SOUTH SEA ISLANDS

W. S. SMART, P.O. Box 120,
SYDNEY, N.S.W.
Showroom : 14, York Street

CANADA

CLARKE, IRWIN & Co., Ltd.
480-486, University Avenue, TORONTO

INDIA

LONGMANS, GREEN & Co., Ltd.,
BOMBAY : Nicol Road.
CALCUTTA : Chittaranjan Avenue.
MADRAS : Mount Road.

SOUTH AFRICA

H. B. TIMMINS, P.O. Box 94, CAPE TOWN.
Showroom : 58-60, Long Street.

Printed in Great Britain for the UNIVERSITY OF LONDON PRESS LTD.,
HAZELL, WATSON AND VINEY, LTD., London and Aylesbury

FOREWORD

THE Clavenger family, whose chronicles are written here, never existed; at least, not under that name. There is no Manor or village of Winford St. Mary on the Hampshire–Wiltshire border or anywhere else in England. Yet both the Manor and the people who lived on it might easily have been real: there is nothing that those people think or feel, or do, eat, or wear, or touch, that could not have been thought, felt, done, eaten, worn or touched in the England of each particular generation. The colours of the picture may be fanciful, but the perspective is true.

For example—the ingredients of the pie eaten by Lionel of Antwerp at the Manor are taken from a cookery-book written by the master-cook of the Prince's nephew, Richard the Second; the details of Queen Elizabeth's visit are mainly borrowed from contemporary accounts of visits which she actually paid to her loving subjects in the southern parts of her realm in the year after the Armada; the siege of Winford by the Parliamentary troops resembles in many respects the siege of Basing House during the Civil War; a play-actor called Robinson, who was killed at Basing House, was the original of Master Endymion; and the Puritan preacher, Hugh Peters, sat for the portrait of Zedekiah Miller—with a half-side of royalist bacon in his embrace. It would have been absurd to try to reproduce the exact manner of speech in each period, especially in the earlier episodes; but I have tried to give something of the characteristic colour, if little of the precise form.

No Chronicles can be both vivid and impartial, and I cannot deny that the seventeenth-century Clavengers were convinced Cavaliers, looking at everything from the royalist angle; but to keep the balance true they had a kinsman on the other side who was both generous and brave. In the succeeding century the family was pro-Hanoverian, and looked at everything from an anti-Jacobite angle; yet one of them had compassion on a hard-pressed " rebel " cousin, and so the balance is kept true again: for the pattern of history is never all white or all black in any part of it.

The rise (and fall) of other families, here traced, will make it possible to watch the gradual process by which a simple yeoman's son might become a prosperous merchant, *his* son, an esquire, and their descendant, one of Marlborough's captains and a member of the landed gentry. It is also shown how an obscure mercantile family could climb into prominence on the ruins of the old religion and finally overtake and outstrip the proud folk whose ancestors had been keybearers to the Dukes of Normandy: and—following a downward instead of an upward curve—the last representative of a line of worthy craftsmen is seen to be a tipsy tinker betraying an old acquaintance in order to save his own skin. Such changes, sometimes for the better, sometimes for the worse, form part of the unrecorded history of almost every family in England. There are few of us who have not among our forebears far greater—and far humbler—figures than we reck of.

An imaginary family, living on an imaginary estate? Yes, of course. Yet while writing their Chronicles I have come to feel that they must have existed; and that somewhere near the place where the Avon broadens out into its estuary I could find—if only I knew where to look—the stately house built by Sir Charles Clavenger on the site of the old Manor wrecked by the Roundheads, and the ancient church with its Clavenger memorials, ranging from Sir Thomas, recumbent in armour, who fought at Poitiers in 1356, to Britannia lamenting for Sir Augustus who fell at Vittoria in 1813. I should like to think that some of my readers feel the same.

D. M. S.

CONTENTS

LIST OF ILLUSTRATIONS

The illustrations on pages 97, 134, and 169 have been based on official postcards, and acknowledgment is hereby made to :
The National Portrait Gallery for the illustration of King Philip II of Spain ; The London Museum for the Embroidered Cap ; and to the Victoria and Albert Museum for the Jacobite Wine Glass.

CHAPTER I

THE LOST SQUIRREL

ON a certain windy morning in the late spring of the year 1357 a small boy was sitting on the top of a hill. It was not a very high hill, but he could see quite a long way as he sat perched on a tussock of rough grass, hugging his knee and gazing dreamily at the landscape spread out like a many-coloured carpet below. To his right, due south, dim ridges of forest faded into a steel-blue smudge that was the sea: to his left stretched a quivering grey expanse of marshland, tufted with willows or patches of yellow iris. Between marsh and forest lay the Manor and the manorial lands of Winford St. Mary, granted by William the Conqueror to his key-bearer, Denzil de Clavenger, nearly three hundred years before and now held by the small boy's father, Sir Thomas Clavenger, Knight, comrade in arms of Edward, most valiant Prince of Wales.

Piers, the younger of Sir Thomas's two sons, was a tall boy for his nine years, and his tight scarlet stockings, reaching from hip to heel, made his legs look even longer than they were. His tunic was of gayest green, with a collar shaped like a monk's cowl and a girdle of dark leather buckled with a clasp of burnished bronze. Denzil, his elder brother by two years, was allowed to wear a small, sheathed dagger at his girdle, and Piers was naturally impatient for the day when he could do likewise.

At that moment he ought not to have sat dreaming on that tussock of grass. He and his brother had been set free by their tutor, Father Oswald, so that they might help in the hunt for their mother's pet squirrel, the bright-eyed, red-coated Russell, who had broken his chain and run away during the previous night. Denzil had chosen to mount his pony and ride with William the Falconer over the marshes; but Piers had preferred to climb the hill with his friend Wat, the yeoman's son, and beat up the gorse thickets on the seaward side. Yet instead of beating up the thickets—which he could trust Wat to do with great thoroughness—here he was quietly playing with himself his own particular game—"*Mappa Mundi.*"

Mappa Mundi—the map of the world; what a marvellous thing it must be! Piers had never seen one; but Father Oswald, who had been educated in the noble northern monastery of Durham, never wearied of telling his pupils about the map that was treasured there. It was an ancient map, already old when the Conqueror came to England, but it was none the worse for that. Nobody doubted that it gave a true picture of the great flat world which—as everybody knew—floated for ever on a vast crystal sea while above it the golden sun, the silver moon, and the bright, mysterious planets moved to and fro. Many strange and terrible lands lay in far-off corners of the world, and strange and terrible were the men and the beasts inhabiting them. About these Piers could never hear enough: and what he loved as much as anything was to make believe that from his perch on the hill he could behold a *Mappa Mundi* of his very own, lying unrolled for his delight.

Then the Manor-house, with its high-pitched central hall, its lily-dotted moat, and its rambling outbuildings, became the golden palace of the Cham of Tartary, and the Norman church in its grove of yews was a temple of that god whom the Saracens worshipped and whose name was "Mahound." Piers imagined that god with a queer, fantastic face, half-grim, half-comical—such a face as that of the carven imp that grinned down from the vaulting of the porch under the Manor gatehouse. Quite often the boy would look up at the imp and say, "Good morrow, Mahound!"

In the *Mappa Mundi* game the village of Winford St. Mary was some famous, far-off city, Babylon perhaps, or maybe Troy. The narrow river that turned the mill was no longer the Win, it was either the Euphrates or the Nile: and the pigs feeding earnestly upon the stretch of common land were dragons if they were not dromedaries. When some familiar figure came into view, broad-shouldered Nick the miller or bandy-legged Hob the thatcher, Piers would have to decide whether he was an Ethiopian, a Saracen or a Trojan—or even a Scot; for if Father Oswald was to be believed the Scots were more terrible than any of these outlandish heathen folk.

WOMEN WORKING IN THE FIELDS, FOURTEENTH CENTURY

Several such figures could be seen that morning, dwarfed by the distance so that they seemed no larger than sheep. Denzil and the Falconer were bobbing on horseback across the marsh, drawing rein now and then by a clump of willow. A woman weeding one of the narrow strips of cultivated land stopped sometimes, straightened her stooping body, and peered right and left under her thickly-gloved hand as if in quest of something; for word had gone forth from the Manor that Dame Eleanor's squirrel had escaped, and there might be a reward for the person who should be lucky enough to find him.

Piers stretched his long legs and gave a shake to his mop of

reddish-brown hair.   Time to be astir, time to stop playing
Mappa Mundi, and join in the chase: but before he could
rise to his feet he felt that someone had come up softly behind
him; and then a voice at once accusing and respectful said,
"You be a-playing Mappy Mound."   Piers swung round
and saw Wat, a sturdy figure in a shapeless garment of hodden
grey and leggings of untanned leather.   Tucked under the
newcomer's arm was Russell himself, with a fragment of
broken chain hanging from his gilded collar.

"Wat—you have found him already! Oh, wonderful!
Where was he?"

"Yonder—he were caught in the gorse, he were."

"Russell, you knave," said Piers, fondling the squirrel.
"Now we must take you home. Are you not glad to go
home? Let us race down the hill, Wat—you can carry
him."

"If we race," remarked Wat, cautiously, "maybe he'll
break loose again."

"Forsooth, that is true. Let us walk—but not too slowly,
for I would fain see Jenkyn bring the jongleur in."

"What—the gleeman with the fiddle and the three balls?
But he went on his way soon after cockcrow, he did."

"My mother would have it that he had borne Russell
away in his bag. That is why Jenkyn was sent spurring along
the Westhampton road to bring him back again."

"I did not know," said Wat, much impressed, "But *will*
Jenkyn bring him back after he sees that Russell is not in his
bag?"

Piers looked disappointed.

"Oh, I had not thought of that. But maybe he will."

"Terrible thievish folk these gleemen be," remarked Wat
wisely.

"So says Simkin the Steward. Yet I would they came
oftener."

"I know one who is of that mind," said Wat.

" Who ? My sister ? "

" Maybe. But it were the French knight I meant."

" Yea, forsooth—he can play flute and fiddle as well as any minstrel when he is merry: but you know, Wat, he is not often merry."

Wat nodded, thinking of the wistful eyes and unsmiling mouth of Messire Olivier de Haubourdin, the French knight whom Sir Thomas had taken prisoner upon the battlefield of Poitiers the previous September and who was still at the Manor, waiting for his ransom-money to be sent from France.

" Do you remember," Piers prattled on, " the day he prayed Nick the Miller to teach him to blow upon his bag-pipe ? First he blew too hard—and the pipe screamed like a pig in pain; and then he blew too soft, and it made no sound at all."

The two boys had now reached the foot of the hill and were turning eastward along the village, almost empty at that hour when the able-bodied inhabitants, men, women and children, were toiling on the long, narrow plots into which each holding was divided. It happened to be one of those days when they were labouring for themselves and not paying rent to the Squire in the shape of work, so they were going about it with greater energy. At the door of one of the tiny wicker-and-clay cottages an aged woman stood with a distaff in her hand steadily spinning; beside a bee-hive in the kerchief-sized garden of another a young crippled girl sat on a wooden stool, peeling reeds to make rush-lights : but the only man to be seen was Nick the Miller himself, striding along with his round white cap cocked over his hairy ear and his broad, freckled hands thrust through his belt. When he recognised Piers he plucked off his cap, then jammed it on again at a more jaunty angle than before, and tucked his hands back into his belt.

" So, so," said he, " Jenkyn's journey was all for naught. We shall have no hanging of a gleeman for stealing of my lady's squirrel. A thievish lot they be. Hearkee, Master Piers, if the good knight your father have a mind for a few fresh eels against Friday—do you tell him with my duty that I caught some in my eel-trap yesterday."

" I will tell him," promised Piers, trying to press past the bulky form that stood astride the way.

" They do say," continued the Miller, " that my lord Lionel—he they call ' of Antwerp '—be taking his sport hereabouts. Biding with the Bishop over yonder he be, with a great train of grooms and falconers and such."

Beyond an idea that Lionel of Antwerp was somehow connected with that valiant warrior, Edward, Prince of Wales, Piers had no very distinct notions about him; but he knew that French prisoners often went hawking and hunting with their English captors.

" Is he waiting to be ransomed, like Messire Olivier? " he asked.

The Miller burst out laughing. " Waiting to be ransomed? He? Why, the Saints preserve you, Master Piers, he is the third son of our Lord the King. He was born in Antwerp— but he is true Englishman and true Plantagenet for all that. So be his brother, my lord John of Gaunt——"

" Oh," said Piers, " I have heard of *him*. He was in the sea-fight called Lespagnols-sur-Mer when he was no older than my brother. But I have never seen one of the King's sons. I would I might."

" My lord Lionel is the comeliest of them all," declared the Miller, who was always chock-full of information, " and the tallest and not the least merry. God wot," he added, suddenly gloomy, " he is like to lack mirth where he is going. As King's Regent he is going to Ireland, and sure I am he will be sad to leave the royal forests of England and all their red deer."

" No one chases the red deer at this season," Piers reminded him.

" It is all one—the seasons come and go, but the red deer still dwell in the green wood. If so be that my lord Lionel is minded to go a-hawking to-day," said the Miller, suddenly gloomy again, " he is like to be misfortunate. This is no hawkers' weather."

" So said William," agreed Piers.

" If so be as the wind drops," continued Nick, " we shall have such a dousing of rain that the Prince will be hard put to it to get back to the Bishop's Palace."

" Oh," breathed Piers, " if he would but take shelter at the Manor-house!"

" Where else should he take shelter if he be stormstaid?" asked the Miller, reasonably.

Piers felt this conversation, however fascinating, had lasted long enough.

" Give you good day, Master Miller," said he. " Wat and I would fain see the gleeman brought in—if indeed Jenkyn have not returned alone."

" Let Simkin look to his stores if there be such folk about," muttered the Miller, drawing aside to let the two boys pass.

" Did you mark that?" Piers asked Wat as they hurried on. " You know Simkin says there are no such thieves as millers beneath the moon."

" So says my father."

" And—Wat—did you hear what Nick Miller said—about the lord Lionel?"

" For sure I did."

" Would you not be fain to see one of the King's sons?"

" I had liefer see the King himself. They do say it brings good luck even to dream of his face."

Piers nodded. " I know. But I have never dreamed that dream. Maybe I might, if I had seen him. He is very tall, my father says, and his beard is very long; and when he is angry his voice is very terrible. If I cannot see him, I would

I might see the Prince of Wales. But the lord Lionel were better than nothing."

"For sure," agreed Wat.

Conversation between the two boys often followed that pattern. Eager questions and a torrent of information from Piers, and brief, stolid answers from Wat; yet they were excellent friends, and both looked forward to the day when the elder would follow the younger to the French wars—or any other wars where a landless lad of gentle birth might seek his fortune. As a younger son, Piers knew he would have to go out into the world and fend for himself while Denzil reigned at the Manor in their father's place ; and Wat, as the son of a yeoman, knew that it would be regarded as right and fitting that he should serve Piers wherever he might go.

They were now drawing near the Manor, leaving behind them the Green with its duck-pond, and the shaggy old oak-tree where the Anglo-Saxon elders had been wont to hold their witenagemot five hundred years before. The last house in the village, the nearest to the church, belonged to Wat's father, and was a little larger and more solid than the others. A pear-tree was trained against the wall; there were three bee-hives in the garden; several hungry hens were pecking round the door. And now the two boys had reached the stone gatehouse of the Manor, built by Sir Humphrey de Clavenger in the troublesome reign of King John and crowned with a fine carved porch added by his grandson, Sir Piers, in the more glorious days of King Edward the First.

Before they reached this gatehouse they had to cross the moat by means of the causeway of turf and stones which for more than seventy years had replaced the old drawbridge. When Sir Humphrey had dug the moat times were so bad and men so lawless that every knight and baron made a stronghold of his home; but when, under the firm rule of one of the greatest of the Plantagenets, Sir Piers beautified the gatehouse he removed both the drawbridge and the portcullis—two most useful things in case of sudden assault—and, though he left water in the moat, constructed a solid way of communication with its western verge.

From the shadow of the porch peered a cluster of faces—there was Simkin the Steward, gaunt and peevish, a fringe of lank grey hair round his bald head; Gillian, the pert young handmaiden of Dame Eleanor; Adam Cook, a ladle in his hand; and, peeping under his elbow, spindle-shanked, shock-pated Jack, his scullion. It was Jack who first caught sight of the squirrel in Wat's arms and let out a cry of " There he be! There be Russell! "

Simkin stepped forward with dignity, and Adam, suddenly aware of Jack's presence, turned upon his scullion crying " There he be, be he? And where be *you*? Gaping like a calf and jostling your betters while the spit stands still and the goose burns. Be off with you."

Much abashed, Jack sped towards the group of low buildings, kitchen, bakehouse, brewhouse, stretching northward from the great hall, while Adam followed with a less hasty tread.

" Simkin," called Piers, " has the gleeman been brought in? "

" Not yet, young Master."

" You see—he did not steal Russell after all. Maybe Jenkyn will ride back alone."

" Then is Jenkyn's but wasted labour," muttered the Steward, who did not share the young Master's anxiety to see (and hear) the wandering fiddler again.

" I will go and tell my lady," said Gillian, gathering up her skirt to avoid the mud of the courtyard and showing a neat pair of ankles clothed in warm red stockings.

" Where is my father? " asked Piers of the Steward. " Nick the Miller says that my lord Lionel of Antwerp is hawking in these parts. Suppose he were stormstaid and sought shelter here! "

" St. Thomas of Canterbury forbid! " groaned Simkin, " We are not furnished forth to feed princes. The hens have not laid these twelve days past—there is no honey in the hives —there is little wine in the cellar—and as for spices and almonds and sunflower seeds! You had best go and seek your noble father, young Sir—and that in haste!"

Gillian soon returned with the squirrel's perch, from which a fragment of broken chain was dangling, and Wat then offered to join the link to that upon Russell's collar. While he was doing so the handmaiden remarked that Sir Thomas and my lady were in the solar chamber, whither Master Piers was to bring Wat immediately.

The group under the gatehouse then scattered, and Gillian, carrying the perch with Russell upon it, hustled rather than conducted the two boys along the rush-strewn hall towards the carved screen beyond which a twisting stone staircase led to the solar chamber. In this chamber Wat had never set foot before, but he had heard his elders speaking of its marvels many times. It had been built and garnished at the behest of Piers's grandmother, Dame Alice, a very proud lady who had been bred up in the royal palace at Westminster among the daughters of Edward the First, and must needs have tapestry on her walls and rugs on her floor, and a hooded hearth, and glass in the windows. It was said that never would she utter a word in the English tongue, but spake ever French, which she called the only tongue meet for knights and ladies of high degree.

For nearly twenty years Dame Alice's painted limestone monument had been one of the glories of Winford Church, but her memory had not faded from the minds of the Winford people. Many of them could recall her in her old age, wrapped in a mantle of mulberry velvet sprinkled with embroidered golden keys—the Clavenger crest—lying in a horse-litter and setting forth on a pilgrimage to the famous shrine at Walsingham in Norfolk. Dame Alice had always loved pilgrimages, and she never forgot that the birth of her only son, Thomas, had followed a journey to the glorious shrine of St. Thomas of Canterbury. In her gratitude she had persuaded her husband to have their child christened after the martyred Archbishop; and everyone at Winford St. Mary, from the lord and lady of the Manor to the humblest serf, felt sure that St. Thomas took a personal interest in his namesake. When the terrible plague known as the Black Death smote England in the year 1348 Winford, in spite of its nearness to one of the seaports from which the infection spread, got off comparatively lightly; and of the forty men of the village who had followed Sir Thomas to France in 1356 all but two returned safely home after the battle of Poitiers. Surely these things must have been the doing of that kindly Londoner, Thomas Becket!

Wat could remember seeing his grandfather wearing one of the twenty black gowns which had been given to as many aged men and women when Dame Alice died: and he had often seen Father Oswald's gaunt shoulders draped in the rich cope made from her ladyship's mulberry-coloured mantle. But never yet had he penetrated farther into the Manor than the great hall, where there was good cheer at Christmas time for everyone, from Nick the Miller and his five red-haired sons to Hob the Hedger and his two pairs of mixed twins. His heart beat a little faster as he followed Piers up the curving staircase.

At the top Gillian stood aside so that Piers should pass first through the half-open door of the solar chamber, at the same time making a sign with her hand that the yeoman's son was to wait until bidden to enter. Nothing loth, Wat halted on the threshold.

What a wonderful room! The wall was hung with that sort of fine tapestry woven at Arras and therefore called arras-cloth. Wat loved the pattern—men leading coupled hounds or galloping on grey or chestnut horses, while a slim white stag with yellow antlers fled before them, all against a background of green trees and flowering turf. The glass in the window was as clear and as gaily-coloured as the glass in the church. Upon the paven floor was spread a Spanish rug, dark red and blue, such as those that good Queen Eleanor brought to England when she came from Castile to wed King Edward of the very long legs.

In the great hall the hearth stood in the centre and the smoke escaped, or tried to escape, from a hole in the roof: but here the hearth was built into the wall, and a projecting hood of carved limestone kept the smoke from puffing outwards. On this hood Wat was able to recognise the Clavenger motto—*Clavem Teneo,* I hold the Key. He could not read, but Piers had often shown it to him on Dame Alice's monument.

On one side of this fireplace, in a high-backed chair of fretted oak, sat Dame Eleanor, lady of the Manor of Winford St. Mary, very noble in a dark blue velvet robe over which was worn a sleeveless jacket of crimson edged with brown fur.

Her hair was braided into a stiff roll on either side of her face, each roll held in a network of golden cords and small pearls, and both kept in position by a band of silver-gilt across the forehead.

Beneath the painted window, on either side of a small table, Sir Thomas Clavenger and his French prisoner sat intent upon a game of chess. Though their

PLANTAGENET GENTLEMEN PLAYING CHESS

garments were very similar—sharply-peaked shoes, long, fine hose, close-fitting, trailing-sleeved tunics girt about the hips with rich girdles of enamelled bronze—their faces and figures were curiously unlike.

The Englishman was long in the shank and broad in the shoulders; his hair was light brown with a reddish tinge; his eyes, very blue, were set far apart under strongly-marked eye-brows, one of which he had a trick of jerking up when he was either annoyed or amused. He had a small mole on his chin; and there was another exactly the same on the chin of his elder son. The left sleeve of his tunic was cut short at the elbow so as not to chafe the recently-healed scar of the wound he had received at Poitiers. In spite of all that Dame Eleanor could do with home-made herb lotions, in spite of the best efforts of Dr. John Gaddesden, the Prince of Wales' own physician, with an ointment of molten gold and bat's grease mixed when the moon was at the full, the injury had taken almost a year to heal. The French knight was of middle height, and though wiry and well-proportioned he looked small beside his English companion. His thin, olive-tinted face had fallen into melancholy lines, and his amber-brown eyes seemed to be searching always for some far horizon over which the messenger might yet ride bringing the ransom that would set him free.

Little did either of the two knights dream that the war which had been raging—off and on—for eighteen years would rage for another eighty-six more: and greatly would Sir Thomas have been dismayed if he had foreseen that its end would not be victory for England and a French crown for an English king. In the interim the knights of the two nations, while fierce foes, could also be courteous and chivalrous companions. They spoke the same language, more or less; they followed the same rules of the same knightly game; they even had the same thoughts and feelings upon every subject except the rightful heir to the throne of France.

As the English King already held large tracts of territory in that land it seemed to his English subjects only just that he, being moreover the son of a French princess, should rule over the whole realm. To this, Frenchmen retorted that by their ancient law no woman could transmit to her son any such claim, and that therefore King John, then ruling over them, was their King and none but he.

Already these disagreements had led to violent clashes on land and sea, and had caused suffering and loss to great folk and lowly on either side: but the Prince of Wales by treating the captured French monarch with gentle courtesy had set an example that his knights were not slow to follow.

Sir Thomas Clavenger, though secretly he may have thought that Messire Olivier was rather foolish to care so much for fiddling and fluting, had a friendly regard for his captive: and Messire Olivier, though secretly he may have thought that Sir Thomas was rather dull to care so little for such things, had become attached to the whole Clavenger family among whom he had lived—in a homesick yet hopeful manner—for the best part of a year. He was especially fond of the children, from the infant Eleanor, still tightly swaddled like a small white chrysalis, to Denzil, the elder boy, the same age as his own firstborn son far away in Touraine.

On that particular morning the two knights, thinking the weather too windy to fly their falcons, had settled down to a game of chess in which they were so deeply absorbed that they hardly glanced up when Piers entered, followed by Gillian. A moment later the squirrel's perch was on its usual bracket near Dame Eleanor's chair, and his delighted mistress was stroking him with her long-fingered hand.

" Russell, you knave," she said. " Foolish one, where have you been? "

Piers answered for him. " On the far side of the hill, so please you, good my mother. Wat found him. He was caught in a gorse bush."

Gillian now put her forefinger on Wat's shoulder and poked rather than pushed him into the room.

"Come hither, Wat," commanded Dame Eleanor kindly.

The boy bowed as low as he could, clutching at his shaggy forelock.

"Do you know what this is, child?" asked the lady, drawing a golden coin from the embroidered pouch at her girdle.

"Nay, lady—for sure."

"Look at it. What can you see?"

"I see a ship, lady. And I do see a man with a great sword—or such-like—in his hand."

"The man is our lord the King. The sword and the ship are a token of the victory he won at sea over against the harbour of Sluys seventeen years since. Take this, child—it is a half-noble—and your father will keep it for you till you are older."

Wat did his best to gulp out some words of thanks, but no word would come. Jenkyn and the gleeman were clean forgotten. He could think of nothing but this marvel, that he, Wat the yeoman's

HALF-NOBLE OF EDWARD III

son, had stood in the solar chamber and that Dame Eleanor had given him a golden gift.

"Take him to the buttery, Gillian," commanded the Dame, "and bid Simkin give him a cake and a draught of ale."

With nose and chin in the air, Gillian obeyed: and Wat, in his confusion, forgot to make another bow before he trotted after her. When they had departed Messire Olivier looked up from the chess board and said, "By my faith, Madame, I cannot choose but rejoice that the poor gleeman was guiltless."

He spoke in French, as did most of his English friends of high degree, and it was in the same tongue, though with a slightly different accent, that Dame Eleanor answered that the children would be of the same mind—if the gleeman were brought back again.

"Without doubt," cried Sir Thomas, cocking one eyebrow. "Everyone here is of that mind, from my lady wife to the newest-hatched gosling on the Green—save only myself. I love none of these jingling, scraping, prancing knaves."

"Ah," said Dame Eleanor, "ah, husband, if you would but heed me and buy a book—such a book as the Queen has at Windsor—with tales of love and war! Then would I never wish to hearken to the old stories of the gleemen again."

"A book!" echoed Sir Thomas. "A *book*—there has never been such a thing as a book at Winford within memory. My mother—God receive her soul—had her Mass-book—the same that you use every day—but such a book as you would have—why, Dame, it would cost as much as three furred gowns, a peregrine falcon, and a surcoat of the newest fashion!"

Dame Eleanor might have said more, but she noticed that the French knight was listening. Any talk of money in his presence suggested the delicate subject of his ransom and was usually avoided by his English friends for that reason.

All this time Piers had been watching for a chance to tell his father what Nick the Miller had said about the lord Lionel, but none came. Every time he opened his mouth it happened that Sir Thomas also had something to say—about Denzil's long tarrying, about Jenkyn's useless journey, or some other matter. And then hoofs were heard. and as they were the hoofs of only one horse it seemed that it must be Jenkyn and not Denzil and William Falconer who now clattered over the cobblestones.

At this moment, just as Piers was making yet another attempt to catch his father's eye, Gillian came in, leading by the hand a seven-year-old girl whose garments were as long, stiff and cumbersome as her mother's, though not made of such rich materials. This was Alice, the elder daughter of the house of Clavenger. The hood of the maid and the bare head of the child were glimmering with fresh raindrops.

" How came you in this plight, daughter ? " asked Dame Eleanor.

" So please you, good my mother, I was feeding the pigeons—and the storm began—and Gillian saw me and brought me hither. And now I would fain go forth again, to see the gleeman."

" Ho," said Sir Thomas, " Jenkyn has brought the gleeman back, has he ? Well then, he can let him go again, as it is clear that he did *not* carry Russell off in his pouch with his fiddle and his three balls."

" Bethink you, husband," whispered Dame Eleanor. " The poor rogue—he has been falsely suspected—and maybe roughly handled. Do we not owe him a dinner and a groat or twain ? "

" And will *he* not then owe *us* another piece of mumming and scraping! Go to, wife. I can see what is in your mind."

" I will tell you what is *not* in my mind," returned the lady, smiling, " and that is to descend and risk a ducking. Gillian can thread another needle for me. Rose-coloured silk. I am embroidering a figure of Julius Cæsar and many threads are needed for his nose."

The two knights had now risen and were moving towards the staircase with Piers still trailing anxiously after his father. Even the excitement of the gleeman's return had not made him forget the lord Lionel. As Sir Thomas vanished round the first bend of the stairs Alice stole forward, caught her brother's hand, and held him back.

"Let me go, sister," urged Piers, "I have something to tell our father. Something very important it is."

"Is that why you have been opening and shutting your mouth like a pike in a pond? Nay, do not frown, sweet brother. Let me come down with you and see the gleeman. Perhaps he will toss his balls—or play his fiddle."

"Not now, you foolish Alice, not now."

"Yet let me come. Denzil never will. He laughs if I want to play with you and him."

"It is something for laughter. A girl cannot run—or jump—or climb. How can a girl play with boys?"

Alice sighed: she knew only too well that it was a thing a girl could not do, however much she wanted to.

The two children had now followed their elders and were standing as inconspicuously as possible in the shadow of the great carved screen. Their father had seated himself in his own throne-like oaken chair on the dais at the other end of the hall, and Messire Olivier sat in a smaller chair on his right. Several dogs, mostly hounds bred for the chase, which had been snoozing round the open log fire in the centre of the room, rose when their master appeared and were now clustering round him, the oldest and most favoured of them all poking his long, wise nose into his hand. The folding oaken doors of the hall stood wide open and through them Jenkyn was in the act of making his entrance, a rather draggled Jenkyn but looking pleased with himself, his chin cocked up and his stomach thrust forward. In one hand he grasped a long cord of which the other end was knotted round the wrist of the woe-begone little figure that entered with him. Piers found it difficult to believe that this was the same gleeman who had danced, and somersaulted, and fiddled, and sung for their amusement only the day before. Rain dripped from his rough hair, his comical nose, his jutting chin; it dripped from his ragged tunic and it made a puddle wherever he set his shabby, crinkled shoes. Slung round his shoulder was a shapeless sheepskin bag, and this he seemed to be trying desperately to protect with his free arm.

From the shadow of the doorway peered Adam and Simkin, with whom were now Ralph the Gardener and Hugh the Carpenter. Jack, however, was not there. He was reluctantly turning the spit on which sizzled a fine, fat goose. It was Wat, clutching a wedge of half-eaten cake, who peeped out beneath the cook's elbow.

"Well, fellow?" barked out Sir Thomas, gruffly. With a lordly wave of the hand, Jenkyn introduced his captive.

"Your orders have been obeyed, noble master," said he. "And forasmuch as this vagabond would neither unstrap his poke nor let me look inside I have brought him hither."

"Undo that cord," commanded Sir Thomas.

Jenkyn stood gaping: he had expected to be praised and now it seemed as if he were to be blamed instead.

"Do you not hear, fellow?" chimed in the gleeman, impudently. "*Undo the cord.*"

Red in the face, Jenkyn obeyed.

"And now," said Sir Thomas to the gleeman, "tell us why you allowed yourself to be dragged back here at the stirrup of my servant. The squirrel was not in your poke— you had but to loose the buckle and no man could have laid a hand upon you."

The vagabond glanced up with an impish grin.

"Having nothing to fear from justice," said he, "had I not something to hope from mercy?"

"By mine own St. Thomas of Canterbury, a bold rogue!" cried the knight.

"Moreover," continued the other, scrabbling in his bag, "it may be that you will need mirth and music when you have eaten to-day. Something I heard by the wayside—

now, if the rain should not cease—who knows? But I will say no more."

Only one person in the great hall could guess what the gleeman had in his mind, and that was Piers. Oh, why had he not been able to tell his father about the lord Lionel!

"You either rave or talk riddles," said Sir Thomas. "Yet, since you have had some wrong at the hands of my servant, you shall fiddle for us when we have eaten and the fiddler's fee shall not be lacking."

"If my fiddle was not broken while I ran at the stirrup," muttered the little man, drawing forth the instrument and scraping a note or two with his short, curved bow.

"Enough, enough," said the knight impatiently; and then he called at the top of his voice, "Simkin! where is Simkin?"

Simkin's bald head poked out from the doorway, and his lean body soon followed.

"Take this fellow away, Simkin," commanded Sir Thomas. "If his fiddle be broken Hugh can mend it for him. Take him to the buttery—feed him well—and he will make you merry with tales of Robin Hood."

The Steward made a sign to the gleeman, who shambled eagerly after him, with Wat, Adam, Hugh and Ralph bringing up the rear.

"Good my father," said Piers, shyly approaching the dais where the two knights were now deep in talk about one of the hounds whose paw had been hurt by a sharp thorn. He spoke so softly that Sir Thomas did not hear.

"Good my father," he began again. Sir Thomas glared over his shoulder at his second son.

"What are you doing here?" he demanded, sternly, "Go to Father Oswald."

"But, good my father—if it please you—Nick the Miller said——"

"It does *not* please me, and I *know* what Nick the Miller said. Get you gone."

Much puzzled, but not daring to disobey, Piers joined Alice, and the two children crept quietly out of the hall. Outside they found that the rain was now less heavy and there were tattered gaps in the black clouds. Jenkyn was skulking in the porch with a frown on his flushed face.

" What ails you, Jenkyn? " asked the boy.

" I did but as I was bidden, young Master," grumped the servant. "How could I know that Russell was not in the bag that the vagabond refused to unbuckle? "

" For my part," said Piers, wisely, " I did not think that anyone had carried Russell away. He always bites strangers. He did not bite Wat when Wat found him on the hill yonder."

" Oh, it was Wat," growled Jenkyn. "For sure it would be Wat—born under a lucky star that boy must have been! "

And with a grunt which showed his low opinion of the star under which he himself had been born, Jenkyn stumped off in the direction of the buttery.

" Hark, I hear horses! " cried Piers.

" And I! "

" It must be Denzil—unless—unless—— "

It was Denzil. A moment later he clattered into the court-yard and swung himself from his panting horse almost before it came to a halt. William Falconer dismounted quite as quickly and—to the astonishment of Piers and Alice—sped towards the kitchen at a pace unusual with him, for, being bandy-legged, he did not find running easy.

The elder of the Clavenger boys was very like the younger, except that he had inherited the small bones, the dark hair and the hazel eyes of their Welsh-born mother. Denzil's garments, too, were much the same, though his girdle was of finer workmanship and at it hung his sheathed dagger. On his gloved hand was perched a hawk whose eyes were blinded by a hood of green velvet.

" Where is father? " he asked as soon as he saw Piers.

"He was in the hall just now. But maybe he has gone back to the solar chamber. What is it, Den?"

"The lord Lionel—he is coming hither—I was sent ahead," stammered Denzil. "Here, take my hawk, Piers——"

"*I* will take her," cried Alice, holding out her arm at the correct angle. "She must go straight to her perch, mustn't she?"

"Of course she must. Here—the glove is too large for you—mind it does not slip. Are you coming with me, Piers?"

Leaving their small sister to carry out her task with anxious care, the two boys dashed headlong into the great hall, only to find that Sir Thomas and his companion were gone.

"Up to the solar," cried Denzil, leading the way.

"Denzil—Piers!" exclaimed Dame Eleanor as her sons tumbled over each other into the room.

Before Sir Thomas had time to invoke St. Thomas of Canterbury, Denzil broke into a breathless explanation. The lord Lionel of Antwerp—hawking beyond the great mere—coming to seek shelter at the Manor.

"How say you?" shouted Sir Thomas. "Coming *hither?*"

"Yes, father—he called to us—William and me—and asked where within a league he might shelter from the storm. And I said that our house was not more than a league away. So he bade us spur ahead, saying he would follow at an ambling trot."

There was at once an amazing bustle and clamour in the solar chamber, Sir Thomas roaring that he must speak with Simkin, and Dame Eleanor crying that she must see Adam Cook, while Gillian should bring forth her richest gear and gown. Meanwhile the French knight went back to the little table by the window and fumbled with the chess men, for the lord Lionel was the brother of the Prince of Wales, the victor of Poitiers, and the thought was slightly painful.

"I do marvel me," remarked Sir Thomas, halting on his way out of the room, "that in this Manor of Winford—where no cock can crow or ass bray without the news running round like sparks in stubble—I marvel me that no one had heard that the lord Lionel was disporting himself in these parts."

Piers plucked up his courage and spoke.

"Father," said he, "that was what Nick the Miller was saying——" he dared not add "and you said you knew."

"Nick the Miller! Ha, I remember—I thought it was of the eels in the traps he had spoken. Ralph had seen them, and told Adam. No matter. What we must do now is to make ready for the Prince."

Unbidden yet unrebuked, the two boys followed their father when he marched forth in quest of Simkin. Even in his cleanest apron a cook was not considered worthy to enter the solar chamber, so Dame Eleanor descended to the great hall to interview Adam, and Alice stayed near her.

CHAPTER II

THE KING'S SON

THE unexpected arrival of so important a guest was bound to cause an upheaval in any household, and both the lord and the lady of Winford Manor were rather anxious and flustered, he about the wines and the spices, she about the roast meats and the puddings and pies. If Dame Eleanor had had her wish, peacocks and cranes, lampreys and larks would have appeared by magic for the entertainment of the lord Lionel:

A FOURTEENTH-CENTURY COOK

but Adam, hastily tying on a clean apron, protested plaintively that none of these things was to be had in the twinkling of an eye. By the mercy of heaven there was a fine goose turning on the spit—if that rogue Jack had not forgotten to keep it turning: there was a good pie in the oven, made of chopped chicken, minced pork, saffron, and the yolks of eggs, and topped with a thick crust that should be the right golden colour in another hour—if that rogue Jack had not forgotten to feed the fire. He, Adam Cook, being a person of singular skill, could no doubt invent and prepare some other little dishes: but Simkin must not stint him of spice and sugar. With this Dame Eleanor had to be content.

Denzil and Piers had a more exciting time than their sister, for Sir Thomas called loudly upon Simkin to produce from the cellar more and richer wines than—according to the Steward himself—were ever in it from the days of King John to that year of grace. Had Sir Thomas forgotten that Spanish and Greek wines were very hard to come by, being brought many leagues by sea in constant peril of pirates and tempests?

" Have we no wine of Cyprus? " demanded Sir Thomas. " None from Alicante? "

" Noble master," snuffled Simkin, " the spigot of the Cyprus cask leaked—and you yourself complained that the Alicante was musty when I served it yesterday. We have red muscadel—enough to make a bowl of hippocras if time served—— "

" But time does *not* serve! " cried Sir Thomas, stamping to and fro. " You know that to make hippocras is a matter of many hours. What else have we, you puff-ball-pated knave? "

" Perry," faltered the Steward, " plenty of perry—— "

" The perry is good," said Sir Thomas, calming down a little, " brewed from our own pears and there are none better—yet it is not prince's brew. No matter. Mix spices with the red muscadel. Let there be no lack of perry. Bring out my finest cups of silver-gilt—and look that you spread my Flemish linen upon the high table."

Simkin hurried away, wishing heartily that he had been more attentive to the spigot and even more heartily that the lord Lionel had not been stormstaid anywhere within reach of Winford St. Mary.

When he had gone Sir Thomas turned to his small sons:

" The rain has ceased," said he, " but when a King's son

says he is coming, he comes. Denzil, do you stay with me. It is fitting that my elder son should be with me when I greet the lord Lionel. And, Piers, do you go and fetch Father Oswald."

Nothing loth, but hoping that in the meantime the Prince would not arrive, Piers set off on his errand.

Most knights of Sir Thomas's rank had their own chaplains and their own private chapels, and Dame Alice had both built a chapel (or " oratory," as it was called) and engaged a priest. But this priest, according to Sir Thomas, was wont to meddle too much in matters that did not concern him, and to quarrel too often with the priest of the parish, Father Oswald's predecessor. So, after Dame Alice died and kindly, simple Oswald came from the north, no other chaplain was sought. It was Oswald who said Mass every morning in Dame Alice's oratory, acted as tutor to the Clavenger boys, and had in his charge the Clavenger chapel in the ancient church. He was also a faithful pastor to the humblest of his flock, faring on foot in all weathers to visit the sick or the dying in lonely, scattered places. Sir Thomas had fallen into the habit of summoning him on many occasions not entirely connected with his priestly duties, but he had two good reasons that day: one was that the chair of the private chaplain should not stand empty and the dignity of the house of Clavenger be thereby in doubt; the other (and kindlier) one was that the old man might share in the general excitement.

The priest's house (to which Piers was now hurrying) consisted of a hall about forty feet long and eighteen feet wide, always open to any wayfarer lacking shelter. The walls were of stone, the high-pitched roof of oaken rafters. Over the door, under the peak of the gable, was his own tiny room, facing towards the church. There was no glass in the window, there were not even rushes on the rough planks of the floor; but on a small shelf at the head of his trestle bed lay Father Oswald's only treasure; a book—not a Mass-book, for the Mass-book belonged to the church and was kept there, but *The Consolations of Philosophy*, by a Latin writer of the fifth century, Boethius by name.

Piers found his good old friend pacing up and down in his narrow patch of garden, his lips moving in prayer and his simple wooden rosary jerking between his knotted, rheumatic fingers. When the excited boy had made him understand that he was wanted—and, even more important, *why* he was wanted—at the Manor, Father Oswald was very willing to come. He begged a moment to thrust a comb of sheep's bone through the fringe of grey hair round his shaven head, replaced his threadbare grey gown by his best one of russet cloth, and declared himself ready: but as he was no longer young or nimble he could not come as fast as Piers might have desired, and the boy was constantly getting ahead, falling back again, and then once more getting ahead.

"Do you not wish, Father, that it were the King himself who was coming?" enquired Piers, hopping three paces on one foot.

"That were indeed a great marvel," answered the deep voice with the north-country burr in it.

"Your grandsire saw *his* grandsire, did he not, Father?" asked Piers.

"Truly—Edward, first of that name. He was borne in a gold-curtained litter through the village where my grandsire dwelt. Towards Scotland he was borne, that mighty King. The hammer of the Scots, they called him. But that was his last journey and from it he never returned. Better if his son, the second Edward, had died before him—his son whom *I* saw."

Piers pricked up his ears. This was something new. He had heard often how a Durham ploughboy looking up from the furrow had beheld a long train of horsemen and baggage-waggons winding northward, and in the midst the prone figure of the dying King; but he had not heard that the son of that King had also passed that way.

"Was he a great King?" he asked. "Did he, too, hammer the Scots?"

"Nay, child, he was a foolish King—God have mercy upon his soul—one that loved the company of grooms and kennelmen better than that of holy bishops and valiant knights. I was a babe, running beside my mother as she toiled in the hayfield—but I can remember seeing a horseman with a fair, feeble face, clad in white velvet, with gold tags to his shoes, and how the cry went up that it was the King."

"What befell after, Father?"

"Defeat and disaster, my son. The blessing of God and His Saints was not with the banners of England at that tide, and the Scots won the day. At a place called Bannockburn it befell."

"Father," said Piers, hopping three paces on the other foot for a change, "have the Scots got black faces, like the men that live near the burning mountain and worship Mahound?"

It was with some reluctance that Father Oswald had to acknowledge that the faces of the Scots were of what he called "the Christian colour."

"Why do they fight against us, Father?"

Father Oswald shrugged his lean shoulders a little impatiently.

"Because they follow a mad dream which they call 'Freedom,'" said he.

Piers found this remark rather hard to understand; but he determined to ask further another time. He and Denzil often heard their elders talking of the wars in Scotland and in France, but they did not pay much heed unless the name of Edward, Prince of Wales, cropped up—as it frequently did. They knew something of the battle of Crécy, in which their father's uncle, Sir Aymer Clavenger, had fought and fallen;

but there was one subject they had never heard their father mention, and that was the battle of Poitiers. This was a matter of constant regret to both of them, for they felt the liveliest interest in the events of that September day less than a year past.

However slowly your companion may walk, you reach the end of your journey in time. Piers and Father Oswald entered the great hall to find Simkin in his best leather tunic and pewter chain directing Jenkyn and another servant as they fixed the trestle-tables upon the dais, unfolded the honey-pale Flemish linen, and set osier baskets full of small, narrow loaves at regular intervals along the board. Then the Steward departed, grasping the key of the great chest, clamped with iron and covered with cow-hide, where the family plate was kept. As he reappeared, with a goblet of silver-gilt in either fist, Sir Thomas emerged from the shadow of the carved screen. The knight was fumbling with the clasp of a richly enamelled girdle which he had donned to do the Prince honour, and behind him came Dame Eleanor, busy with the pearl-studded brooch that held her embroidered mantle in place.

Messire Olivier appeared next, his arms folded, his eyes upon the ground; he was still wearing the same shabby tunic as before, and had not attempted to make himself look more gay. Hard on his heels trotted Denzil and Alice, both breathless with excitement.

They were only just in time. Voices, horses' hooves, jangling of stirrups, buckles and bridles told that the royal visitor was outside Sir Denzil's gatehouse. Thither hurried Sir Thomas; and his three children, running eagerly after him in spite of Father Oswald's warning hand, saw him bow low and then take hold of the gilded stirrup of a grey horse whose high-pommelled scarlet saddle was sprinkled with leopards wrought in bright gold.

Lionel of Antwerp was then nineteen years of age. Though

his great height made him look older, there was something boyish about his face and manner that made him seem younger. The hood of his green velvet shoulder-cape was pushed back, showing his thick crop of russet hair—the true Plantagenet hair, almost the same colour as Russell's coat. His close-fitting tunic was barred with broad, slanting stripes, alternately white and crimson; his shoes, tied at the ankle with thongs of gold, were the same vivid scarlet as the trappings of his horse. A great mantle of purple velvet had protected both rider and steed from the storm; and as he drew rein the prince shrugged this off his broad shoulders so that one of his servitors could catch it and carry it away. Like the two older knights of his band, he bore upon his gloved left hand a hooded hawk. Another member of the party was a falconer, across whose saddle see-sawed two long wooden perches.

"God save you, good Sir Thomas Clavenger," said Lionel, speaking in English. "I have come hither to seek shelter from "— he glanced up at the sky and smiled—"from the storm which has now passed."

"Mine honoured lord," Sir Thomas made answer, still holding tight to the golden stirrup, "if it will please you to tarry a little—to put on fresh raiment—to partake of meat and drink—my falconer will aid yours to care for the hawks——"

Even as he spoke William was drawing near as fast as his bandy legs would carry him. It was a proud moment for William when he helped Prince Lionel's falconer to collect the various hawks, settle them upon their perches, and carry them to the Manor mews.

After the Prince had dismounted and entered the great hall there was much bustling and babbling. Sir Thomas was leading his guest towards the dais, Dame Eleanor offering a cup of wine, the children keeping as close as they dared to the magnificent figure, the hounds approaching with questioning eyes and noses, and Father Oswald getting in the way just because he was humbly anxious to get out of it. When

Lionel had drunk the wine, at the same time courteously refusing a change of raiment, he was installed in Sir Thomas's high-backed, throne-like chair and his host made ready to wait upon him.

It was more than twenty years since Thomas Clavenger had been a young esquire skilful in handing wine-cups, carving large, bony birds, and performing the other duties of that condition. His hand shook as he offered a brimming goblet and several drops of the red muscadel fell on the royal sleeve. Worse still, while he was carving the goose he had to grip its leg with his left hand as he wielded the huge, grey knife with his right, and, owing to the injury to his left arm, he could not grip firmly enough. The goose, as if it were again the possessor of a pair of wings, escaped from his fingers, and slid off the silver dish, and would have shot straight into Prince Lionel's lap if Messire Olivier had not spiked it on the tip of his dagger.

Sir Thomas, crimson in the face, swore by his own Saint Thomas of Canterbury that he was a clumsy loon: but the Prince took it as a huge joke, and soon made the whole company laugh with him by relating how the first time he had carved before the King his father at Windsor the same thing had happened, only there had then been no one quick or clever enough to catch the bird on the wing.

" It was a peacock," he explained, " with all its plumes— and it landed fair in the lap of the Queen my mother to the no small mirth of everyone save herself—and me. You remember, do you not? " he added, turning to the elder of the two knights who had come with him.

" Truly, my lord—a sight not easily forgotten."

" And one I was loth to have missed," interposed the younger knight, smiling.

The talk then passed lightly and easily to the various tasks an esquire must learn to perform, and when Lionel drew the French knight into the discussion that pensive person made them all laugh again by confessing that the knight whom he had squired was so exacting about the way in which his hair was curled before a tournament that he, Messire Olivier, had often wished that his master either had naturally curly hair or none at all.

All this time Denzil and Piers had been standing stiff, straight and silent on either side of the Prince's chair, Denzil holding a shallow gilt bowl half-full of rosewater and Piers with a neatly folded napkin over his arm. Their great moment was soon to come, and their minds were so earnestly fixed upon it that they had hardly a thought to spare for the roast goose or the golden pie.

And then the great moment came. The repast was done. The goose was a mere huddle of bones, only the least fragment of the pie remained, and the goblets held nothing but the dregs of muscadel and perry. Sir Thomas made a sign to his sons, and the elder, hastily dropping one knee, offered the rosewater to the Prince that he might dip his royal (and greasy) fingers in it. There were as yet no such things as table-forks.

Very carefully Denzil rose from his knee, when the lord Lionel had rinsed both hands—especially the left, which was used to grasp portions of roast or pieces of pudding while the right hand plied a small, sharp knife. The bowl swayed perilously as the boy struggled to his feet, but no drop lapped over the brim. Then it was Piers' turn to kneel and do his duty as a well-taught page.

As the Prince took the napkin from the younger boy he turned to Sir Thomas and said :

" By their likeness to yourself I do perceive that these two varlets are your sons, Sir Thomas."

" They are, my lord. And it is high time that they were in the household of some more worthy knight than their father, learning more of the lore of courtesy than they can learn in this rude Manor of mine."

"None so rude, Sir Thomas," returned the Prince good-naturedly. "A man might well send his son hither to be taught."

Sir Thomas was pleased.

"Well, my lord," said he, "that is what a good friend of mine, Sir Walter Warren, proposes to do next year. And my boys are to be in the care of Sir Giles Mowbray—a valiant warrior who fought beside me at Poitiers."

There was a sudden bustle at the hall door, and Simkin's voice was heard asking in a hissing whisper whether it were now time that the gleeman should come in.

THE GLEEMAN

"Will it please you to hear him scrape a jig or two, my lord?" enquired Sir Thomas. "How he comes to be here at all is a strange chance. It is a tale of a lost squirrel."

"Let us," returned the Prince, "let us hear both the gleeman and the tale."

At a nod from Sir Thomas the gleeman came tripping in. The sheepskin pouch still hung across his shoulder, but he was now wearing a tunic of apple-green satin, stained and shabby yet sparkling here and there with spangles. In one hand was his fiddle, in the other his bow.

"Scrape us a jig first," commanded the knight, and, while the minstrel obeyed, he related to the Prince the story of Russell's escape and Jenkyn's errand.

Then the gleeman sang, in a rather wheezy and yet not unpleasant voice, an old song of April, daisies in the fields and cuckoos in the copses. And after that he drew from his poke three painted balls, a green, a yellow and a blue, and these he tossed in the air and kept spinning all at once, to the no small admiration of the group of serving folk clustered round the door. Alice watched, too, from her place at Dame Eleanor's side: but Denzil and Piers had eyes for no one but the Prince now.

Presently Messire Olivier begged leave to speak a few words to the little man who, it seemed, knew enough French to carry on a simple conversation. They plunged into a lively discussion of ballads and lays, and the French knight even borrowed the fiddle and produced from it a small number of rather uncertain sounds.

Dame Eleanor chose this moment to crave the Prince's leave to withdraw, and the reluctant Alice had no choice but to follow her mother out of the hall and up to the solar chamber. No sooner had they departed than Lionel turned suddenly to his host and asked if he would grant him a grace.

"If it be in my poor power—right gladly, my lord."

"Tell me something of that battle at Poitiers where my brother of Wales fought so valiantly."

Sir Thomas hesitated, twisting his empty goblet between his finger and thumb.

"Is there anything that I could tell you that you have not heard already?"

"Nay, there is much. We do not speak overoften of such matters in the company of our gentle foes of France. From my brother himself I have heard—and shall hear—nothing. Moreover, he has but lately returned to England, bringing the French King with him."

"Yes, my lord; that I know. And I know that upon the road from Sandwich to London they halted and made orison together before the shrine of mine own St. Thomas of Canterbury."

The Prince did not ask—as Sir Thomas half hoped he

might—why he called the saint his "own St. Thomas." Instead, with unaffected eagerness, he said:

"To your story, good Sir Thomas, to your story. I know the place—near Poitiers. I know the day, the nineteenth of September in the year of grace 1356. A great host against a small—a fresh host against a weary—and then victory—*not* for the great host but for the small. But I would fain know more."

"Truly, my lord, we were very few and very weary, both horse and man. Yet, by the grace of God and St. George——"

Sir Thomas paused, uncertain what to say next, and the Prince prompted him.

"You were marching through France—from Bordeaux northward—up the valley of the Loire?"

"Yea, my lord. For the Prince your brother had gathered round him in his own faithful city of Bordeaux an army of some seven thousand men, English and Aquitainian—men-at-arms, archers, lightly-armed foot-soldiers. It was there I joined him with my own two-score men, good bowmen all."

The Prince made an approving murmur, and then remarked that he had heard that the French had taken to crossbows of the Genoese fashion instead of the longbows still favoured by the English.

"That is so, my lord—and Genoese bowmen are hired to handle them. A cumbersome matter it is to wind up and unwind a crossbow, and though the bolts they shoot are heavier than our arrows they do not fall so true or pierce so deep."

Lionel nodded.

"The longbow for me!" said he. "And now let us return to the valley of the Loire."

"If we must, my lord. But I have no skill in telling the tale as it should be told."

" What! Must you borrow that fellow's fiddle to help you along? "

The two boys standing erect by the Prince's chair had some difficulty in biting back broad grins at this idea, but Sir Thomas did not find it so amusing.

" I leave fiddles to fiddlers," said he. " And if they tell their tales better, it is not because the tales are more true. Let me see what I can do in my own plain way."

" There is no better way, and none more to my mind," the Prince assured him.

Thus encouraged, the knight began again.

" The Prince of Wales expected to be met in Normandy by the King his father; or, if that plan failed, he was to join hands with an English force mustered in Brittany. We started in high hope, for some of us had fought at Crécy, and all of us remembered the outcome of *that* battle."

Again Lionel made the murmuring sound that Sir Thomas seemed to find cheering. As for Denzil and Piers they were listening without budging—almost without breathing. In the distance could be heard a gentle scraping as Messire Olivier and the gleeman took turns in playing upon the gleeman's fiddle.

" King John of France," explained Sir Thomas, " to defend those stretches of the Loire where crossings might be made, had collected a large army at Chartres. And before long the Prince our Captain, seeing that he could neither cross the Loire nor win his way to Brittany, gave the word that we must needs march back to Bordeaux."

" A word that must have stuck in the gullet of my brother of Wales," remarked Lionel.

" We retreated," continued Sir Thomas, not heeding the interruption, " towards Poitiers. The French pursued us : they crossed the Loire at Blois. A week later they crossed the Vienne—still in pursuit. Then King John outflanked us and his army lay athwart our road."

" What of our forces in Brittany ? "

" They set out to join hands with us but the French headed them off at a place called Pont-au-Cé."

" How many men do you reckon marched beneath the golden lilies ? I have heard talk of twenty thousand."

" Twenty—nay, fifty—fifty thousand would be nearer the mark. Moreover, we were—as I have said—leg-weary. And retreating takes the very heart out from beneath a man's ribs."

" Tell further, good Sir Thomas."

" Maybe I should now say something of the Cardinal of Perigord. You know, my lord, that his Eminence tried to stop the battle ere it began ? "

" Yes—but tell further."

" You must understand that we had taken up our position on ground chosen by the Prince our Captain. On the right bank of a little river it was. We were astride a narrow lane with high hedges and sloping vineyards on either side. There we were to fight, if fight we needs must."

" A wise choice of my brother of Wales."

" Ah, my lord, when has he been proved other than wise ? Let me see—what next ? Upon the eighteenth day of September—a Sunday it was—the Cardinal sought the King's leave to try to patch up a truce. Messire Olivier yonder—who was in the King's tent—says that the Cardinal swore we English were already beaten men."

" Ha! " said the Prince, snorting like a war-horse. " Said he so ? "

" It seems also, my lord, that reinforcements were on their way to join the French : so a day's delay was better for them than for us."

" What! were their fifty thousand—you said fifty thousand, did you not ?—were they not thought enough to crush our poor seven thousand ? "

" My lord, they too remembered Crécy."

" Tell, further, I pray you, good Sir Thomas, tell further."

" All that bright Sunday the Cardinal jogged to and fro between the camps. On a white mule he rode, with a chaplain ever riding behind him to carry his great red hat with the red tassels. And the Prince our Captain, mindful of the peril in which we stood, said at last that he was willing to swear a truce upon honourable terms."

" Such as—— "

" Such as these: that he should surrender all the castles and all the captives he had taken—and promise not to fight against the King for seven years."

" Bitter bread for the mouth of my brother of Wales."

" Ay, my lord—if he had had to eat it. But the King was not content. The Prince himself must yield, with a hundred of his knights. And if he would not, and a battle followed, no quarter would be given."

" No quarter! That means no prisoners—and no ransoms. Small gain to the victorious side! But say on."

" While these parleys were going on we were busy digging ditches and making wattle fences. By dawn on Monday all was as the Prince had planned."

" How was his army divided? "

" Into three divisions, of which the second was under his personal command."

" What of the French? "

" From the top of our little hill we could see them, not stretched out, but in four divisions, one behind the other. The Genoese cross-bowmen we knew by their steel caps, which shone in the morning sun."

" How were our three divisions placed? " asked Lionel, leaning eagerly forward.

" On either side of the narrow lane—the lane I spoke of, bordered with hedges and vines. We had archers on foot, their horses tethered near by. Then there were three hundred mounted archers and as many men-at-arms waiting—in ambush as it were—to fall upon the second division of the French."

"Were you near my brother that day, good Sir Thomas?"

"Almost as near as I am to you now, my lord. And with him were Sir John Chandos and Lord James Audley, both Knights of the Most Noble Order of the Garter—and a Gascon knight, one of his loyal liegemen from Guienne——"

"I know whom you would say—the Captal de Buch. Tell me more of him before you end your tale."

"Needs must I, my lord. Yonder gleeman with his old rhymes of heroes and dragons has no such heart-warming story."

"How did the battle begin?" prompted Lionel, as Sir Thomas paused.

"Three hundred chosen men-at-arms tried to rush the little hill and take it by storm. Up the narrow lane they hurled themselves—and right and left, from the cover of the hedges and the vines, our arrows rained upon them. And as they crashed down the slope their first division was thrown into disorder."

"And then?"

"The flank of the second division was laid open—and the Prince gave the word—and the mounted archers attacked. And then that division began to waver and to give ground—and as it fell back it carried with it the third division, immediately behind."

"What folly—so to place them that if one retreated the next must needs do likewise!"

"So the Prince our Captain said. And you can guess, my lord, how we chafed to spur in pursuit when we saw them thus falling back. But the Prince had warned us that he would not have it so. The longbowmen and the men-at-arms held firm—our line was neither weakened nor split asunder. And that was well—for we had still to meet the fourth French division, large, fresh, and full of fight, com-manded by the King in person."

" Ha! And what next ? "

" We saw them marching upon us—their blue banners with the golden lilies unfurled as if to defy us."

" What said my brother of Wales ? "

" Nothing much at first, except to bid his esquire to tighten the buckle of his sword-belt. Then a certain English knight—by your leave I will not name him, for he would now wish his words to be forgotten—this knight, looking on that forest of French banners, cried aloud, ' We are lost, poor wretches that we are!' And the Prince turned upon him and said with a terrible voice, ' Thou liest, dastard—we are not lost while yet I live.' And we that were about him cried that it was so, our cries making a hollow sound within our helmets which for the most part had the visors down."

" Yet," said Lionel thoughtfully, " to see so great an army all bristling with banners might make even a stout heart turn a little cold."

" Truly, my lord," agreed Sir Thomas, who had himself felt an uncomfortable chill beneath his steel breastplate and embroidered surcoat.

" And what befell after ? "

" Sir John Chandos was for making a counter-attack. The Captal de Buch sought leave to take a small company of archers—with *their* banner—and fall upon the French rear. At this plan the Prince laughed a little, for it was wild enough, God wot, but he did not say ' No.' And when the Captal had dashed away to gather his archers together the Prince turned to Sir John Chandos and touched him on the shoulder. ' John,' said he, ' do you go forward. You shall not see me turn my back this day.' And to his standard-bearer, Sir Walter Woodland, he gave the word of command, ' Banners advance, in the name of God and St. George!' "

Sir Thomas paused for breath and his royal listener sug-

PRINCE LIONEL WASHES HIS HANDS (*see page* 40)

BOANERGES BIRCH REHEARSING HIS PUPILS (*see page* 71)

gested that he might care to drink a draught of wine, but
the knight, remembering that there was a dearth of red
muscadel and being a little tired of home-brewed perry,
bowed his thanks and began again.

"Then we swept down the hill—we and the Prince our
Captain. I remember how
the sky was dark with our
yard-long arrows and the
shorter bolts of the cross-
bowmen—and how above
the beat of hooves and the
moans of the wounded and
the clash of steel we could
hear our archers crying that
the grey goose was biting
well that day."

Denzil and Piers grinned
to each other. How often
had they heard the men
who had fought in France
talking of Gammer Goose
whose grey quills plumed
their arrows for the fray.

"Laud and honour to my
lady goose," said Lionel,
laughing. "And what after,
pray?"

"Why, my lord, the two
armies were so tightly inter-

A CROSSBOWMAN

locked that it seemed as if nothing could rend them asunder.
And then—suddenly—beyond the French rear—we saw the
white-and-red banner of St. George above the blue banners
of France."

"It was the Captal de Buch!" cried Lionel, bringing his hand
down on the table with a smack that made the goblets leap.

" It was he, my lord. And the French—little recking how small was the force he led—fell into great dismay. Their centre was broken—their right and left wings had crumpled up. They ran hither and thither, with loud cries."

" Where was their King? Did he also run and cry? "

" Nay, my lord—he bore himself right kingly that day. He was recognized by the golden lilies on his surcoat and the golden circlet upon his helm—and he was hemmed in by a crowd of men-at-arms, some Gascon, some English."

" Who took him prisoner? I have heard talk of a French renegade serving us for gain."

" Denis de Morbecque, my lord—a French knight who had been banished from the realm of France."

" For what cause? "

" An affray at St. Omer. By evil chance—and from no evil intent—he had stabbed a man to death. Being an outlaw from his own land, he took service with the English. When he drew near the French King and called upon him to yield, the King answered—as the manner is with Princes—' Tell me first to whom I yield.' And he was fain to unfold the truth—that he was a Frenchman, but an outlaw, fighting against France."

" What said the King? "

" I cannot tell. During this parley the crowd about him had grown thicker. The English and the Gascons, each eager to make sure of so great a prize, tugged him to and fro between them so that he stood in grave peril of being torn in twain."

" What of my brother in the meanwhile? "

" It was about this time, my lord, that Sir John Chandos began to cry aloud that, since the day was ours, it were well that the Prince's banner should be displayed in some place where his followers might see and rally to it. This being done, the Prince's minstrels were bidden to play—and they played with such good will that they could be heard above all the shouting."

" And after? "

" The Prince doffed his helmet, and shook the hair from his forehead, and cried with a great voice, ' Where is our cousin of France? Where is the King? ' So, no man answering, he sent two English lords in quest of him. And while they were about that business certain of his knights pitched his own pavilion near the place where his banner was displayed."

" Ha! I should know that pavilion," interrupted Lionel. " Is it not of goodly scarlet red? "

" It is, my lord."

" And while these things were afoot, Sir Thomas, where were *you*? "

" My lord, when I saw the banner and heard the trumpets I made my way as best as I could towards the banner. I had taken one prisoner—— " he glanced at Messire Olivier, who was still hobnobbing with the minstrel—" whose horse's bridle I had buckled to mine, and the wound in my arm was bleeding so fast that my gauntlet was filling with blood. My captive of his courtesy unarmed me when we drew rein, and the Prince's own leech came and tended me. And while he was binding up my hurt the two English lords rode slowly towards the scarlet pavilion with the King of France between them."

Neither Prince Lionel nor Sir Thomas Clavenger had noticed that the minstrel had now slipped away and that the French knight had quietly placed himself next to Denzil behind the chair of honour. When the Prince uttered his usual quick, " And what after? " it was Messire Olivier who answered. " By your good leave, my lord, that will I tell— for the telling concerns your brother, the Prince of Wales. The curtains of the scarlet pavilion being drawn back, we that were outside could see—— "

" What could you see? " prompted Lionel, as Messire Olivier paused. " Tell on."

" The Prince of Wales kneeling on one knee—unbuckling

the armour of the King of France. And we heard our King say, ' Fair cousin, you have this day won great honour and much glory.' "

" And what said my brother then ? "

" He made answer full gently, ' Not I, my lord—the victory was not won by me—it was given by God.' "

" Do you take up the tale," said Sir Thomas. " You were at the supper-table that night as well as I."

" Not at the high table," corrected Messire Olivier, modestly, " but—it is true—where I might, by some stretching of my neck and cocking of my ears, see and hear something of what passed."

Lionel turned to him with a good-natured nod and a movement of the hand that encouraged him to continue.

" At the high table sat the King of France and Philip his youngest son: but the Prince of Wales would not sit with them. He called himself unworthy: and therewith he spake many gentle and consoling words for the which we—his French captives—praised him greatly."

" Surely," said Lionel, " my brother himself served the King with meat and drink, as an esquire serves a knight, with all reverence and ceremony due ? "

Sir Thomas answered, with a twitch of his eloquent eyebrow, " Yea, my lord, and that with better grace and more skill than were shown at this table not an hour since."

They all laughed at this except Denzil and Piers, who knew that they must not join in a joke against their father, and Father Oswald, who, having eaten much more heartily than was his wont, nodded peacefully in his corner.

The rain had ceased now, the clouds had all rolled away to the landward leaving a clear, gleaming sky. As the sunlight slanted through the high, narrow windows Lionel rose, smiled, and said that it was time that he should take his leave. A moment later, as if pulled by some invisible cord, Dame Clavenger and little Alice emerged from the shadow of the screen, and in the courtyard outside there was a sound of mingled human feet and horses' hooves, human voices and horses' neighing. One of the two knights in attendance on the Prince hurried out to give the signal to the falconer to bring the hawks from the mews.

Then the gaily-harnessed horses, with their high-peaked saddles covered with velvet and their bridles hung with bells, were led up to Sir Humphrey's gatehouse and the Prince emerged. From a respectful distance the Manor servants, including Jack the scullion, were watching everything he did.

Sir Thomas took hold of the gilded stirrup, but before the Prince mounted he turned to the knight and said courteously,

" Good Sir Thomas, I give you and your Dame most hearty thanks for your gentle welcome: and when next I see my brother of Wales I shall tell him that I have had my wish at last—my wish that I might hear the true story of what befell at Poitiers last year. If there were any grace I might do you—— "

Sir Thomas hesitated for a moment and glanced at Dame Eleanor, who was standing in the shadow of the porch.

" Such a grace there might be "—he began.

" Name it, name it," urged the Prince.

" My lord, if my own St. Thomas of Canterbury should grant me a third son—and if that son might be called Lionel— in remembrance of this day—— "

" With all my heart," said the Prince.

It was at this moment that Father Oswald awoke with a jerk, blinked, peered right and left, and, suddenly remembering where he was and why, made his way as fast as his rheumatic legs would carry him after the vanished company. He was just in time to see Prince Lionel spring lightly into the saddle, wave his hand and ride away.

As soon as the royal cavalcade was out of sight the various groups in the Manor courtyard broke up. Sir Thomas, Dame Eleanor and the French knight returned to the solar chamber to talk about the events of the day; Father Oswald started off on his halting homeward walk; the servants dispersed to their various duties, Adam Cook driving Jack before him with a firm hand; Denzil decided to go with William Falconer to see if the hawks were settling down comfortably after the excitement of strange hawks in their quarters; and Piers was left alone with his friend Wat, the yeoman's son.

A MEDIEVAL BANQUET

"Oh, Wat," cried the boy breathlessly, "has this not been a marvellous day! We have seen a real Prince—one of the King's own sons—the tallest of them, they say—he has sat at meat in the great hall—he will tell the Prince of Wales that he has been at Winford St. Mary—did you hear him say so, Wat? Were you near enough to hear?"

"For sure," said Wat.

"Shall you ever forget this day?" asked Piers. "I never shall—I know I never shall. Shall you ever forget it, Wat?"

"No," said Wat.

And with that Piers had to be content.

CHAPTER III

MASKS AND MONSTERS

" 'Most fair Eliza, orient pearl of morn,
  Whom virtue, beauty, grace and worth adorn,
    Before thy feet we scatter golden lilies—— ' "

" Not ' golden ', brother; ' silver '."

                                    . . . " ' silver lilies
  And golden daffadillies— '

Alack, I can remember no more."

        " ' In wisdom, Pallas; Beauty, she of Troy—— ' "

" Forsooth, so it is. But, Sue, I shall never get these lines
by heart in time—or, if I do, I shall forget everything when
I see *Her*."

" Why, then, do not look at her."

" What! And tumble over her footstool? "

Susannah Clavenger burst out laughing at this picture of her
twin-brother, Harry, tumbling over the footstool of the
Queen; for it was Queen Elizabeth who was the " fair Eliza "
of the poem that Harry was trying in vain to commit to
memory, and in the course of a summer progress through the
southern parts of her realm she was coming to dine, sup and
sleep at the Manor of Winford St. Mary.

The twins were sitting on the low stone ledge of a long
terrace with which their father, Squire Francis Clavenger,
had beautified the eastern front of the ancient Manor House.
Beneath curved the hollow of the now dry moat, gay with
flowering shrubs and sweet-smelling herbs: beyond stretched
orchards and vegetable gardens, flanked on one side by a

velvet-smooth bowling-green and on the other by what was known as a knot-garden, a maze of winding paths bordered by clipped hedges of hornbeam and yew. Between the children was perched Susannah's doll, Lucrece, stiff and gorgeous in a hooped gown and peaked bodice not unlike the equally stiff but rather less gorgeous garments worn by the little girl herself: at their feet lay Blanche, the younger and more affectionate of their mother's two pet spaniels.

From the tower of Winford village church came the sound of a clock striking the hour of three.

There had been no clock in that tower in Plantagenet days; indeed, there had been none until twelve years before, when Squire Francis had installed one to mark his thankfulness for the birth of his much-desired son and heir. The Winford people were proud of their clock: for the neighbouring villages of Little Bunstead, Haverley and Churp were clockless all. It is true that among the nettles in the ruined cloisters of Haverley Abbey there lay rusting some fragments of cog-wheels, bars and chains which rumour said had once formed parts of a great clock made by one of the monks in the olden times; but nobody thought of gathering them up and trying to fit them together again.

The Squire, too, was proud of the Winford clock. When the wind was in the right direction he could hear its deep chime as he lay in bed—even when the bed-curtains were closely drawn and his quilted linen night-cap was pulled well over his ears. To express his delight at the defeat of the Spanish Armada a year before, he had had the hands and the numerals freshly gilded—otherwise he might have thought that a new coat of gold paint should be applied in honour of the Queen. The ancient bells, once known as Gabriel, Mary and John the Baptist, had been taken down and re-cast in the year of Elizabeth's accession, losing their old names and their old cracked voices in the process. They were in good trim to ring a peal of welcome to the Tudor Queen.

Two hundred and thirty-seven years had passed since the last royal visitor came to the Manor of Winford St. Mary and during those years many things had altered much. The memory of that visit had faded; neither Harry nor Susannah had ever heard how Lionel of Antwerp, son of King Edward the Third, had sat at meat in the same great hall where preparations were now being made for the reception of his very distant kinswoman, the daughter of King Henry the Eighth. The Plantagenets had vanished; their Tudor supplanters would soon vanish also, and make room for a dynasty of Scots. Father Oswald would have been both shocked and sad if he could have foreseen that a day would come when England would be forced by fate to turn to Scotland for a King. Indeed, it was well for his peace of mind that he did not possess the gift of prophecy.

In the Norman church where, robed in richly-coloured vestments, he had once celebrated the rites of the old faith, a black-gowned, bearded clergyman now ministered to the villagers as directed by the Prayer Book called " King Edward the Sixth's." The humble parsonage-house where he had led an almost monkish life had been replaced by a neatly-timbered, lattice-windowed Vicarage which—though larger than the earlier building—was hardly large enough to hold the numerous children of the Vicar. Instead of a solitary, hand-written book upon his bedside shelf, Father Oswald's successor had half a dozen printed ones, or more; and he would have laughed at the *Mappa Mundi* in which the simple priest had so firmly believed. Nearly a hundred years had passed since the Continent of America was discovered, and nine since Drake had sailed right round the world in his famous ship the *Golden Hind*. Up at the Manor there was a map showing that Continent, and the East and West Indies as well: and, though some people still believed that very strange monsters lived in distant lands, nearly everyone knew that the earth was shaped more like a tennis-ball than a pancake, and, moreover, that it hung in space instead of floating upon a crystal sea.

Between the first royal visit in 1357 and the second in 1589 the Clavengers of Winford St. Mary had played their parts not unworthily in the pageant of English history, though without leaving any particularly brilliant patch upon its pages. Sir Thomas, as you will remember, fought at Poitiers and lived to tell the tale; his grandson fell at Agincourt. When the bald-headed, hook-nosed Duke of Bedford won the battle of Verneuil there was a Clavenger serving under him, leading a band of archers from his own manorlands: and when Joan of Arc compelled Talbot, Earl of Shrewsbury, to raise the siege of Orleans, there was a Clavenger among those retreating English Captains who were so astonished and indignant to find themselves in retreat that they vowed the Maid must have been aided by witchcraft.

Then came the Wars of the Roses, and the two sons of that Clavenger Captain ranged themselves on opposite sides. The elder chose the Red Rose of Lancaster and fought manfully for gentle, pious King Henry the Sixth and his warlike Queen, Margaret of Anjou: the younger, declaring that he liked neither King Dove nor Queen Eagle, sported the White Rose, and fought no less manfully for the House of York. What happened to those two brothers is another story—it may be told some day: in the end they were reconciled, and the Yorkist brother bequeathed to the second son of the Lancastrian a certain thickly-wooded estate bestowed upon him by King Edward the Fourth as a reward for his loyalty to the White Rose. The name of the estate was Brackenden, and it lay between twenty and thirty leagues south-west of Winford in the direction of the sea. For a time the two branches of the original Clavenger tree remained good friends enough; but Clavenger of Brackenden espoused the cause of Richard the Third, the last of the Plantagenets, while Clavenger of Winford St. Mary sided with Henry the

Seventh, the first of the Tudors. After that neither branch
cared to claim kinship with the other, and presently the only
bonds between them were their far-away ancestors, their
crest, and their name.

Meanwhile the descendants of Wat, the yeoman's son,
had been rising slowly but steadily in their little world.
One of them, commonly called Edward the Falconer, had
gained the good will of Sir Lionel Clavenger, him who fell
at Agincourt, by his skill and care in tending the falcons in
the Manor Mews. Sir Lionel showed his approval by a
grant of land, larger in extent and more fertile in character
than the holding occupied by the same yeoman family since
Norman times; and Edward's grandson came to be called
" Falconer " as a surname. Already two generations of
Nick the Miller's offspring had borne the name of " Miller ".
Now, in 1589, there was a Miller at the mill and another at the
forge: there was a Falconer at Upper Field Farm, a Falconer at
Long Copse Farm, and yet another in business as a shipwright
at the seaport town of Westhampton not many miles away.

The feudal system, with all that was good in it and all
that was bad, had come to an end; the people of Winford
were Squire Clavenger's tenants, not his serfs; yet they still
looked up to him as their natural leader and protector, and
in times of public peril or public rejoicing it was always to
him that they turned first. When word was brought that
Don Philip of Spain was making ready to launch a mighty
fleet against England, it was to the Squire that the villagers
went for guidance: it was he who planned to have the alarm
sounded and the warning beacon lit, and bade the men
burnish and sharpen their bill-hooks and their scythes lest
the Spaniards should land at Westhampton and march upon
Winford St. Mary. Then, when the Armada had been
scattered and broken by fire and tempest, it was he who
provided from his own cellars and storehouses the beer and
beef for a feast in his biggest barn.

The news that the Queen proposed to visit the Manor was received by every tenant as a personal honour to himself; for Francis Clavenger was much liked, and he was a more kindly landlord than were some of his neighbours who had

longer purses and shorter pedigrees. A whisper went round that maybe "She" would dub him knight; "and who more worthy?" asked many voices: "and where," asked others, mostly women's voices, "would you find a handsomer boy than Master Harry, or two prettier children than his sisters?" Mrs. Clavenger was a fine gentlewoman, to be sure, but inclining a little to pride, and more puffed-up with being the grand-daughter of old Sir Miles Clavenger on the mother's side than Squire Francis was with being his grand-son on the father's.

The whisper about the knighthood reached the ears of the twins, who, having been brought up by their nurse on tales of Guy of Warwick and Bevis of Hampton, wondered whether, if once their father were a knight, he would have to leave them and go away to hunt dragons. But Susannah pointed out to her brother that neither great-grandpapa Miles nor their neighbour Sir Gresham Fenworth had gone dragon-hunting, and that therefore one could very well be dubbed knight without being obliged to do it. Guy and Bevis had lived a long, long time ago; even before the yew-trees in the churchyard were planted, and Parson Graves said that *they* were five hundred years old or more.

It was not of these things that Susannah was thinking as she sat with Harry and Lucrece on the terrace and listened to the church clock striking the hour of three. Her whole mind was fixed upon one point: how could she help her twin to acquit himself reasonably well, to remember his lines, to keep his head-dress from falling askew, and to escape the beating (or beatings) which he would assuredly receive if anything went wrong!

In her hand the little girl held a large sheet of paper upon which Boanerges Birch, the Winford schoolmaster, had written out the verses composed by him and to be recited by Harry. With clenched fists and crumpled brows the boy was trying to fix these verses in his memory.

"Look you now," urged Susannah, kindly, "do not spur so fast. Begin again."

"Unless I spur fast, the words fly right away," confessed Harry, ruefully. "I wish Ned Falconer were to be Renown instead of me. And—if needs I must take part in this mum-ming—I would I might play the Monster in his place. I am much better at remembering the Monster's lines:

'Lo, I am slain—I fall—I faint—I die!'"

"Nay," interrupted Susannah, firmly, "leave the Monster's lines to Ned: I'll warrant he knows them well and will speak them as they should be spoken."

"It is cake and pudding for Ned," grumbled Harry, kicking his heels against the stone ledge. "He saw the players when the Lord Chamberlain's company came to Westhampton and Farmer Falconer took him to see them. And you know father would not take me."

"No, that would he not," agreed Susannah. "He said the players were rogues and vagabonds fit only to be put in the stocks. If it be so, why should the Queen take such pleasure in their playing? For it seems they play often before her."

"Yes, and there is one company wherein all the players are children—those that our Uncle Mark saw when he was in London."

"You would not do for that company," said Susannah, with sisterly candour, "your beard would have grown before you had learned your part."

"Who said I wanted to be one of them?" retorted Harry. "I would as lief be a dancing bear."

"Come, now—to your task, brother Harry—begin afresh—

'Most fair Eliza——' "

"Give me time to get my breath again," pleaded Harry.

"Time, forsooth—and in ten days the Queen will be here."

"For my own part," said Harry, dropping his voice to a whisper, "I were better pleased if she were not coming hither."

"Hush, Harry—if someone should hear!"

"Nay, who would be abroad? Mother is in the still-room with Audrey, busy about the syrup of roses and the eringo. And Father is in his closet, busy with those long lists of matters needful. And I'll tell you something, sister. Father himself is not all joyful over her coming."

"Oh, Harry!" cried Susannah, round-eyed.

"Oh, Sue!" he mimicked. "But it is truth! Oh, Sue! Have you not marked how he tugs at his beard, and his eyebrows twitch? And how his finger is ever going up and down those lists—fish and fowl, and ale and wine?"

"Ah," said Susannah, sagely, "that is not because he is not

blithe at the Queen's coming hither—it is because all these things are very chargeable. And you have heard him say a score of times that we are much the poorer for those gold pieces that he gave to fit out a ship to fight the Spaniards last year."

" Yes, forsooth—more than a score of times. But that is not what causes Parson Graves to tug at *his* beard."

" Is he tugging at it ? " asked Susannah, interested.

" Ay, he is. Yesterday—when he was saying to Master Birch how he could not sleep o' nights lest some evil hap should befall the Queen while she tarries here. And again to-day I saw him tugging it."

" But why should any evil hap befall ? "

" They were speaking of what they called that nest of Papists at Brackenden."

" Brackenden—where the *other* Clavengers dwell. But they would not harm the Queen, brother. They were ready to fight for her against King Philip."

" So said Master Birch. He said that for all he knew our kinsfolk yonder were as honest and peaceable folk as need be, barring that they are re—re— "

" Recusants, brother."

" Ay, that is the word. And he said, moreover, that they had never been caught plotting for the Queen of Scots— nor for the King of Spain. But Parson Graves said that for his part he would sleep better o' nights if Brackenden were a hundred leagues from here and another hundred from the sea."

" Why, what a strange thing to say! "

" Not strange at all, if so be that there is at Brackenden great coming and going of all manner of men—and you can never tell for sure whether the poor tinker by the wayside, or the pedlar with his pack upon his shoulder, is what he looks to be, or a Mass-priest from over the sea."

Though the little, ancient manor-house of Brackenden was

a good twenty leagues from Winford, deep in the green shadows of the forest that stretched towards the coast, Harry and Susannah had heard marvellous tales about the place: how it had sliding panels, and hollow walls, and niches up in the broad chimneys large enough to harbour a grown man. And there was word, too, of a vaulted chamber where hung a silver lamp that was kept burning both by night and day. At Winford was just such a chamber, but it was used mainly for storing crossbows and fowlers' nets and hawking gear, and only a small iron staple in the roof showed that just such a lamp had hung there for more than twice a hundred years—from the time that Dame Alice built the little oratory in the reign of King Edward the Second to the time that her descendant, Miles Clavenger, adopted the reformed faith in the reign of boyish, bookish King Edward the Sixth.

It is true that the Winford lamp was rekindled for a while during the next reign, when Queen Mary Tudor set fiercely about restoring the old religion in her perplexed and divided kingdom : but soon after her half-sister, the red-haired, demure Elizabeth, came to the throne, Miles Clavenger died, and there was no doubt about the sturdy Protestantism of his son and successor, Henry. This Henry was the grandfather of Harry and Susannah. They could not remember him, but they often gazed at his monument in the Clavenger chapel of the parish church. It was of skilfully carved and painted alabaster, showing him in plate armour, with a weeping lion at his feet wiping away its tears with one paw.

"If," remarked Susannah, pensively, "if our kinsfolk yonder at Brackenden were not recusants, maybe the Queen would have tarried there instead of at Winford, and then you would not have had to play Renown before her, or Ned——"

"Look, there *is* Ned!" cried her brother, jumping up so

suddenly that he knocked poor Lucrece to the ground. While Susannah, with loud cries of indignation, rescued her darling, Harry ran to meet Ned, glad to see his friend, and glad of any excuse to forget " most fair Eliza."

Edward Falconer was not, as Harry Clavenger was, a handsome boy. His nose had an upward tilt, his mouth was wide, and the hair on his head was more like tow or hay than human hair: but he had what Harry lacked, a look of alert intelligence and good humour. Except that his belted, full-skirted coat was of brown instead of blue stuff, and the clasp of his belt pewter instead of silver, there was little difference between his garments and Harry's. Together they attended the small grammar school vigorously conducted by Boanerges Birch, and together they hoped to pass into one of the great Universities, probably Oxford. Ned's father was a prosperous man, who combined the crafts of wool-merchant, leather-seller and farmer very successfully. His first-born son had no bent towards book-learning and needed none, for he would in course of time carry on the family business in all its branches; but, being an ambitious man as well as a shrewd one, he hoped to see his second boy a lawyer or a parson, or, in any event, a good scholar and a credit to his folk. Rumour said that Master Falconer had a mind to apply to the College of Heralds in London to devise a Coat of Arms for him and grant him and his descendants permission to bear it: but the Squire refused to believe that his tenant would fall into such folly, and waste his money on heralds' fees simply so as to be able to write " Esquire " after his name.

When Ned saw Harry coming towards him he let out a terrible growl—so terrible that it tickled his throat and made him choke.

" How now, goodman Monster," cried Harry, " are you going to dine upon our bones ? "

" Nay—but I am come to tell you, in all monsterly gentle-ness, that Master Birch would have you go to the great hall—

c.c.—5

your trumpet and your veil and your wings are there, and you must learn to blow the one and wear the other."

" My trumpet, my veil, my wings," groaned Harry. " Was there ever such foolish mumming! Yet if I had a grinning mask like yours, and gloves with long green claws upon them, I would not mind so much."

" The mask is hot and smells of glue," returned Ned. " Come, now, and you had better be perfect in your part, for our dominie is in no dovelike humour."

" Shall I come also?" asked Susannah, who had joined them.

" Nay—the strewing of the garlands cannot be rehearsed till the garlands are ready."

" They will be ready soon," said Susannah, " Tib and Prue are busy with the leaves at this hour—and I *ought* to be busy with the buds and the blossoms."

With these words she whisked Lucrece under her arm and, lifting her long and wide cherry-coloured skirt with her disengaged hand, she trotted away, her close-fitting white linen bonnet bobbing like a lily-bud in the breeze, and Blanche scampering excitely after her.

If the Clavengers of Plantagenet times could have returned to their old home in that year of grace 1589 they would have found it greatly changed but not out of all recognition. The ancient gatehouse remained, with its quaint imp grinning down from the vaulting of the porch—" Don Philip " was the name given to it by the children of this generation; many of the outbuildings, bakehouse, brewhouse, kitchen and stables were much as they had been of yore: strong outer walls still encircled the Manor, giving it the character of a fortress-dwelling-place as in the days when the first de Clavenger dug the moat and reared the masonry: but the traceried window of the gatehouse had been replaced by an oriel and the whole of the eastern side had been completely rebuilt by grandfather Henry, partly in rich, dark red brick laid herringbone-wise and partly in what was called magpie-work, black-and-white. The white was smooth plaster, the black, beams of wood painted with pitch and arranged in complicated designs.

It was in front of this new wing that Squire Francis had constructed his fine terrace. On the first floor he had knocked three rooms into one, to form that long gallery without which no gentleman's house was thought worthy of him. The solar had vanished, but where it had been was a room called the

GRANDFATHER HENRY'S WING

dining-parlour, panelled in chestnut wood with a design of masks and scrolls, and ceiled with exquisite plaster mouldings with the Clavenger arms surrounded by wreaths of oak-leaves. In the great hall the hearth had been moved from the centre to the side, and the old screen of fretted lace-like carving had been replaced by something in the new classical design, similar to the panels in the dining-parlour.

That dining-parlour was the room in which the Squire and Mrs. Clavenger took most pride. The polished table rested on four swollen-looking, barrel-shaped legs: along it lay a strip of Turkish carpet, red and blue; and there were woven mats upon the floor. For the children and other people of no particular importance square stools with leather seats were provided; but for the lord and lady of the Manor and any guest of high degree there were broad and stately chairs upholstered all over in Genoa velvet, shagged with fringe and studded with round, glittering brass nails. At

ELIZABETHAN FURNITURE

either end of the apartment was a sideboard or " court-cupboard " of walnut and rose-wood, adorned with various pieces of plate, flagons, salvers and salt-cellars, some of them dating from the days when Lionel of Antwerp had dined in the great hall, others of more recent date and workmanship. On the wall hung a large map of the world, printed upon linen and varnished over—Mercator's famous map, the first to show the East and West Indies.

This dining-parlour would not be large enough to hold the Queen and all her train, so, for the time being, the table was to be set forth again on the dais in the great hall, but with this difference—other tables would not now run the length of the hall so that the whole household might sit at meat under the same roof of ancient, smoke-seasoned oak. In front of the carved screen a rather creaky and shaky platform had been erected by the estate carpenter and upon its planks *The Triumph of Renown,* a pageant devised and written by Boanerges Birch, Bachelor of Arts, was to be played for the delight of Her Majesty.

When Harry and Ned entered from the garden they found Boanerges himself in the centre of the stage. In one hand he clutched a sheaf of crabbed-looking script, in the other a trumpet painted yellow. At his feet, in a confused heap, lay a grinning mask, a robe sewn with green scales, two swords of lath painted to resemble silver, a gold-coloured veil, a pair of wings fashioned of swans' plumes dyed pink, and a zig-zag strip of gilded wood—this last was to represent a thunderbolt, and when it was thrown a drum was to roll behind the scene. Huddled in one corner, shuffling their feet and looking much abashed, were three of his pupils, Jeremy, Joshua and Martin, the two first the sons of the carpenter who had rigged up the scaffolding, the last, the son of the blacksmith who had helped to make various small objects for use in the performance, including the iron frame-work supporting the pink wings. Joshua, dressed as a man, and Martin, in his sister's best gown, were to impersonate Wisdom and Virtue, while Jeremy, all in black, was to be Evil Intent, the Monster's servant.

Boanerges, a withered, hard-featured person in a close-fitting skull-cap and a long robe bristling with pewter buttons, was certainly *not* in his mildest mood, and his pupils were glad that he had left his rod in the school-room.

"Haste ye, haste ye," he roared, when he saw Harry and Ned. " On with your wings, Renown—on with your mask, Monster. Come, come, take your places, dispose yourselves

in your degrees. Wisdom, if you gape so, the Queen's Grace [1]
will think you are Folly—Virtue, look not so dismally, or
they will say that Virtue is punished instead of Vice. As
for you, Evil Intent, I would have you frown—and heave up
your shoulders to your ears—and walk with your knees
somewhat bent. So! That is better."

In the centre of the stage hung a pair of green curtains
to which was fastened a large label—*The Fortress Impregnable*:
to the right a piece of old arras-cloth (the same that had decked
the great hall more than a century before) was draped over
a bench supposed to be what Boanerges described as a " bosky
hill."

" Get you behind the curtains, Virtue, Wisdom and
Renown," he commanded his actors. " Listen for your cues—
have you your swords and your trump ? "

When they had obeyed, he made a sign to the Monster and
Evil Intent, who were to utter the opening lines. The subject
of their conversation is a certain fair Maiden-Queen dwelling
in the Fortress Impregnable.

" All maidens," growls the Monster, after a good deal of
flowery dialogue,

> " All maidens in such strongholds are my prey;
> Them to devour with me is holiday.
> Such was the nature of that Minotaur
> Who dwelt in Cretan Labyrinth of yore,
> And such mine is. Come, varlet, to your task."

Evil Intent expresses his readiness to obey his master, who then
gives him his orders in these words:

> " Go—with infected vapours foul and fell
> Blast her bright beauty; from the smoke of hell
> Distil a poison that shall do such hurt

[1] In Elizabethan days the sovereign was more often described as ' Her
Grace ' than as ' Her Majesty.'

As unto Hercules did Nessus' shirt;
Then with your thunderbolt of fearsome sound
Lay that proud fortress level with the ground,
What time I lie upon this bosky hill
Watching to see how well you do my will."

Evil Intent hurls the thunderbolt, but it falls harmlessly aside; then from the Fortress Impregnable—that is to say, from between the green curtains—emerge Virtue and Wisdom, with their swords. After a great deal of poetry, they slay the Monster and Evil Intent: the curtains part, and Renown, daughter of Wisdom and Virtue, is seen, perched on a small table covered with flame-coloured velvet. She blows her trumpet before descending, coming forward, and kneeling at the Queen's footstool, where she recites her " Fair Eliza " poem, while from right and left advance groups of little girls strewing tinsel flowers.

That was the plot of Boanerges Birch's little pageant: but if the story was simple, the dialogue was not. Every stanza was packed with classical allusions designed to please a learned Queen: and the Epilogue, spoken by Ned in the character of King Arthur, was in Latin. The ancient Celtic King was introduced as a compliment to the Tudors, who, tracing their descent from Cadwallader, were very proud of their Welsh ancestry.

During the rehearsal the unfortunate author was in a pitiful plight. None of the actors—except the Monster—remembered or spoke the lines correctly or used the right gestures. Evil Intent was so sheepish, Wisdom and Virtue were so awkward, Renown stammered so badly and blew the trumpet so half-heartedly that Boanerges sank down speechless with fury upon the bosky hill. He had threatened them with the rod, he had tried to encourage them with promises of cherries and comfits if they did better, but all to no purpose; and (if he had dared to do it) he would have informed Squire Clavenger that *The Triumph of Renown* would not take place after all.

While Boanerges was struggling with his cast another struggle only a little less fierce was going on in the old oratory where, among a jumble of hunting gear, the Squire kept his few books and papers, his vellum scrolls of ancestral shields and his estate accounts. With his elbows on the table and his hands supporting his head, Francis Clavenger was conning the list (thoughtfully provided by the Queen's Master of

Think your Country your home, the'inhabitants your neighbours, all freinds your children, and your children your own Sowli endeuouring to surpass all these' in liberality and good nature.

QUEEN ELIZABETH'S HANDWRITING

the Household) of the meats, drinks and delicacies habitually served at her board.

Except for a chapter from the Bible every evening and reports from his steward once a week, the Squire did little reading. The books forming his small library had been bought not because he cared much for them but because it was the fashion to possess them: *The Paradyse of Daynty Devises,* a collection of rather serious poems by a choirmaster; *A Posie of Gillo-flowers,* less serious poems, some translated from French and Italian, mixed with riddles and anagrams; *Euphues, the Anatomy of Wit,* and *Euphues and his England,* by John Lyly, two long romantic tales in language which honest Squire Francis secretly thought far too artificial and sugary, though, knowing that it was much the fashion at Court, he kept his opinion to himself. At least, having peeped into each volume, he was not bound to read them all through—nor did he try. Now, with a long sheet of closely-written paper in his hand, he sat conning line after line of close, difficult writing, his lips shaping each word as he puzzled it out. Though the Queen herself could—and often did—write the clear Italian hand then coming into favour, many people preferred the more angular, obscure " Old English " script and the Master of her Household was one of those people.

Old Squire Henry had held that his son had no need of bookish learning if he could manage a horse, wind a horn, and train and fly a falcon; but Francis Clavenger, though he seldom regretted his lack of such learning, determined that his son should be bred up as befitted the subject of a Queen who encouraged—and sometimes even rewarded—fine gentlemen who were also fine scholars. At this moment, wrestling with the spidery script, he wished that he could enlist the aid of Boanerges Birch or Parson Graves, neither of whom was at that moment within hail.

" Larks," he muttered, " partridges, plover, capon, pheasants, pigeons—blessed be Heaven Her Grace brings her own kitchen gear, for we have not above half the number of pots and cauldrons and roasting-spits that will be needed! What next—ah, lamb and kid: and then swan and goose—well, our poultry-yard will furnish the goose if not the swan."

He laid down the paper and heaved a deep sigh. Would his neighbours, the Fenworths of Haverley Abbey, make a better show than he? It was a painful thought.

" What comes now? " he asked himself, returning to his reading. "Carp and pike, salmon and tench, lamprey, haddock, sole. Why, the ocean-sea is not wide and deep enough to

hold so many fishes! And there is more to come—tarts,
fritters, syrups, eringo, pippins, cherries."

With something like a groan he turned the paper over
and tackled the other side.

" White wax for candles—rushes for the floor of the hall—
herbs, bitter and sweet—ginger, vinegar, mustard—fodder
for twenty horses—litter for the same. And there remains
Master Ribblestraw."

Tossing the large sheet aside, he picked up a smaller one,
inscribed in a delicate Italian hand.

From our shop in Cheapside, this V day of June, 1589.

Item: for one rich jewell of golde, being a Swan of mother-
of-perle on the one syde, the other syde ennammled white:
one of the wyngs garneshed with small diamonds: about the
necke a collar of small rubies clasped with a sparke of opall:
the said jewell to be despatched by a sure hande to the worship-
full Master Francis Clavenger, Esq.

By me, Ralph Ribblestraw, Alderman and Goldsmith of
London   ...   .   £57.

The worshipful Master Francis Clavenger began to do a little
arithmetic, putting down Alderman Ribblestraw's bill in
order to have all his fingers to calculate with.

"Heaven have mercy on me," he groaned at last. "Between
the King of Spain, whom God confound, and the Queen's
Grace, whom God save, and Master Ribblestraw, whom God
help me to pay for his handiwork, I am like to find myself
the poorer by two thousand pounds, not counting the twenty
that I paid to the College of Heralds for finding me a Welsh
ancestress."

Meanwhile, in one of the attics under the gables of Squire
Henry's wing, Susannah was helping the two maidservants,
Tib and Prue, to twine garlands of small tinsel flowers, yellow,
white and pink. With them was the twins' younger sister, six-
year-old Lettice, also doing her best to help—though without

much success, for she pricked her small, unskilful fingers on the wires round which the tinsel threads were wound.

Mrs. Clavenger was in the still-room, surrounded by trays of dried herbs, pots of honey, flasks and phials of various cordials, and piles of eringo—the candied roots of sea-holly then much prized as a sweetmeat. Beside her was old Audrey, wise, wrinkled, rheumatic old Audrey, who had been Francis Clavenger's nurse and was now housekeeper at the Manor.

"Have we remembered everything, good Audrey?" the lady was asking for the twentieth time that day, and for the twentieth time the housekeeper answered soothingly, "Rest you content, Madam, rest you content; nothing has been forgotten—no, nor will be."

"There is naught amiss with the eringo," said Mrs. Clavenger, twisting her hands in her beautiful apron of fine lawn embroidered with threads of black and silver. "We have the trick of making it crisp and sweet—I'll warrant there will be none such at Haverley. But it is the syrup of roses that I mislike."

"Tush, Madam," returned Audrey firmly. "It looks good and will taste better. Go to."

While they were thus employed the Squire joined them, his ruffled hair and furrowed forehead showing how much his recent occupation had upset him.

"Husband, husband," cried his lady, as soon as he appeared, "look at this syrup of roses—here in this crystal phial—is it as clear as that was that we made when your sister Deborah visited us? She swore she had never seen any so clear: but is not this something clouded?"

Her husband hardly glanced at the phial.

"Less clouded than my wit was when I was led into this undertaking," he said gloomily.

"Nay, sweet Frank, you could hardly have done otherwise. You could not stand aside when it became known that the

Queen's Grace was making a progress in these parts. Moreover, those upstart Fenworths of Haverley Abbey would have crowed over us if she had gone there and not come hither—and *they* have dwelt there only since King Harry the Eighth drove the monks forth and *we* have dwelt here since the Conqueror came. And, moreover——"

"And, moreover, there is still much to be done," interrupted the Squire, "and only ten days to do it in."

Some fourteen miles away, at what had once been the great Benedictine Abbey of Haverley, the family whom Mrs. Clavenger scornfully called "those upstart Fenworths" were also busily preparing for a royal visit. Gregory Fenworth, merchant, Member of Parliament for the seaport of Westhampton, had attracted the favourable notice of Henry the Eighth by stoutly supporting that fickle monarch in everything he chose to do—or to undo. While Miles Clavenger changed his faith partly from conviction and partly upon the family principle that a Clavenger must always follow his King, Fenworth had only one motive—self-interest coloured by ambition. Under Edward the Sixth he had received a grant of the Abbey of Haverley and all the rich lands that had once been the pride and care of the learned and charitable monks of St. Benedict. When the old religion was restored during Queen Mary Tudor's reign, he had shivered lest his new possessions should be taken from him and given back to the monks—as no doubt they would have been if the reign had lasted longer. As things fell out, he was left in undisturbed enjoyment of the royal gift. No one rejoiced more than Gregory and his grown-up sons when the half-Spanish Queen died and her half-Welsh, half-English younger sister, Elizabeth, reigned in her stead.

These Fenworths were pushful folk. While the Clavengers were well content to stay quietly at home, the Fenworths sat in House of Commons and on the bench of the Hampshire Justices of the Peace, and invested money very successfully in some of the daring sea-adventures of Drake and Hawkins and Frobisher. They also discovered that they had a Welsh great-grandmother ; a timely discovery, for the Queen seldom failed to show favour to loyal subjects who—like the House of Tudor itself—could trace their origin back to the land of Wales. Gregory's elder son, Gresham Fenworth (named after that famous merchant, the founder of the Royal Exchange) received a knighthood in 1587: and now, in the summer of 1589, the whole family were resolved to outshine everyone else in the south of England in the splendour of their entertainment to the Queen.

By turning the monks' fishpond into a lake they were able to arrange a water-pageant, with tritons, mermaids, naiads and nymphs. Sir Gresham, his brother and his two elder sons were to sing madrigals arranged for four voices by their own choirmaster and music-maker, Christopher Welbye, who also wrote the words for the water-pageant, and the music to accompany it, to be played upon the lute and viol. The small boys of the family were to enact the part of water-sprites—a task which they undertook with alacrity.

News of all these preparations reached Winford, and caused Squire Clavenger to clutch at his hair while his wife wrung her hands. They had no lake: they had no musician attached to their household: and the fashionable craze for part-singing had not yet invaded the Manor. The only person quite undismayed was Master Birch, who confided to Parson Graves that he was sure the poetry to be spoken by all those finny and scaly creatures would be far inferior to *The Triumph of Renown,* and much poorer in classical allusions: for Kit Welbye, though an honest fellow enough, had never studied either at Oxford or at Cambridge, and could not be expected to vie with one that was a Bachelor of Arts.

Parson Graves for his part had no desire to push himself forward in connection with the royal visit. Everyone knew that the Queen disapproved of the clergy marrying; and he was a married man, with a large family of small children. This was rather hard on Mrs. Graves, who had to choose between keeping well in the background or risking a sharp snub from the Queen's Grace: and there was a good deal of argument in the Vicarage—a house full of worldly noises, from the creaking of the cradle, the cooing of the baby and the whirr of the spinning-wheel to the contending voices of the clergyman and his wife.

At last the great day dawned, cloudless and clear. Thanks to the loyal labours of the Winford people the road from Haverley had been drained and levelled to some extent, and was less full of ridges and hollows than it was wont to be. Less dusty they could not make it, and the alternative between being choked with dust or spattered with mud remained. As the weather was dry, dust was the travellers' portion; and the approach of the royal cavalcade was visible a mile away by the clouds of chalky powder that were raised by the hooves of the horses and the wheels of the chariots.

The Queen's coach came first, escorted by pikemen on foot ; then three or four other coaches, less magnificent, conveying her ladies in waiting and one or two of her courtiers who were too old or too gouty for horse-riding. On either side trotted about half a dozen gentlemen of the neighbourhood, among whom Sir Gresham and his sons were conspicuous; and bringing up the rear was a large, lumbering waggon full of kitchen gear, and crowded with cooks, turnspits and scullions, all of whom looked exceedingly dignified.

When the procession reached the fringes of Winford village, the escorting horsemen, with many becks and bows and hand-wavings and hat-raisings, wheeled round and rode back in the direction whence they had come.

Meanwhile, beneath the old gatehouse of the Manor a breathless group awaited the coming of the Queen. The best tailor in Westhampton had been entrusted with the important task of providing the garments in which the Squire, his lady and their children were to welcome her: the best shoemaker in that town had been ordered to make shoes for them after the latest London fashion, with high cork heels.

Francis Clavenger was buttoned into a doublet of tawny velvet slashed with white satin and ornamented with loops of gold: his padded trunk-hose were of the same velvet, tied at the knee with broad ribbons to match the slashings. Slung over his left shoulder was a short cape of black brocade striped with rows of seed-pearls. His gloves were of white leather, fringed with black silk and so heavily perfumed that he had only to move his hand for everyone standing near to get a whiff of fragrance. The hat which he clutched nervously had a high crown and a narrow brim, was made of velvet to match his suit, and sported at one side a tuft of small white feathers. Nothing could have been stiffer or more snowy than the linen ruff encircling his neck unless it were the collar of gauze and narrow lace rising from Mrs. Clavenger's shoulders and forming a sort of fan-shaped screen behind her head.

The dress to which that good lady had devoted many hours of anxious meditation was of black velvet slashed with primrose yellow and quilled with much silver ribbon. Her farthingale—the drum-shaped hoop over which her skirt was draped—had not its equal for size in the whole county of Hampshire. In one hand she held a long-handled fan of yellow feathers and in the other a pomander—a silver-gilt ball with a pierced top containing aromatic vinegar, attached by a long chain to her girdle. She wore no hat, but a small wreath of flowers made of gilt wire and seed-pearls crowned her smoothly combed and tightly coiled hair.

As for the children, they made a delightful patch of colour, Harry all in white and the two little girls in sea-blue. Beyond them was a dingy patch, where Parson Graves and his wife,

Boanerges Birch, and one or two of the principal tenants were standing, wearing, it is true, their Sunday best, but tending to dull and sober greys and browns.

Everyone was ready and ranged in position much too early, and, in consequence, everyone was getting hot and peevish before the eagerly awaited moment came. The younger spectators suffered particularly, for their clothes were heavy and (in places) tight, and they found it difficult either to move about or to stand still. Harry's ruff gave him a lot of trouble, being wider and stiffer than the one he usually wore. Robin, the Squire's personal servant, had to come more than once and rearrange the folds with an implement made for that purpose and known as a poking-stick.

Among the elders every heart was beating faster at the thought of beholding the Queen. With the exception of Boanerges Birch, who had caught a far-off glimpse of her when she visited Oxford in his student days, none of them had ever seen her. All of them knew that her age was fifty-five; yet there was a general conviction that she was a sort of immortal goddess, a "Faerie Queen", as Master Edmund Spenser was to call her only a year later, for ever radiant, truly "an orient pearl of morn." To her people she represented security, prosperity, and national pride. It was her pleasure to pose as a poor feeble woman; but great Kings were outwitted by her, and strong men quailed beneath her eye—she would have been surprised if they had not. Later ages, looking back at her reign, may have seen more clearly than her subjects could see that she was completely unscrupu- lous, grimly avaricious, and capable of relentless cruelty. Yet she was also stout of heart, keen of sight, and to England as she herself claimed—"a most loving Prince." Only a small section withheld their loyalty—the Catholics, to whom she was a murderess as well as being a usurper. Two brief years had passed since she had sent to the block her kins- woman, Mary Stuart, Queen of Scots, whose claim to the

throne of England was rather better than her own. Even
Catholics like the Clavengers of Brackenden who held aloof
from plots against her life and were, at a pinch, ready to
fight in defence of the Protestant England over which she
ruled, regarded her without enthusiasm. But to the Clavengers of Winford St. Mary she was almost a divinity upon
earth.

Word had been sent from Haverley Abbey that the Queen,
having breakfasted at six-thirty on beef, manchets of bread
and brown ale, would reach Winford in time to partake of
dinner at the usual dinner-hour—eleven o'clock in the
morning. By ten-thirty the ringers were all in the belfry of
St. Mary's Church, grasping the ropes ready to ring a welcoming peal. The parish beadle, after desperate exertions, had
cleared the high road and the village of all beggars, pedlars,
cripples, gipsies, and other tattered wayfarers—only too
numerous since the dissolution of the monasteries had deprived
them of their ancient centres of succour and places of shelter.
A new class of vagabonds had come into being, desperate
and dangerous, and beadles were busy all over the land,
harrying, hunting and rough-handling them.

When, at last, the look-out on the top of the church tower
spied the dust-clouds upon the Haverley road and gave the
signal to the ringers, a joyous peal clanged forth. The crowds
lining the village street strained and swayed. The Squire
clutched his hat in one hand and the hilt of his sheathed
rapier in the other: his lady held her pomander to her nose
and sniffed vigorously. Lettice grabbed at Susannah's sleeve;
Harry stood rigid and solemn, flushed to the tips of his rather
sticking-out ears. Boanerges Birch first fixed his cap more
firmly on his skull and then hastily plucked it off: Parson
Graves folded his palms together as if about to pray and did
his best to look as if Mrs. Graves and three or four of their
children did not belong to him at all.

In spite of loyal efforts to level the road it was still scored by ruts which made the coaches jerk and bounce, and rise and fall, like small boats in a rough sea. The Queen's coach was the largest, the gayest with painted shields and gilded moulding: the harness of its six sturdy dappled horses was dangling with tassels and tinkling with bells. Such of the villagers as were not giving a helping hand to the ringers in the belfry or to the servants at the Manor had brought forth their wives and families and stood in excited groups in front of their lath-and-timber houses—small and flimsy houses enough, but larger and more solid than the little huts that had contented the villeins of Plantagenet days. The men had their flat woollen caps in their fists, ready to toss them in the air as the cavalcade passed: most of the women had swaddled babies in their arms, or toddlers in bunchy skirts whom they held up that they might see—and perhaps be seen. Every neck was craned, every foot stretched tip-toe, and cries of " God save Her Grace! ", " Long live the Queen ", broke forth in a variety of tones, deep and shrill. From the inside of the coach a loud, emphatic voice answered them: " I thank you," said the voice, " I thank you, my good people."

The Queen sat bolt upright, her unchanging smile leaving uncovered a row of teeth which reminded nobody of orient pearl, for they were discoloured by too much eating of sweetmeats. The swaying of the coach had tilted slightly to one side her wig of closely-curled reddish-golden hair over which were festooned strings of large pearls, emeralds and diamonds. Could this indeed be the fair Eliza, fabled to be lovelier than Helen of Troy? Her dead white, hollow cheeks were criss-crossed by a thousand tiny wrinkles: her high-bridged nose was as sharp as a bird's beak: no eyebrows over-arched her small, dark hazel eyes, and no lashes shaded them—those piercing, quelling, terrible eyes. Even the smile stretching her thin lips could not soften the sharpness of her glance.

Nobody had time to take in the details of her costume, and little was remembered later but a shimmer of jewels and a glow of silken stuffs, peach-pink and lily-pale. If anyone could have stolen a glimpse at the official list of her dresses they would have found the garments she wore that day described as being of " peche collored satten al over covered

with white cut-work." She sported both a ruff and a fan-shaped, lace-edged collar. This ruff, instead of encircling the whole throat as Mrs. Clavenger's did, was open in front, and the bodice, cut low, left bare Elizabeth's withered throat and chest. How many ropes of pearls dangled round her it would have taken some time to count. From the shortest rope swung a cross of gold set with three enormous emeralds, the gift of the Earl of Leicester—that ambitious Earl whom she would neither take as her husband nor allow to take Mary Queen of Scots as his wife, and whose emerald cross she wore often—and often touched sentimentally with the tips of her delicate fingers.

Almost before the people of Winford had realised that she was in their midst she had passed on: but the excitements of the day were not over, for there was to be a supper for all the Squire's tenants in the old tithe-barn, with plenty of beef and ale, prunes and raisins, rice and ginger; and the only vagabond whom the beadle had *not* driven away, an aged but active fiddler, was to play after the trestle-tables had been raised, so that all the lads and lasses might dance to their hearts' content.

When the royal coach heaved itself to a standstill before the old gatehouse, Squire Clavenger took a long step forward and then stood stock still. A simple country gentleman, he had had no courtly training to instruct him what he should do. Yet instinct served him well. As soon as the dazzling figure had descended and stood upon the crimson velvet spread for its golden-shod feet, he dropped upon one knee and bowed his head as if blinded by the brightness of the vision.

CHAPTER IV

"MOST FAIR ELIZA"

AFTERWARDS the Clavenger children used to try earnestly to recollect exactly what happened at every stage of the Queen's visit to their home. It was strangely difficult to do so. They—and their elders, too—had been so excited that it all seemed like a dream: but Harry remembered how a deep voice from between the narrow lips had called him "a likely sprig," and Susannah and Lettice how she had flicked their cheeks very gently with her fingers. Poor Parson Graves would gladly have forgotten how the royal eyes had rested disapprovingly upon Mrs. Graves and the children, and how the royal comment had been "a parson married is a parson marred." The Queen, who always liked good-looking gentlemen, was exceedingly gracious to the Squire; and though she paid comparatively little attention to Mrs. Clavenger, she at least did not—and could not—object to her existence. Her Master of the Household had mentioned the fact—thoughtfully communicated to him beforehand by Francis Clavenger—that one of the ancestresses of the family had been a Welshwoman, Dame Eleanor, wife of Sir Thomas, the same who had entertained Prince Lionel of Antwerp.

"Ha!" said the Queen, "methinks our ancient principality stands in no peril of being either forgotten or dishonoured in these southern regions of our realm. Here be leeks springing up among roses!"

As the Squire could think of nothing to say in reply, he contented himself with another very low bow, hoping that the allusion was more for *his* ancestress than for the Welsh great-grandmother whom the Fenworths had somehow hunted up. The Queen then requested to be shown the knot-garden, as she desired to compare it with the one planted by her kingly father at Hampton Court; and while she was inspecting it Mrs. Clavenger had an opportunity to seek the opinion of the Mistress of the Queen's ladies as to whether the sleeping-apartment prepared for Her Grace contained everything that she was likely to need or accustomed to have.

As the Manor had not been planned with an eye to royal guests the finest bedchamber was naturally that set aside for the Squire and his lady—and it was this bedchamber which was prepared for Elizabeth. The great four-post bedstead was hung with its noblest needlework curtains, embroidered by Mrs. Clavenger in a bewildering variety of tiny stitches and rich colours. Upon a carved coffer of walnut wood were set forth a silver-gilt ewer and basin and a little bowl of tawny-white soap balls. And the Venetian mirror which was the pride of Mrs. Clavenger's heart had been carefully moved from the long gallery and fixed upon the tapestried wall of the bedroom.

The Mistress of the Queen's ladies admired the bed-hangings, felt the huge feather mattresses and pillows and nodded, expressed herself as satisfied with the washing-arrangements, and cast an approving eye at the panel-backed oak chair and the velvet-covered footstool by the hearth; but when she caught sight of the mirror she frowned and shook her head.

"Nay," said she, "no such toy must come within Her Grace's sight. 'Tis seven years since she hath seen herself in a looking-glass—and now you will find none at Richmond or at Windsor, at Nonsuch or at Hampton Court. Have it taken speedily down and away, Madam."

"Alack, alack, where can it be stowed!" moaned Mrs. Clavenger, in a sad fluster.

"Some place where the Queen is not likely to go," hinted the older woman. "Have you no attics or lumber-rooms?"

"There is the nursery," said Mrs. Clavenger, brightening.

" I will tell the children to put away their balls and battledores while it is up yonder. And I thank you for the warning—heartily."

And she bustled off, calling loudly for Justin, one of the heftiest of the younger menservants.

Very soon the beautiful mirror was unhooked from the wall and carried up the narrow, twisting stairs which no one wearing a farthingale could possibly have climbed. Unlike their young ancestors in Plantagenet times, the little Clavengers of Tudor days *had* a nursery, a room of their very own, where they could keep their toys and play together as noisily as they pleased. Justin balanced the mirror carefully on the top of a great oaken cupboard, gazing with some interest at the reflection of his own red-cheeked face and his best jerkin of russet frieze. It was seldom that he had an opportunity to do so undisturbed.

Meanwhile the Queen was tripping on her high-heeled brocade shoes along the sanded path of the knot-garden. By a gracious wave of her hand she had invited Harry, Susannah and Lettice to follow her, and she made some smiling remark to Squire Francis about an " escort of innocents." At certain points the path was so narrow and the clipped hedges so high that Mrs. Clavenger could hardly squeeze her way through when wearing her largest farthingale, and the Queen's was larger even than that; but the Squire, with great gallantry and with some peril to his tawny-velvet tunic and his fringed gloves, contrived to make a way for her.

After the knot-garden and the bowling-green had been seen and commended, the Queen hinted that she would like to visit some of the main rooms of the house, which her host was only too glad to show her. Mrs. Clavenger joined them in the long gallery, where, among other treasures, there was a musical instrument of the kind called " the virginals." It was a keyboard instrument with a double row of ivory keys, black and white; its case and the inner surface of its up-tilted lid were painted in gay colours, little figures of men and women disporting themselves among rocks, waterfalls and willow-trees. The Queen paused, admired the painting, declared that one of the feminine forms was assuredly the goddess Diana, "whom," she added with a simper, "I account mine own, being that she was a huntress and a virgin. You love music, Clavenger? You have a musician in your household, as have the Fenworths at Haverley?"

Mrs. Clavenger darted a reproachful glance at her husband, for, although she cared for music as little as he did, she had long lent a curious ear to tales of the musical activities of the "upstart Fenworths." The Squire, slightly confused, explained that for his part he knew more of hunting calls than of madrigals, but that he had a mind to make his daughters skilful upon the virginals, when he could find an honest fellow apt to teach them.

"Let it be soon," said the Queen. "Young fingers move nimbly and young wits learn apace."

As she spoke, she touched some of the keys as if hardly aware of what she did, and everyone recognised the air she was playing—the old fiddler was practising it in the barn at that very moment, and it was often heard when the villagers danced round the maypole on the Green. No one had the courage to speak until Lettice, clapping her hands in excitement, cried "Sellenger's Round! It is Sellenger's Round!"; and then, terrified at what she had done, hid her face against her mother's farthingale.

"Do not chide her," commanded Elizabeth, seeing the faces of both father and mother grow stern; "she speaks truly—it is Sellenger's Round; and—did they but know it—the milkmaids keeping time to it on the grass are happier than their Queen—their hearts are as light as their heels, and heartsease is not for her."

With these words she cast down her eyes and sighed; after which she observed that she herself played the virginals most commonly when she was alone, "the better to shun melancholy." Melancholy—that, said Susannah to herself, that means sadness—or what old Audrey called "doleful dumps." Was it possible that a great Queen could ever need to shun it?

Meanwhile, the Queen's own cooks, eagerly aided by the Manor servants, had prepared a dinner the like of which had never been seen within those walls. There was hardly room upon the high table for all the dishes of each course, and Mrs. Clavenger, watching her royal guest, felt that nothing could be amiss, so heartily did the royal jaws work. When this good lady saw anything new and strange she was wont to clamour loudly to the Squire, demanding that it should at once be introduced at the Manor; but now she looked without enthusiasm at the unfamiliar object placed beside the Queen's place by the Master of the Household. It was a graceful two-pronged fork of silver-gilt with an enamelled handle.

Not only Mrs. Clavenger but the Squire and the three children watched with awe while Elizabeth speared portions of meat or fish, lifted them on the prongs and then thrust them into her mouth. What skill! What steadiness of hand! How was it possible to perform that feat without any danger of thrusting a morsel against one's cheek, one's chin, one's nose—or even pricking one's face! Mrs. Clavenger confessed her astonishment to the Mistress of the Queen's ladies, who explained that this new-fangled notion had been brought from Italy and had delighted the Queen as it enabled her to enjoy her dinner without dirtying her hands. Last Christmas she had graciously presented a similar implement to one or two highly favoured friends: but not all of them had had the courage to make use of her gift.

Much to the content of the Squire and his wife, the syrup of roses was gravely commended and the pippins from the Manor orchard were pronounced to be fully as good as those that were so well loved by King Harry the Eighth. Then the trestle table was removed, a footstool was brought for the Queen's feet, and she was informed that if it were her good will and pleasure the boys of the Winford grammar school would forthwith enact before her a brief interlude or pageant, invented and composed by their master, and entitled *The Triumph of Renown*.

"Let us share in this triumph," said the Queen, with a bend of her head—upon which the wig had been put straight by now. On either side of her chair were grouped the Squire and Mrs. Clavenger, the gentlemen and ladies of her household, and a few privileged friends and neighbours of the family: from the shadow of the doorway peered the miller, the carpenter, the blacksmith, and other worthy villagers who, with their wives and their elder children, were mercifully permitted to catch a one-sided glimpse of the performance.

Behind the curtains of the Fortress Impregnable Boanerges Birch was grouping Wisdom, Virtue and Renown in their correct positions and hissing desperate instructions into their ears. Ten days of hard labour had made the young actors word-perfect, but another ten minutes of delay might well have driven every syllable from their minds.

By ringing a small silver bell the Squire was to give the signal for the Monster and Evil Intent to advance from either side of the rickety little platform and begin the play, but, in his good-natured desire not to dismay the actors by doing this too soon, he put it off so long that there was some perplexity behind the scenes. At last, however, the tinkle made itself heard, and the Monster, drawing a deep breath, began to crawl forward. To meet him came Evil Intent, garbed in black and walking with his knees bent—as desired by the author.

"Behold in me a monster fierce and fell——"

The first words came forth a little unsteadily, for through the eye-holes of the mask Ned could catch glimpses of a blur of brightness which he knew must be the Queen. Soon, how-

ever, he plucked up courage and uttered his alarming lines
with a vigour which brought a smile of real amusement to
the lips of "fair Eliza."

"Who doth inhabit yonder island tower,
    Whose chalky walls defy old Neptune's power?"

To answer him Evil Intent crept nearer.

"What, Monster, wot you not there dwelleth there
    A royal Maid as wise as she is fair?"

And at great length, with many allusions to famous beauties,
and goddesses, and nymphs, Evil Intent described the astonish-
ing loveliness of the lady in the Fortress Impregnable, while
the Monster kept up a low growling.

"'Fore Heaven," remarked a deep voice, "a very fearsome
Monster—yet methinks Evil Intent is a gentler beast than he is
wont to be."

It was the Queen who spoke, thus showing that she was
paying close attention to the performance and also that she
was struck by the contrast between the roars of the Monster
and the bleats of his companion.

Boanerges Birch, lurking behind the green curtains, tried
to convey to the quivering Jeremy that he must play his
part with more fire: but a glimpse of the schoolmaster's
clenched fist and angry face only made the boy quake more.
He nearly forgot the lines in which he declared his readiness
to obey the Monster's orders, and when he hurled the thunderbolt it fell short of the target and flopped foolishly down on
the stage. Boanerges in his fury peered forward so far that
the Queen could see his head poking out between the
curtains.

"Nay, goodman dominie," said she, with a gruff chuckle,
"be not wroth—this is an allegory—the thunderstones of
malice must ever fall short of any Fortress truly Impregnable."

Then she chuckled again, for a sudden loud drum-tap from
within the Fortress showed that someone had remembered

rather too late that a peal of thunder should follow a thunder-bolt. At last the curtains parted and Wisdom and Virtue came forth, each with a band round his brow bearing his name in silver characters, so that there might be no mistake about it. Wisdom wore a doublet and hose of grey laced with silver and Virtue a gown of violet damask sewn with golden spangles. Each waved a wooden sword shimmering with silver paint, and it would have been difficult to say which of the two put more energy into the task of slaying Evil Intent and his terrible master. It is true that poor Jeremy was only too thankful to be slain; indeed, he laid himself down quite flat before Virtue's sword had touched him.

"Sharp is the sword of Virtue," remarked Elizabeth, " it slays before it smites! "

Ned was resolved that he would be more difficult to kill. At the rehearsals he had crumpled up as soon as Wisdom's blade clattered against his mask, but now, excited by the presence of the Queen and by her comments, which were so emphatically spoken that he could hear them even through the flaps of his headgear, he introduced some action entirely new. To the amazement of Boanerges, he grasped the sword between his paws and very nearly tugged it from the hands of the startled Joshua. Then he pretended to gnaw it with his long teeth; and then he slapped it right and left in spite of Joshua's efforts to keep it steady. Virtue, seeing Wisdom hard pressed, now came to his partner's aid, but the Monster continued to struggle and—only just out of the sight of the audience—Boanerges continued to bob to and fro in much agitation.

The Queen, who realised that she was witnessing something not included in the original plan of the interlude, checked herself in the middle of one of her barking laughs and called out, "Die, Monster, die—when Virtue aids Wisdom what else can a poor Monster do ? "

Ned, a little frightened at his own audacity, obediently

flopped quite flat and spoke the lines which ought to have announced several minutes earlier that the terrible beast had been overcome.

"Vanquished beneath these conquering blades I lie;
    Lo, I am slain—I faint—I fall—I die!"

"By my faith," said Elizabeth, "I would all Monsters were as mannerly."

Now it was time for Harry, his pink wings waggling on his shoulders, his azure robe wrapping itself round his ankles, to step down from the inner part of the Fortress Impregnable blowing his trumpet as he did so. Wisdom and Virtue, both out of breath as the result of their tussle with the Monster, drew back the green curtains and summoned their daughter to come forth:

"Draw near, thou mighty maid yclept Renown,
    Thou wingèd guardian of Eliza's crown——"

and a great many more lines of the same sort, which they recited "turn about".

Meanwhile the unfortunate Harry stood stiff with fright, his perch rocking slightly beneath his feet. With wide-open eyes he gazed at the row of faces, especially at one face apart from the others and higher than they—a chalk-white face under a wig of gingerbread-coloured curls. Then, remembering what he had to do—and also what would happen to him if he failed to do it—he raised the trumpet to his lips and blew into it all the breath he had in his body. At the last rehearsal he had produced a blast which, if not ear-splitting, was reasonably loud and clear: but now only the faintest and feeblest of toots was heard. What must he do next? The boy lowered the shaking hand that held the trumpet and began, in an equally unsteady voice:

"Renown am I—my trump with brazen sound
    Awakes the echoes all the globe around."

The Queen had good-naturedly restrained her mirth at the

faintness of the trumpet-blast, but to hear it described as waking the echoes all round the world was too much for her gravity. Out pealed the jolly, boisterous laugh that she had inherited from her father, King Henry, and down from his perch tumbled Harry Clavenger, turning an involuntary somersault across the stage and ending up with his heels in the air directly opposite the Queen's footstool.

A gasp rose from the audience and a groan broke from the lips of Boanerges Birch. The Squire turned purple, his wife turned pale: and when Wisdom and Virtue had helped Renown to rise it was seen that Harry was in tears, not only because he had bumped the back of his head but also from sheer terror and shame. The veil of golden gauze which had hidden his close-cropped hair had fallen off, and in scrambling to his feet he had gathered up his robe so high that everyone could see a definitely boyish pair of stockings and breeches underneath. Instead of a graceful and stately allegorical figure there stood before the Queen only a flushed, ruffled and abashed small boy.

Boanerges Birch could contain himself no longer. Frowning horribly he emerged from the Fortress Impregnable, only to be hailed by the Queen as "Goodman dominie" and bidden to advance. At the sound of her voice his eyebrows relaxed and he came forward bowing low.

"God's death, goodman dominie," said Elizabeth, loud enough for everyone to hear, "we have seldom seen a better fable. Renown—was not that your meaning, goodman dominie?—Renown may tumble headlong, but if Wisdom and Virtue be at hand to raise her up, she will not lie long in the dust."

Master Boanerges Birch bowed even lower than before. He dared not contradict the Queen, or tell her plainly that his meaning had been quite different. Suddenly realising that he was an intruder on the scene, he withdrew again into the Fortress Impregnable.

Harry, hardly knowing what he did, picked up his veil and his trumpet, envying the Monster and Evil Intent who for the moment had nothing to do except remain prone upon the planks. And then from right and left the little girls with their tinsel garlands, three of them on either side, began timidly to advance. Susannah led the right-hand group, and as she drew near her twin she whispered to him the first words of his final speech :

" Most fair Eliza, orient pearl of morn! "

Harry heard, gulped, drew himself erect, repeated the line in a voice which startled him (and everyone else) by its high pitch, and finished the speech at a brisk gallop without many stumbles on the way.

Meanwhile the Monster had crawled quietly out of sight and was hastily replacing his mask and scales with the tinsel diadem and crimson doublet of King Arthur. At the right moment, and without a trace of shyness, he walked to the centre of the little stage and recited in a steady voice, with the correct gestures, the Latin epilogue in which King Arthur greeted his sister-monarch " *Elizabetha nitidissima, pulcherrima, speciosa,*"—Elizabeth, the most brilliant, the most beautiful, the most splendid. To all these compliments the Queen listened with a smile in which there was neither amusement nor bashfulness, though she held her fan up before her face in a modest manner once or twice. And then *The Triumph of Renown* ended with all the players kneeling in a drift of glittering blossoms, silver, gold and pink, and raising their hands in salutation with a cry of " *Vivat Regina!* "

From the day—thirty-one years before—that she ascended the throne, Elizabeth had possessed the truly royal and very useful knack of bestowing much pleasure and winning much love by uttering a very few skilfully-chosen words. She mastered her queenly craft so thoroughly that it became second nature, and the most appropriate phrases rose effortless to her lips. Added to this graciousness was a kindly desire that the schoolmaster should be spared humiliation and his scholars a sharp dose of the rod.

"Come forth again, goodman dominie," she commanded: and Boanerges obeyed, with his skull-cap in his hand.

"They serve us well," proclaimed the Queen, "and well deserve our princely commendation, that breed up the youth of our realm in good Latinity and other branches of humane letters. Your interlude has contented us, master dominie, and we find the allegories therein both apt and dutiful. Therefore we make known our pleasure that your scholars should enjoy a long day's holiday to mark this our visit to Winford St. Mary."

Yet again Boanerges bowed: and from the kneeling groups of small boys and girls grateful eyes were lifted to the unforgettable face inclined graciously towards them. The interlude was done—for which Harry was quite as thankful as he was for the prospect of a holiday from school: and Mrs. Clavenger came forward to offer comfits and spiced wine to the Queen upon a salver of silver-gilt while the Squire presented an embroidered napkin for her fingers.

Scarcely glancing at the lady, Elizabeth fixed her keen unwinking gaze upon Francis Clavenger, his well-shaped nose, his fine eyes of a deep greyish-blue, under strongly-marked brows of which one sometimes jerked upwards, his particularly neat and handsome leg in its flame-coloured stocking. Without averting her glance, she stretched out her hand for a comfit and nibbled it between her discoloured teeth.

"It suits well," said she, still nibbling, "with the love we bear our subjects that we both heed their virtues and reward the same. You, Clavenger, belong to one of those ancient families that are the surest prop of a lawful throne: there runs in your veins some vagrant drop of Welsh blood, drawn from the venerable stock whence we ourselves derive. Moreover, we are informed that when Don Philip's fleet was making ready to put to sea you were among those of our trusty lieges who furnished forth ships to oppose his proud galleons. The napkin, if it please you."

The Squire, who, in his confusion at this royal discourse, had forgotten all about the napkin, hastily presented it. Instead of returning the oblong of embroidered linen to him when she had wiped the tips of her fingers she laid it across the arm of her chair and said, with a sort of gruff graciousness, "And now, if it please you, your sword."

With a fumbling hand—for he knew what this meant—Francis Clavenger tugged his rapier out of

PHILIP II OF SPAIN

its sheath and offered the hilt to the Queen; and his wife nearly dropped the salver and all its comfits and crystal phials upon the floor, for she, too, understood. A great day, a memorable day! No longer would the upstart Fenworths imagine themselves to be of more account than the Clavengers: no longer would the Squire—nay, a Squire no

more—groan at the cost of entertaining royalty. Like a
person in a dream she watched her husband kneel, saw his
own blade tap him briskly upon his puffed and padded
shoulder, and heard the voice of Elizabeth saying, " Rise up,
Sir rancis Clavenger! "

The twins also understood: had they not heard such matters
spoken of many times? But Lettice was too young to understand, and she felt nothing but alarm when the Queen touched
her father with the sword. Looking wildly at her mother, she
was surprised to see her smiling with such an air of joy that
she forgot her terror and smiled back again.

At six o'clock the high table was again garnished and
spread, and the handiwork of the royal cooks—aided by the
Manor cooks—was set before the Queen. There was joy
among the serving-men, the tenants and the villagers, for
with the news of the knighting of the lord of the Manor
had spread the information that seven casks of the best ale
were to be broached that they might all drink the health of
Her Grace and of Sir Francis. Justin had even started a
rumour that an ox might be roasted whole upon the Green
as had been done when the twins were born.

Though Elizabeth liked good looks she also liked quick
wits, and she did not find both these qualities in the new-
made knight. Growing a little weary of his brief, awkward
answers to her remarks and convinced that his lady would
be even less interesting, she summoned Boanerges Birch
to come and sit near her, and plunged into a learned conversation with him about the Latin poets. When she heard
that he was an Oxford man, she reminded him how she had
visited his University some twenty years before and Latin
plays had been enacted before her by the scholars.

" May it please Your Grace," said Boanerges, proudly,
" I was then in the groves of learning. I was one of the mad
wags that did make noises as of a cry of hounds beneath your
windows—the hunting of Duke Theseus it was."

" Were you so, in faith? " cried the Queen. " Why then, it seems that even as the acorn grows into an oak a mad wag may grow into a grave and reverend dominie."

After supper the company betook themselves to the long gallery, where Elizabeth played a game of chess with her Master of the Household and then called for her needle and continued the piece of stitchery upon which she was at that time engaged—a book-cover of blue velvet embroidered with threads of silver and gold, and set with tiny rubies and pearls. It was to serve as the binding of a small Bible— " a book," said the Queen, " that I love ever to have at my pillow."

This remark alarmed Mrs. Clavenger, who had not thought of putting a Bible—or any other book—on the walnut-wood table beside the bed destined for the Queen. She made a sign to Harry to come to her, and whispered in his ear that he must run forthwith to his father's closet, and fetch thence the larger and finer of the two Bibles kept there—the one with the picture at the beginning in which King Henry the Eighth was shown distributing copies of God's Word among his kneeling subjects. This he was to bear in his own hands to the great bedchamber and set upon the table by the bed.

Nothing loth, the boy sped away. He was growing weary of sitting bolt upright, motionless and mute, watching the Queen's needle rise and fall as she stitched. When he had carried out his mother's behest he did not return to the gallery but crept off to see if he could find Ned. It was not yet nine o'clock and the light lingered in the sky. From the barn by the Green came the scrape of one busy fiddle and the tap of many dancing feet. On the Green itself a small group of boys was playing leap-frog, and Harry saw at once that Ned was the boy who was at the moment " giving a back."

" Ned," he cried, " when that course is run, come hither! "

"I will come!" Ned called back cheerfully.

A few moments later he joined his friend at the edge of the Green.

"How, Harry," said he, "still in doleful dumps? Why, what ails you, man? You are not to be beaten—the Queen's Grace took heed thereof—and we are to keep holiday to-morrow."

"Nay, it is not that. But, Ned—you heard what they said—about the playing of Latin plays at Oxford. I did not know."

"Why, what if they do? That will be rare sport."

"For you, maybe: but not for me. I have had my fill of play-acting now and for ever. And if I must needs begin again when I go to Oxford, I will pray my father that I may go to Cambridge instead."

"For all you know they have Latin plays there also. I'll warrant they do. And I am for Oxford; so I will thank you not to wend otherwhere. If they have Latin plays, you need not bear a chief part; Master Boanerges spouted no Latin—you heard what he said—he made noises as of a cry of hounds."

"I could do that," agreed Harry, more or less consoled.

An hour later Sir Francis, carrying a great branched candle-stick with a cluster of flickering candles, escorted his guest with much ceremony to her bedchamber and respectfully wished her good night.

"Such nights," returned the Queen, "are for such as you. For such as me, who bear the weight of the whole realm upon my brows, the hours of sleep must be few."

And, with a pensive shake of the head, she entered the room.

Before Sir Francis had reached the head of the staircase he heard the bolts of the bedchamber door being drawn on the inside.

"Dame," he said to his wife, when he joined her in the second-best bedchamber, "I marvel that Her Grace should bolt her door. What does she fear? I told her that four of my trustiest servants would keep ward all night. Is it because I am akin to those Popish knaves at Brackenden that she is so unquiet?"

"Nay, Sir Francis, nay," returned his lady, wrestling with the clasp of her ruff. "If she had feared them of Brackenden would she have visited us at Winford?"

"True, dame, true," agreed the newly-dubbed knight. "Maybe it is because she would fain read God's Word before she lays her down to sleep."

Lady Clavenger had her own ideas upon the subject, not wholly unconnected with the royal wig: but she felt that so profane a suggestion would not be well received and contented herself by remarking that she was thankful now that she had persuaded her husband to buy that silver-gilt ewer and basin last Martinmas-time. It was well for Harry's peace of mind that he could not hear her next remark.

"And *now*, husband, *now*, Sir Francis, you must act as befits a knight and one that will shortly be a Justice of the Peace—for a Justice of the Peace you cannot fail to be named —you must act as befits a gentleman of that quality—truly you must, Frank."

"What does *that* portend?" asked Sir Francis, uneasily. "When you call me 'Frank' I know that you wish to win me to your own way of thinking."

"You must have your own musician—as the Fenworths have—and there must be singing of catches and madrigals in the long gallery here as there is in the long gallery at Haverley."

Sir Francis groaned, but did not say Nay.

"If you will spare *me* the task of strumming on a lute or hallo'ing in a chorus——" he muttered.

"No need, no need," said Lady Clavenger, quickly. "Why, you need not even *listen*, unless you have a mind. Harry can learn to play upon the lute or the viol de gamba and to sing. Poor child, he fared ill to-day, but it was no fault of his. And Susannah, I warrant, will be an apt scholar upon the virginals—and we can find some sweet-voiced neighbours to join us in learning to make harmony."

"I do perceive," growled Sir Francis, pulling on his nightcap, "that I am to pay for my new honour for the rest of my mortal life."

Meanwhile the Queen had retired to rest and, propped up against Lady Clavenger's largest and softest feather pillow, she was reading by the light of one slender, unsteady candle. The book she held in her hand was not the Bible but a small volume of philosophy in the Greek tongue.

Presently all the candles in Winford Manor were quenched, and silence—except for a snore here and there or the squeak of a mouse behind the wood-work—filled its rooms and galleries. Twenty leagues away, over the Wiltshire border, in the home of the Popish Clavengers, a small, spare man dressed like a pedlar of the poorer sort, was holding an earnest argument with the head of that family.

"It is time for me to go, my son," said the small man, gently but with an air of authority, "I am waited for else-where."

"But, good Father," protested Ambrose Clavenger, "wait only till the Queen has returned to London. If you were caught upon the road, who would believe that you— that we—meant her no harm? You would be carted to Tyburn and hanged—and this ancient stronghold of the true faith laid in ruins."

The two men, one tall and good-looking, dressed in rich though sober-coloured array and the other puny, insignificant, almost in rags, were standing beside a gap in the panelling of the dining-parlour at Brackenden. An oblong of wood, skilfully concealed by the carving, had been slid back and inside could be seen a narrow staircase of brick. This com-municated with a tiny, windowless cell in the thickness of the chimney. From this cell the disguised priest had just descended and to it Ambrose Clavenger was pressing him to return.

"I know, Father," continued the Squire of Brackenden. "that death has no terrors for *you*—and I know that loss of worldly gear ought to have no terrors for *me*. But I beseech you—for the sake of my son Philip whom you baptised—so that he may hold this house and these lands when I am gone, and keep the lamp of the true faith burning at Brackenden——"

The priest seemed touched by this appeal, but hesitated still.

"Bethink you, Father," pleaded Ambrose Clavenger. "It is not yourself alone—nor myself and my son. While the Queen is in these parts this house will be watched night and day. At any moment a magistrate may come and question me. Up yonder in the chimney they will never find you—the trick of the panel is too subtle for that—but if you were at large—if you were taken—alas, is there a Catholic family for fifty leagues around that would not be punished, and that most cruelly?"

"That is true, my son—that is most unhappily true."

"Then you will go back to your hiding-place? You will? You will go now?"

The priest nodded, and without another word slipped through the opening and began to ascend the stair. Clavenger touched a spring hidden in the carving, and the panel slid back into its place. When, barely an hour later, Sir Gresham Fenworth arrived, with a small troop of horsemen, to search the house for perilous visitors, he could find nobody answering to that description.

By that time it was broad daylight, and breakfast was being prepared for the Queen at Winford—manchets of wheaten bread, flagons of brown ale and platters of beef. Sir Francis and his wife could hardly realise that the royal sojourn would soon be over, for Elizabeth proposed to dine at Mere Castle, ten leagues on the road to London, and her departure was fixed for nine o'clock. Punctually at that hour her coach-horses were harnessed, her household were in readiness, and the ringers were back in the belfry to ring a farewell peal. The quaint stone imp who now bore the name of Don Philip looked down upon the patch of brave red velvet spread for the Queen's feet as she walked under the gatehouse to her waiting coach. All the Clavengers came with her, but she paid little heed to any of them except Sir Francis.

"Ha, man," she said to him, with a tap of her fan on the shoulder that had felt the tap of the sword, "ha, man, did not the head of a knight make a deeper dent in the pillow last night than the head of a squire could make the night before? Nay, look not so foolishly—we thank you for your good cheer, and here is our hand upon it."

Feeling little less foolish than he looked, Sir Francis took the hand she held out to him and kissed it with such vigour and devotion that a small pink patch remained for a moment upon its whiteness. Then he assisted her to climb into the coach before mounting his favourite dapple-grey and wheeling round to form part of her escort on the first stage of her journey northward.

Lady Clavenger and the children stood in the porch until the sound of hoofs and wheels died away. It seemed impossible that the Queen had gone: but then it seemed equally impossible that she had ever come. When they returned to the great hall it had a bleak and shabby air—the empty stage, the vacant chair of state, the tinsel garlands and the painted swords. Even Blanche and Sweetheart, the two spaniels that had frisked so gaily round the Queen's farthingale as she came forth, now drooped their tails and seemed depressed.

"The bells have ceased, Mother," ventured Harry, with a slightly apprehensive glance at her ladyship. What would her humour be? Would she chide him because of his head-long tumble from the Fortress Impregnable the day before, and the sorry figure he had cut as Renown? But she did not feel like chiding. This was her only son. Five daughters God had sent her, Susannah, Katherine, Lettice, Judith and Joan, and of these, three—dark-eyed Katherine, ailing Judith, and merry, golden-haired Joan, had died in early childhood and would one day be carved in a solemn row kneeling behind their mother's effigy on her tomb of painted alabaster in Winford Church. She was an affectionate mother according to the stern notions of the times, but she would have given all her little girls, the living and the dead, rather than lose her handsome, sturdy boy.

"The bells, mother," said Harry again, "they have ceased."

"That means," returned Lady Clavenger, "that her coach —the Queen's coach—is now out of sight. We must be ready to welcome Sir Francis—your father—when he turns back and rides home. I would I might bid the ringers ring again, but I fear me they have quitted their ropes by now."

"Mother," said Lettice, emboldened by the unusual softness of Lady Clavenger's expression, "did—did the Queen's Grace eat all the eringo—all the pretty comfits?"

"Nay, child—there are enough left and to spare. It is fitting that ye should regale yourselves upon this great day, now that your father is made a knight. If comfits were lacking, more could be brought—yea, enough for Blanche, and for Sweetheart, and for Lucrece, too—had Lucrece any teeth to bite withal."

"Lucrece is to have a new name as she cannot have any comfits," announced Susannah, smoothing down the doll's stiffly-pleated taffetas gown. "She is not to be called Lucrece any more—she is to be called ' most fair Eliza! ' "

CHAPTER V

THE SKY DARKENS

" MASTER ENDYMION, think you there will be fish in the moat when it is full of water?   Shall we be able to drop a line from the window of the dining-parlour and draw up a dace or a trout? "

" Or a sturgeon or a whale! "

" Nay, Master Endymion, do not mock me.   It would be rare sport."

" Do you fear we may go hungry when there is moat-water between us and the orchard? "

" Nay, Master Endymion—not with all those flitches of bacon and barrels of meal that are stored in the cellar, and——"

Master Endymion silenced the speaker with a warning glance, for a third person had quietly drawn near—a sour-faced, stiff-necked man with closely cropped red hair. His plain linen bands, dull grey raiment and high-crowned black hat formed a curious contrast to the gay colours worn by the other two.

It is true that Master Endymion's claret-hued doublet was faded and frayed, his crimson velvet breeches patched and his white stockings darned; but there was about him a sort of lightness, carelessness and grace that made many people forget the poverty of his attire. As to his companion, seven-year-old Denzil Clavenger, he was clothed as befitted the only son of Sir Piers Clavenger, second baronet of that name. His doublet and breeches were of parchment-coloured satin, his wide collar was of rich Venetian lace, and the blue rosettes upon his shoes had been renewed that very day by Justin, his father's valet, barber and cobbler, the busiest and not the least important member of the household at Winford Manor.

The newcomer halted without speaking, and turned his small, pale eyes in the direction where Denzil and Endymion had been gazing—the farther or eastward end of the moat, where a group of sturdy fellows, stripped to the waist, were busy digging to reopen the old culvert which would let the waters of the Win once more surround the outer walls of the house. Centuries had passed since moats went out of fashion and the Clavenger of that time had had *his* dried up and turned into a herb garden; but now Sir Piers had given the word that the Manor was to be a moated Manor again, and his neighbours and tenants in the village asked each other why. Some of them knew why: many of them guessed why: few of them agreed with broad-shouldered Wat the blacksmith that what Sir Piers did was his business and nobody else's. The person who disagreed most emphatically with the smith was his first cousin, Zedekiah Miller—the same person whose approach had ended the dialogue between Denzil and Master Endymion. The red hair of their jovial ancestor of Plantagenet times, Nick the Miller, had been inherited by both Wat and Zedekiah, but it was Wat only whose heritage included a cheerful disposition.

Denzil, having been taught courtesy from his cradle, wished the man "Good afternoon" in a polite voice: Master Endymion did the same, hailing him as "most sweet Master Zedekiah" and making him a low bow, though without rising from the grassy bank where he and Denzil were sitting. Disregarding this mockery, Zedekiah saluted the boy with a stiff bend of the head and said, in slow, twanging tones, that he had come to seek speech with the worshipful Sir Piers Clavenger.

"My father," explained Denzil, "is from home to-day."

"Does he purpose to return at the setting of the sun or to abide in the tents of strangers till the rising up thereof?"

"Of a surety he will be home to-night," said Denzil, who loved to impart information, "for he has but ridden some twelve leagues to——"

He stopped short, for Master Endymion had kicked him—quite gently—on the shin.

Zedekiah noticed the action, and an angry flush crept over his whey-white face.

"It is unseemly," he exclaimed, "it is unfitting—that a son of Belial, a godless play-actor, should come between this babe and me—*me*, who can remember him in swaddling bands."

"Why, as to that," retorted Endymion, "I am of opinion that to try to draw knowledge out of lips too innocent to withhold the same is a trick at which even my 'father' Belial would boggle."

"They are all alike," muttered the other, clenching his hands ; "graceless, godless, making a mock of holy things. But the Lord Jehovah shall yet arise in His might and they shall fly as dust before the wind."

"Why, as to that," said Endymion, "I might find flying easier than walking as things are with me now."

He rose as he spoke, supporting himself on the stout stick that had been propped against the bank, and it then became evident that his left leg was shorter than his right.

"Wherefore," demanded Zedekiah, "wherefore is it that things *are* so with thee ? Even because of thy profane leaping and skipping like unto a he-goat upon the mountains. It was in an evil hour that good Sir Piers took pity upon thee instead of letting thee depart with the rest of thy painted band."

Endymion's dark eyes flashed, and it seemed as if he were going to drive his clenched fist at Zedekiah's jaw: then he recovered himself, with a laugh and a shrug.

"Marry," said he, "I am glad my last caper was cut in so worthy a cause."

"So worthy a cause!" echoed Zedekiah, amazed.

"Ay, Master Puritan—to make Sir Piers and his lady laugh a little when God wot there is now scant food for laughter among loyal subjects and honest men."

" The laughter of fools," quoted Zedekiah rudely, " is like the crackling of thorns under a pot. Your doings are known—your masques and your mummings, your idolatry of a profane writer, Shakespeare by name. These things, I say, are known to God and man. Let all heed what shall follow."

Then, adding over his shoulder that he would return ere the going down of the sun, Zedekiah stalked away in the direction whence he had come.

Everyone in Winford knew that Endymion (whose surname no one knew) had been a member of a troupe of strolling players that had visited the district two years before, and that when he broke his leg in the course of a performance at the Manor Sir Piers and his lady had insisted that he should remain there until the hurt was healed. It seemed very strange to most people that, when once he could hobble about, he did not hobble away for ever. But he had won the good will of his benefactors, and he had found many ways of being both useful and agreeable to them. Young Lady Clavenger, Denzil's mother, had been a Maid of Honour to Queen Henrietta Maria, and had taken part in many of the masques devised to help the bright-eyed little French queen to learn the language of her husband's subjects. These innocent amateur theatricals were severely condemned by the Puritan party, whose power grew greater every day: and when Penelope Clavenger, with the aid of Master Endymion, began to amuse herself in the same way in her own house there was much head-shaking and brow-knitting among the villagers of the Zedekiah Miller persuasion. They had already felt some misgivings when Sir Piers brought home his light-hearted young bride in 1632. That she was charitable to the poor, skilful with her needle and a devout churchwoman availed her nothing. " What," asked the Winford Puritans, " what would Old Squire and Old Parson have thought of it all! " And when it became known that Master Denzil was receiving lessons in Latin grammar from this mysterious vagabond there was hardly any doubt as to what those two worthies would have thought and said.

"Old Squire"—that was Sir Harry Clavenger, the same who as a small boy had played in *The Triumph of Renown* before Queen Elizabeth. He had grown up into a rather solid, stolid kind of gentleman, not precisely a Puritan but inclining a little that way. Perhaps his early and unlucky experience of play-acting [1] may have given him a distaste for such amusements. At all events, when he entered Parliament in 1616 he soon gained the reputation of being opposed to all new-fangled notions as well as to anything in the form of frivolity. By marrying a rich wife, the only child of a Kentish gentleman, he brought fresh prosperity to the Clavenger family; and by coming forward as a violent critic of the habit of tobacco-smoking he attracted the attention of that amiable oddity King James the First and Sixth. Invited to the royal palace of Whitehall and permitted to walk once or twice up and down the long gallery in conversation with His Majesty, Harry Clavenger wisely suppressed the fact that he did not share the King's desire to see maypoles set upon all village greens and young lads and lasses dancing round them after church-time on Sundays. The monarch's strong Scottish accent made it difficult for the subject to understand everything that he said; but when once Clavenger realised that by "tobaikie" James meant "tobacco" they got on very well; for as soon as he heard the word, the M.P. nodded respectfully, thus showing that he, too, abhorred the loathsome weed, and His Majesty shuffled along in his old loose shoes, quoting Greek and Latin and gabbling like a gander.

Not long after this, it happened that the King was casting about for some gentleman suitable to be promoted to the new order he had recently invented—that of baronet, or hereditary knight. Each person thus honoured had to pay down one thousand pounds, and candidates had therefore to be well-to-do in addition to being gently born.

[1] See Chapter IV.

"Babie Charles," said His Majesty to his grave-eyed son, the Prince of Wales, "d'ye mind that Hampshire carle that was sae weel groundit in the arguments against tobaikie? I'd like fine to ken if he has disposable the sum o' siller needful to make a baronet o' him."

"No doubt your Majesty will have little difficulty in obtaining the information," returned Prince Charles, without much enthusiasm. The King, having ascertained that the "Hampshire carle" was worthy of the honour—and capable of paying for it—decided to add the name of Clavenger to the Baronetage, and Sir Harry, solemnly gratified, began to take a warm interest in the ancestors in whom, hitherto, he had taken but little. The College of Heralds was set to work upon the family tree; and the old family names of Piers and Denzil, Humphrey and Lionel, came into favour again. It was about this time that the heralds granted a coat of arms, with a falcon as a crest, to Edward Falconer, mercer, of London; but Harry Clavenger had lost sight of his old playmate after they both left Oxford, and would not have recognised the Monster of the Winford interlude if he had met the cheerful-looking, prosperous inhabitant of Cheapside who had once answered to the name of "Ned."

No one was better pleased at the granting of the baronetcy than "Old Parson"—otherwise the Reverend William Burdock, Vicar of Winford St. Mary, who promptly preached a very long sermon on the text: "The righteous shall see it and rejoice." He was a clergyman of the more austere and puritanical type, and even the Archbishop of Canterbury could not prevail upon him to wear a surplice instead of a black Geneva gown or to put railings of brass or oak round the communion table in the church. While he lived, Zedekiah and the rest of the Winford Puritans listened with satisfaction to his lengthy sermons, mostly from the fiercer portions of the Old Testament; but the case was altered when, upon his death in 1631 (a year after the death of his friend and patron,

Sir Harry) young Sir Piers appointed a parson of a completely different kind.

Edmund Aubrey was as gentle, as charitable and as friendly as his predecessor was fierce, narrow and stern. Like Father Oswald three hundred years before, he loved gardening, and he encouraged his parishioners to cultivate many sorts of flowers and vegetables that they had never tried to grow before. He also loved music, and the village choir improved with every Sunday that went by. Only a few of his flock frowned when he wore the white surplice and set up the brass communion rails that Archbishop Laud decreed; but those few, led by Zedekiah, decided to meet for worship in a barn. There a sermon was sometimes delivered (at immense length) by their leader, and sometimes by some other layman who had seen what *they* called the New Light, and had much to say on the subject of sin—not their own sins, but those of the King, the Queen, the Archbishop, and the loyal nobility and gentry of the realm.

Mild though Parson Aubrey was, there had been some expectation that he might object to Denzil receiving his first lessons from a play-actor whose surname nobody knew. But, after a long, quiet talk with Master Endymion, he told Sir Piers that, for the present at least, it was as good a plan as any. He himself felt no envy, for his favourite studies were Greek and Hebrew, and the task of teaching a small boy the first elements of Latin did not attract him at all.

From where that boy and his strange tutor were sitting that summer afternoon in the year 1641 they could see Parson Aubrey working in his garden, wielding the hoe with right good will. Endymion remarked that his industry was a reproach to their idleness, but Denzil made no reply. As soon as Zedekiah was beyond earshot, he asked rather resentfully, " Why did you kick my leg, Master Endymion? "

" To remind you of what Sir Piers has told you many times —that you should use few words or none if people ask questions about his movements, or about what is going on in the Manor. In such days as these, child, it behoves the King's friends to take heed lest they help the King's foes."

"I am sorry," said Denzil. "I did forget—but I will remember another time."

It seemed very strange to the small boy that King Charles should have any foes—King Charles, whom he had been taught to love and honour, and in whose defence it would be a noble thing to fight, even to die. Other boys of his age— whose parents had different ideas—were learning to look upon His Majesty as a sort of monster, whose one aim was to trample down the liberties of the people of England.

There was something else that puzzled Denzil very much. The King, he had been told, was good: and yet he had done something that grieved Sir Piers and Penelope. They had both looked very sad when news came from London that the Marquis of Strafford had been beheaded on Tower Hill— Strafford, the faithful servant whose death-warrant Parliament had forced his royal master to sign.

At first the Clavengers would not believe that the news was true: and then a letter came to Lady Clavenger from one of the Queen's Maids of Honour to tell her—at the Queen's own behest—that it was to save Her Majesty from the fury of Parliament that Strafford had been sacrificed. For Parliament hated Henrietta Maria, a foreigner and a Papist, and threatened that, if the death-warrant were not signed, she would be the object of their next attack.

Parson Aubrey mourned, but almost in silence. Master Endymion, being pressed for his judgment, said that he could answer only in the words of Will Shakespeare—" It will have blood, they say—blood will have blood ": whereat Lady Clavenger shuddered and Sir Piers cried out hastily, " God grant that may not be the way of it! "

Denzil, puzzling over all these things, decided that though the King was a very good man he did not always do right;

and that Parliament consisted of very bad men, who always did what was wrong.

Even in that small Hampshire community those who were " for Church and King " and those who were against them were eyeing each other with growing distrust. Life was becoming less friendly, easy and secure. Up at the Manor Endymion was too busy writing at Sir Piers' dictation to have any time for masques and mummings, and if the lads and lasses still danced round the maypole, or sang the old songs of Chevy Chase and Robin Hood, Zedekiah and his followers would come and rail at them and spoil their sport entirely.

To Denzil and his elder sister, Lucasta, the results of all these changes were not altogether disagreeable—the younger children, Humphrey and Henrietta, were too young to know what was going on outside the nursery. Of course the flooding of the moat was a great excitement; and it was fun to watch the estate-carpenter fixing stout oaken shutters on the windows and strengthening various doors with iron bands provided by Wat the smith. Wat was one of the most skilful dancers and powerful wrestlers in the neighbourhood, and he hotly resented the efforts of his cousin Zedekiah to put down dancing and wrestling.

It was true, as Denzil had remarked, that barrels of meal and flitches of bacon were being stored away in the cupboards and cellars of the manor; and other things were being collected there which he was not allowed to see, for they were brought after dark along the Haverley road—muskets, gunpowder, tubs of pitch. Sir Piers, after taking counsel with that great royalist and chivalrous hero, Amyas Paulet, Marquis of Winchester, was doing at Winford as the Marquis was doing at his own Manor of Basing—preparing to defend a tract of country valuable to the King if war should break out between him and Parliament, and to stand a siege if surrounded by the King's enemies. Though Winford was not more than a large village, its position near the main road from London to Westhampton might make it important.

Luckily the Clavengers of Tudor times, when beautifying their property according to the fashions of the period, had neither filled in the dry moat nor weakened the thick walls which it encircled. The large, rambling house, with its patchwork mixture of buildings, was still what it had been under the Plantagenets—a stronghold as well as a habitation.

Denzil was roused from his meditations by the voice of Master Endymion, asking him if he had learned a certain passage of Virgil beginning *Sunt geminæ somni portæ*—there are twin gates to Sleep.

The boy flushed.

" Nay, Master Endymion—I watched Wat at work in the long gallery—putting iron bands on the shutters—and I played awhile with brother Humphrey—and Lucasta and I went to the fruit-garden to gather berries for the syrup old Nan is making —and then I came hither to see how the digging of the moat had sped."

" And here we have both sat, doing nothing," said Endymion, trying to look stern, " nothing, that is to say, except watch others at work."

" Be not wroth, Master Endymion," Denzil pleaded, " I will do better to-morrow. Did *you* always mind your book ? "

" No, child. Had I done so I should never have come hither wearing mummer's motley."

" Sweet Master Endymion," said Denzil, drawing nearer, " was it because you would not mind your book that you had to quit Oxford ? Or was it for some madcap prank ? Or for some great wrong-doing ? "

The question startled Endymion—and well it might.

" Who told you that I had ever been at Oxford ? " he asked. " And why do you think I had to quit that place ? "

" Nobody told me, Master Endymion. But Cambridge

is not loyal to the King and Oxford *is*—so I had liefer you were from Oxford. And I once heard Parson Aubrey say that scholars are driven thence for madcap pranks as well as for great wrong-doings."

Endymion sat silent for a moment, with folded arms and lowered eyes. Then he said: "Child, it is true—both as regards Oxford, and as regards the madcap prank. Let it be a lesson to you to mind your book and to play no pranks—or few."

He smiled a little sadly as he spoke and then, grasping his stick, began to limp towards the causeway of turf and flag-stones running from Sir Denzil's gatehouse to the edge of the Green. Denzil was just about to follow him when he heard a thud of hooves on the Haverley road and peered eagerly in that direction, hoping that the horseman might be his father, and that he might be taken up on the saddle and given a short ride on Bevis, Sir Piers' Flemish steed.

It *was* his father; and when Bevis caught sight of the boy he whinnied eagerly, expecting an apple. A sturdy beast was Bevis, with a barrel-shaped body, a long, wavy mane and tail, and a neat, narrow head: he had been foaled in the royal stables at Windsor, and was very like the horse upon which Sir Antonio Van Dyck painted the King. His master stooped down and lifted the delighted Denzil up before him, but no word was spoken till they overtook Master Endymion —as they soon did.

"I had speech with Colonel Carless," said Sir Piers, bending down and lowering his voice. "If need be, he will send us a score or so of men. There was a message from my kinsman. I am to ride over to Brackenden on Friday—after dusk but before moonrise."

"Do I ride with you, sir?"

"That might be well—yes, you shall ride with me."

Great would have been the astonishment of the first Protestant Clavengers if they had known that within less than

KING CHARLES AND QUEEN HENRIETTA MARIA WITH THEIR TWO ELDEST
CHILDREN

117

a hundred years the head of their line would not only acknowledge a Popish Clavenger of Brackenden as his kinsman but would also propose to ride over to that lonely Manor " after dusk."

Several things had happened to bring about this better understanding. Piers Clavenger, visiting the Court of King Charles and Queen Henrietta Maria as the accepted suitor of Penelope Vernon, the Queen's Maid of Honour, had been surprised to find that nobody stood higher in the good will of His Majesty than a certain dark, serious gentleman, a Catholic from Hampshire but educated chiefly in France, Philip Clavenger by name. He had married a French lady and was already a widower, with two small sons whom the kind-hearted Queen Henrietta had placed in the nursery with her own baby boy, Charles, Prince of Wales.

Another thing which went far to overcome any prejudice Piers may have felt was the fact that the Marquis of Winchester, one of the King's devoted servants, was also of the ancient faith. And, finally, as the King's enemies became more powerful, his friends tended to draw closer to one another.

None the less, the kinsmen had seen little or nothing of each other for some years, Philip having been absent on frequent missions to the Continent, and Brackenden having been left dusty and desolate in the care of a handful of old servants. The two boys had been sent to their French grandmother in 1637, when the clash between the Crown and the Commons began to look serious.

Now, at the suggestion of Lord Winchester and Colonel Carless, Sir Piers was trying to get into touch with his cousin so that they might take counsel together. It was very important that men of the Zedekiah Miller breed should not get wind of this, and Endymion hastily informed the baronet that the leader of the village malcontents had been seeking him not long before.

" Devil take the fellow! " cried Sir Piers ; " there is no end to his carping and complaining—but we must not arouse his suspicions. I had better see him the next time he comes a-whining."

The next time was the same evening. Sir Piers received the Puritan in the old vaulted oratory, now a book-room fitted with oaken shelves and well garnished with books of many sizes. While Zedekiah snivelled out his complaints his eyes travelled disapprovingly over the titles on the backs of such books as were nearest to him—Shakespeare—Ovid—Jonson— play-acting, and paganism and profanity. The three P's— an excellent subject for his next sermon: and he could make them four by adding prelacy, government of the Church by Bishops, a thing which he regarded as equally deplorable.

Up in the nursery—a long room with a sloping roof under the gables of the half-timbered wing—old Nan was rocking the carved oak cradle in which baby Henrietta was cosily falling asleep while Lucasta was amusing her small brother Humphrey by cutting out funny little figures from a sheet of stiff white paper.

" Who is that, Humphrey ? " she asked him, laughing and holding out a thin-legged man with an absurdly high-crowned hat.

" I know! " cried the boy, clapping his hands. " Zed-e-ki-ah."

" Hush, sweeting," said old Nan, lifting up a warning finger, " not so loud. You will wake the babe! "

" Sister, could you cut out a likeness of Par-la-ment ? " whispered Humphrey, who always divided long words into separate syllables, with a pause between each.

" Nay, brother, that can I not. Parliament is not one man— it is many men."

" All wicked ? "

Lucasta thought that they were all wicked, but could not be sure.

" But the King, sister," said Humphrey, " the King is good. Cut me out a likeness of the King."

Lucasta reflected for a moment. The King. She had never seen him—at least, not to remember it. There was no picture of him at the Manor, though she knew that it had been His Majesty's gracious intention to bestow upon Sir Piers a copy of one of the lifelike portraits painted in happier times by Sir Antonio Van Dyck. Presently the little girl nodded, and took up her scissors and paper again. She *had*

GREAT SEAL OF KING CHARLES THE FIRST

seen—" Mam " had often shown her—a tracing upon parchment of the Great Seal of England. On one side you saw the King sitting on his throne, crown on head, sceptre and orb in hands, a lion to his right, a unicorn to his left, the lion clutching a flag with the cross of St. George, the unicorn a flag with the cross of St. Andrew. It would be quite impossible to cut *that* out; but the design on the other side was simpler and easier, and Lucasta got to work at once, snipping away busily while her small brother looked on.

" He is on horseback," she explained in a low voice. " He has a shield on his arm and a sword in his hand. I don't *think* I can cut out the greyhound that runs beside him, and I *know* I can't do the view of London with the bridge and all the spires and houses. I will begin with the horse."

" Begin with horse," echoed Humphrey, approvingly.

His sister did not speak again for several minutes; she was too busy trying to remember the exact outline of that horse and his royal rider, and giving a careful snip to her paper now and then. Presently it became plain that the object she was cutting out *was* a horse, a fat horse with a long tail—not unlike Bevis.

" No bridle," said a small voice, reproachfully, " no bridle—King tumble off."

" Alack, I had forgot! And it is too late now. But Mam says the King is a wondrous skilful horseman. Maybe he can ride without. Or—maybe—I could give him a bridle of silken thread from one of Mam's pretty skeins. Now I come to *him*. He is raising his sword above his head as if he were going to chop hard at someone."

" King chop at Zed-e-kiah," murmured Humphrey, " King chop *hard* at Zed-e-kiah."

Lucasta paused again.

" This is not easy to do, brother. I must cut carefully round the great plume that hangs from the helmet. Peace, now—or my hand may slip."

With an anxious frown she bent over her task, turning the paper this way and that as her scissors snipped their way round.

" Oh, brave! " cried Humphrey, too excited to hold his peace.

Then—as she had feared it might—his sister's hand *did* slip.

" Oh, alack," she cried almost in tears, " the King has lost his head ! "

" King lost head," repeated Humphrey, placidly. " But do not weep, Lu. Cut out another King. And I will be good."

"Nay, I have not enough paper for another King. Only this little piece. I might cut out the greyhound—all by himself. But do not stir—or *he* will lose his head, too—*and* his little turned-up tail."

This time Humphrey *was* good; and for his reward he had a charming hound, a lifelike hound, scampering along with its nose as well as its tail in the air; but Lucasta sighed as she retrieved from the nursery floor the plumed and helmeted head of her sovereign lord, King Charles.

On Friday evening Denzil lay awake in the damask-curtained bed which he shared with Humphrey. When he heard the clatter of hooves on the cobble-stones of the courtyard he remembered that his father and Master Endymion were to ride to Brackenden that night. He got up without waking his brother and poked his head out of the window, which looked across the moat towards the village. Presently two horsemen emerged from under the old gatehouse and set off at an easy trot: and a moment later the boy saw with surprise a figure rise from the deep grass beside the causeway and follow them, running fast and stooping low. Even without the high-crowned hat Denzil could recognise Zedekiah Miller.

Lady Clavenger was in the still-room with old Justin, busy about jars of healing salve and phials of herb cordial. In the fashion of her garments and the way she did her hair she imitated her royal friend Henrietta Maria as closely as she could. Her dress was of sea-green satin, with full sleeves to the elbow and a collar of mechlin lace round the shoulders: and her dark hair was arranged in long and short curls, the long on either side of her face, the short across the forehead. Both she and Justin looked round with surprise when the door opened and a small barefooted, night-capped figure came in, holding up his linen nightgown in both hands, so that he should not trip over it.

"My sweeting, what is amiss?" cried Lady Clavenger. "Were you frightened by a dream?"

"Not a dream," faltered Denzil. "But I looked forth—when father rode away—and there was one hiding by the causeway—watching—and then he rose and followed after."

"Could you see who it was, my son?"

"It was Zedekiah Miller. He is not going to hurt father, Mam—is he?"

"God forbid, my darling. But now Justin will carry you back to bed."

Nothing loth, Denzil submitted to being picked up in the still powerful arms of the old servitor, into whose wrinkled ear he whispered as they withdrew, "It was Zedekiah—I *know* it was."

"For sure it were, Master Denzil. Always a knave he were. Played truant from school—robbed orchards—spoke pertly to his betters. I'll tell 'ee what, young Master—if I'd a-knowed he were skulking yonder I'd ha' opened the sluice and let in the moat-water a day sooner nor we reckoned! Drowned them lean shanks o' his I would."

Not until the east was flooded with pearly light did Sir Piers and Master Endymion return. They found Lady Clavenger still awake, waiting for them in the book-room with a flagon of Rhenish wine.

Sir Piers followed the fashions set by the King as closely as Penelope followed those set by the Queen. The wide-brimmed black hat, worn pulled down at one side and cocked up at the other, the grey velvet tunic braided with silver and slashed with pale tawny silk, the full breeches held in at the knee by close-fitting buff riding-boots—all these details were copied from a royal original, but with this difference—that the King was of small, slight build and the subject was broad of shoulder and long of shank.

As soon as he had drunk a little wine, Penelope told her husband Denzil's story.

"Ha," said Sir Piers, "so that was the way of it! You were right, Endymion."

"An easy road for a pursuer," remarked Endymion; "many high hedges—many sharp turns."

"What does it mean?" cried poor Penelope, clasping her hands.

"Mischief—if he can work any. But let us speak of other matters. Are you not curious to know how I fared at Brackenden?"

"Yes, Piers—very. What is the house like? And what said your kinsman?"

"The house, sweet Pen, is little better than a ruin. It could not be held for six hours against as many stout fellows armed with muskets: but kinsman Philip has no mind to hold it."

"Alack, Piers—has he turned traitor? I thought him loyal to the core."

"Why, so did I—and so I do. But he has promised the King that he will hold himself in readiness to go with the Queen—if she should have to quit this realm for a time."

"The Queen—quit England!" repeated Lady Clavenger, in dismay.

"Be sure, dearest Pen, that she would never go unless it were the better to serve the King. And do you not know that we cannot all serve our royal master as we ourselves would choose? If the worst should befall, I had liefer lead a charge than defend a house. But the way of it is that I must defend a house."

"And a noble, goodly old house, too," said Master Endymion. "Unless I mistake, it is this very day, sir, that the moat is to be again a moat in truth as well as in name?"

It was that very day. All the Clavenger children, from Lucasta, wearing a satin gown very like her mother's, to baby Henrietta, crowing and cooing in the arms of old Nan, gathered on the causeway to see the Win pouring through the old culvert and spreading into a sheet of amber-coloured, glassy water all round the Manor walls.

Zedekiah and his friends had a great deal to say about this

event when they assembled in the barn that same day: and
not long after they met in much excitement to discuss the fact
—reported by one of their spies—that two small cannon and
several stacks of muskets had been smuggled into the Manor
after dark. It was decided to send a trusty messenger—
Zedekiah himself—to London: and questions were asked in
Parliament upon the subject soon after. Rumours flew wildly
all over England, but the time was near when news-letters or
news-sheets, the forerunners of the modern newspaper, would
be printed and circulated, each side in the great quarrel having
its own.

The year 1641 did not end cheerfully. Though Parliament
blamed the King's Counsellors for such matters as seemed
amiss in the governance of England, a determined attempt was
being made to shift the balance of power from the Crown to
the Commons. Then in January 1642, King Charles went
down to Westminster in person to arrest five of the most
troublesome members—only to find the birds flown and
himself looking foolish. It was soon after that he quitted
London, never to return to it as a free man, and the Queen,
broken-hearted, sailed for Holland, where she hoped to get
some help for her husband through their widowed eldest
daughter, the Princess of Orange. Philip Clavenger went
with her, and Brackenden, being of no use either to the
Royalists or the Roundheads, was left empty except for the
old servitors.

" Roundhead," thought Denzil, was an excellent name for
people like Zedekiah, whose hair was cut so short that their
ears stuck out like the handles on a pipkin. Master Endymion
said that, " as to that," those gentry reminded him of nothing
so much as the pelican carved on a certain sundial at Oxford—
a bare skull and a long beak.

More than ever was Denzil convinced that Parliament consisted of very wicked men. He imagined that all the Members
must look like Zedekiah Miller, gaunt and grim, tight-lipped

and frosty-eyed, with high, steeple-crowned hats. Very many of them were like that: but some of them were a little different. Oliver Cromwell, Member for Huntingdon, wore his hair untidily long, and his features were clumsy and ruddy instead of being pinched and pale. Denzil, gathering from the conversation of his elders that " Noll " was one of the worst rebels, decided to bestow his name upon the ugly imp grinning down from the vaulting of the ancient porch. It was very comforting to be quite sure that the real Noll and his linen-drapers and 'prentice lads could never stand up against King Charles's army, manned by the yeomen and led by the chivalry of England.

The Parliamentarians next tried to force the King to transfer the control of his armed forces from himself to Parliament and, upon his refusal, declared that they proposed to appoint and dismiss his ministers, garrison all fortified places, reform (by which they meant destroy) the Church of England and choose guardians for the royal children. A Committee of Public Safety was set up, and the Earl of Essex, one of the very few anti-royalist lords, was placed in command of an army.

" They have lost their wits," cried Sir Piers, " and that is the way of it."

He desired nothing so much as to go to Nottingham, where the King had raised the royal standard, but word was brought to him that he could best serve his master by holding Winford Manor against his enemies. That Manor was not yet formally besieged, but the two boys were already " playing sieges," riding their hobby-horses, beating their drums, and flourishing two wooden swords to which clung traces of silver paint— they were the same swords that Wisdom and Virtue had wielded fifty years before, and Master Endymion, finding them among a jumble of old stuff up in the attic, had used them in one or two of his masques.

Lucasta felt very much left out of all this, and was only a

little consoled when " Mam " told her that she might make for her father one of those quilted and embroidered linen caps which the gentlemen of that time wore always by night and sometimes by day. When Lucasta showed her stitchery to Master Endymion such a queer look flickered across his face that she wondered for a moment whether he grieved because there was no one to make such a cap for *him*.

The King held most of the northern and western parts of the realm, but between him and his supporters in the south lay London. Whoever held the capital had command of the nation's money-bags, and it was stubbornly held by the Parliamentarians. After his partial success at Edgehill the King's brilliant young nephew, Prince Rupert, wanted to march on London, but the counsels of his more cautious elders prevailed, and an opportunity was missed which never presented itself again.

Meanwhile, many of the farmers on the Winford estates, with their sons and farm servants, had sought and obtained Sir Piers's leave to enlist in the troop of horse which Sir Peregrine Fenworth of Haverley was raising for the King. A few of Zedekiah's followers rode away to join Sir William Waller, the nearest Parliamentary Commander, but Zedekiah himself had other plans, and remained behind. Parliament had now set about " reforming " the Church of England, and he was waiting with impatience until Parson Aubrey should be ejected, as many other clergymen had been ejected whose only crime was that they would not break the solemn vows they had made when ordained.

The good parson himself wanted to go and join the King, who was now at Oxford, and to act as chaplain to the royalist army; but Sir Piers besought him earnestly to do no such thing. If Zedekiah could have resisted the temptation to brag, the blow that fell upon Winford Church might have fallen quite suddenly; but, meeting Aubrey on the Green one day, he informed him triumphantly that a Parliamentary

Commission was on its way from London " to cleanse yonder temple of Baal from the abominations therein and to set up some godly preacher in the pulpit too long profaned by false doctrine."

There was much indignation at the Manor when these words were repeated there. Denzil and Humphrey offered to go and drive away the Commissioners with their silver swords, and Sir Piers, rightly concluding that among the " abominations " the tombs of his ancestors would be numbered, wished very much that he himself could sally forth with a sword of steel. All he could do was to entreat the perplexed clergyman to bring as many of his books as he could carry, and take up his abode with his friends in the Manor.

" Mark my words," said he, " we shall need your prayers soon. When these rogues have struck at the Church in *your* person they will not tarry ere they strike at the King in *mine*."

Stipulating only that he should not quit the vicarage until compelled by force to do so, Edmund Aubrey sadly agreed. The same night he managed to convey a chest of books and a barrel of his famous russet pippins into his place of refuge. Zedekiah was holding a prayer meeting in the barn and so was safely out of the way.

With deep snuffles and high snivels did the Roundhead address his admirers that night. Though he did not say so in so many plain words, he felt convinced that the next time he addressed them it would be from the pulpit of the parish church.

On the following afternoon the three Commissioners arrived, stern men, in leather coats and steel caps, at whom the villagers gaped in some dismay. With them came a wisp of a little lean man with an enormous beaky nose and a slight cast in his prominent light brown eyes. Zedekiah, eagerly welcoming the three bearers of the Parliamentary warrant, wondered idly who the fourth stranger might be: but nobody enlightened him at first.

QUEEN ELIZABETH (*see page* 87)

DENZIL AND HUMPHREY GOING THE ROUNDS OF THE SENTRIES
(*see page* 141)

Having refused to renounce his oath of allegiance to the King and to abjure prelacy and the Book of Common Prayer, Edmund Aubrey was called upon to give up the keys of the vicarage and of the church.

"Master Commissioner," said he, as he obeyed, "your warrant is not God's. May He have mercy on this flock, left shepherdless with so many wolves abroad!"

The fourth horseman shot an angry glance at the parson out of his crooked yellow eyes and opened his mouth as if to speak, but the leader of the Commission spoke first.

"Shepherdless!" he repeated. "Wolves! Yea, verily, they have been shepherdless too long and thou art the wolf that has preyed upon them. But thy time is come: thy power is spent. And they shall be shepherdless no longer, for Parliament in its wisdom has sent the worshipful and godly Master Agag Witherpoon to be their minister."

Zedekiah could hardly believe his ears. This shabby stranger and not himself was to supplant Parson Aubrey! It was a bitter moment for him and a heavy humiliation. He glanced round to see if his adherents would show either surprise or regret, but they were all clustering about their new minister and urging him to take possession of his house and set about purifying the temple of Baal without further delay.

That same evening a loud tumult from the direction of the church drew the Clavengers and Parson Aubrey to the windows of the dining-parlour. Ancient yew trees partly screened the building from their sight, but there was no mistaking the significance of the noises that reached their ears—and the crash and clatter of breaking glass as Master Witherspoon's new congregation drove hoes and bill-hooks through the stained windows.

Sir Piers proved himself to be a true prophet. Little more than a week after these events a messenger from Colonel Carless's headquarters made his way to the Manor to announce that the Colonel, having received a report from his spies that an assault was intended upon that house, proposed to send a troop of twenty men under Cornet Langton to aid in its defence. Westhampton, after some wavering, had declared for Parliament—a serious blow to the King's cause, making it all the more important that Winford should not fall.

When the twenty men arrived they were seen to be a queerly mixed collection. The oldest, a scarred warrior, Corporal Phineas Dobb by name, had fought in Pomerania

THE PURITANS ASSAULTING THE CHURCH OF WINFORD ST. MARY

and Bavaria under King Gustavus Adolphus of Sweden: the youngest were either raw recruits or young yeomen and farm lads whose only taste of real war had been the battle of Edgehill and some skirmishing in the country about Oxford. The garrison of the Manor, consisting mainly of the men-servants and some volunteers from the village, mustered another twenty: so that defence numbered about forty men all told. There were just enough muskets to go round, and enough bandoliers to hold the ammunition for each musket;

but only Corporal Phineas had a proper steel cap of the kind
known as a "morion," with side-flaps protecting cheek and
jaw. The others were rigged out in a variety of metal
head-gear, some specimens dating back to the days of Queen
Elizabeth, and some looking suspiciously like iron pots
borrowed from the kitchen-quarters.

To receive Cornet Langton with due ceremony, Sir Piers
doffed his new quilted day-cap—which he planted on the top
of the Elizabethan buffet in the dining-parlour—gathered his
family round him, not forgetting Master Endymion and
Parson Aubrey, and bade Justin set out a flagon of the finest
wine in the cellars. The Cornet was a pleasant-looking man
of about twenty-five or six who wore his fringed scarf—the
badge of an officer—at a jaunty angle and made a good deal
of jingling with his spurs. He bowed low to Sir Piers and
Penelope, a little less low (but most respectfully) to Parson
Aubrey, and then swung round towards Endymion, who was
doing his best to slip behind the tall form of the baronet.

" Why," he exclaimed, " is it thou, Endymion Warner?
Well met, thou old wag! What hast thou been about since
Corpus Christi would have none of thee? "

" Playing the fool in other places," returned Endymion, by
turns red and pale in the face. " And paying dearly for my
folly, too."

" He was ever a gay wag," remarked the Cornet to Sir
Piers, " but those dusty old Fellows of our College took too
grave a view of the prank for which they sent him away."

" You speak in riddles, sir," said Sir Piers, torn between a
good-natured desire to spare Endymion's feelings and a lively
curiosity to hear more.

" What! has he not told you the story? I marvel——"
here the Cornet broke into irrepressible laughter—" I marvel
that he can look at yonder day-cap and forget how he planted
its fellow on the pate of the pelican on our College fountain! "

" Was *that* the way of it? " cried Sir Piers. " Nay, Master

Endymion—look not so shamefaced. I remember that pelican——"

"So do I," interposed Parson Aubrey, "and I hope the Cornet will now tell us the story, which I have already heard—but promised *not* to tell."

"Well, sir," said the Cornet, turning again to Sir Piers, "you must know that our Warden—good, worthy man—was accustomed to don such a cap—though not so bravely embroidered—when he took his ease under his pet mulberry tree on a summer afternoon."

"I remember that tree," interposed Parson Aubrey, as the narrator paused.

"Marry, so do I!" added Sir Piers, not to be left out.

"At such times," continued the Cornet, "he would make a show of reading some learned book, or Latin, or Greek. But soon the book would drop from his hand, the spectacles would slip down his nose, his head would sink forward, and he fell into so deep a slumber that he would scarcely have known it if one of us had tweaked him by the nose."

"And one of you did so?" prompted Penelope, with a smiling glance at Master Endymion.

"One of us, madam, did worse than that. One of us twitched off the Warden's cap as he sat snoring, crept away with it, and fixed it upon the bald pate of the stone pelican on the fountain in the quadrangle."

Everyone laughed except Endymion.

"Never hang your head, man," cried Sir Piers; "it was no small feat of skill to climb up that same fountain; and I'll wager it was not the first time some mad fellow had made a mock of that pelican."

"You say truly, sir," agreed the Cornet, with a grin. "But—by your leave—and yours, madam—what befell after you were thrust forth, Endymion Warner?"

"Maybe," hinted Lady Clavenger, with a glance at Endymion's face, "maybe he would rather not tell."

" Nay, madam—I thank you; it is a tale more foolish than merry, but if you care to hear——"

" Tell on, then," prompted Sir Piers, while Denzil, Lucasta and Humphrey crept nearer so as to hear better.

" My friend Langton," began Endymion, " may remember my uncle, Dr. Nicodemus Warner, Rector of St. Polycarp-by-the-Tower——"

" Only too well—and I remember thanking heaven that he was your uncle and not mine: a mighty grave and grim churchman he was."

" He being my sole kinsman," continued Endymion, " to him I went. If I had stolen the college plate he could not have been more shocked. So behold me driven forth a second time, to earn my bread as best I might."

" And how did you set about it? " asked Sir Piers, interested.

" Well, sir, I took service with a certain scrivener in the city of London—one of Master Zedekiah Miller's persuasion, no light taskmaster and no good paymaster, but, as the proverb says, ' Need makes the ass to trot.' "

" And why did you quit that learned employment? " asked the Cornet.

" Because, one fine morning, my master, coming softly in, found me at the window instead of at my desk—ay, and found me looking forth to see the morris-dancers go by, and —worse still—heard me humming the tune played by the pipe and tabor."

" And what followed? "

" A long sermon, sir, upon the exceeding wickedness of dancing, and of watching dancers, and of humming a morris tune. After which your humble servant found himself driven forth a third time, and flung upon the cobblestones without one poor groat in his pocket."

" Alack," said Penelope, " that was a heavy punishment for a small sin ! "

" And then, madam, to end the story, I joined a troop of

strolling players. One day I must stamp and roar in some old tragedy—and another day I must caper as a clown. And between-times it was my duty to look after and lead about the poor old dancing bear that was the best Christian and the kindliest creature in that company."

"What happened to the bear ? " asked Sir Piers, "I remember none when you—when the players came hither."

"Poor old Solon—I gave him that name because he looked  so wise—poor old Solon died at Westhampton not long before. And beshrew me if I did not weep more tears for him than I would have shed for my Uncle Nicodemus ! As for what befell after I came hither" —he faltered, and then added in a lower voice— "you, my merciful lord and lady, know as well as

EMBROIDERED CAP

I do, and Langton must wait to hear another time."

"I wish," whispered Lucasta to Denzil, "I wish the bear had not died—I wish it had tarried here with Master Endymion."

"Cut bear out of paper for me, sister," urged Humphrey.

"Well, Endymion," said Sir Piers, clapping him on the shoulder, "you have returned to your scrivening craft, for my quill is none of the readiest, and there will be much writing and reckoning to be done."

"And," added Penelope, smiling, "you shall not be punished if you quit your task sometimes and peer out to see the morris-dancers on the green. Alas "—the smile faded from her face—" alas, I had forgot—they dance upon the green no more."

They were all merry enough after that, drinking health to

the King and confusion to the Roundhead rogues, and talking confidently of the day when the King would be back in his palace at Whitehall and Parson Aubrey in his vicarage at Winford. Then they asked the Cornet about Prince Rupert, and he told them of his reckless valour, his immense height, his dark, handsome face, the scarlet plume he wore in his steel cap, the white dog that followed him everywhere, even on to the field of battle.

Early next morning, under the directions of the Cornet and the Corporal, the final preparations were made, and barrels of gunpowder were placed in pits dug for that purpose beneath the causeway: and later in the day a troop of Parliamentary soldiers, horse, foot and artillery, marched up the village street to the beat of a drum and proceeded to encamp themselves on the Green. Agag Witherspoon and Zedekiah Miller both hurried to greet them, each scowling at the other but smiling at the newcomers. Sir Piers, the Cornet and the Corporal watched these doings through loopholes in the gatehouse shutters. And presently they saw a clumsily-built, red-faced personage ride slowly towards them, accompanied by two men, one carrying a small trumpet and the other a large white flag.

" Heaven be my witness," cried Sir Piers, " that fellow on the horse is little Simpkins, the butcher of Westhampton! "

The trumpeter sounded a few notes, and Simpkins looked expectantly towards the gatehouse.

" That is the call for a parley," explained the Cornet.

" No parley," said Sir Piers, firmly.

The red-faced Roundhead, seeing that the gates were not going to swing open, then shouted at the top of his voice that Parliament demanded that the Manor and all its stores of arms, food and valuables should be surrendered and all those persons delivered up to justice who were in arms against Parliament's righteous authority.

Having done this, he rode back to his troop. Five minutes later

Corporal Phineas—eagerly aided by the two small boys—hoisted the blue flag upon which Lady Clavenger and her daughter had embroidered in gold the crest and motto of the family—the hand holding the key and the words, *Clavem Teneo*. At the same time other members of the garrison ran out the noses of the cannon from the loopholes commanding the causeway.

"They are answered," said Sir Piers, with satisfaction, as he applied his eye to the loophole. "When do we blow up the causeway?"

"Not until after dusk, sir—if indeed we may do it then—for by every rule of war they should now fire upon us."

But the watchers saw no flicker of the flaming linstock that, thrust into the touch-hole of the cannon, would ignite the powder and send a missile the shape and size of a tennis-ball speeding through the air.

"Nay, I was wrong," confessed Langton. "And here comes another of those knaves—on foot, this time—carrying a white-fringed scarf tied to a silver-headed cane. Marry, he looks less of a churl than the other—what say you, sir?"

"A very proper gentleman," agreed Sir Piers, "but for the height of his hat and the great flaps on his jackboots. What's to do now?"

The Cornet explained that "by every rule of war" he must now go down and talk to the "very proper gentleman" through the little wicket in the great main door below. When he came up again he looked exceedingly amazed. The Puritan demanded speech with Sir Piers, whose kinsman he claimed to be. His name was Francis Fielding.

"Fielding," echoed Sir Piers. "To be sure—my Aunt Susannah married a Squire of the Welsh Marches—one Fielden or Fielding. What evil fruit has this grafting brought forth! Better the tree had been blasted. Yet I must needs receive him. Bring him hither. Stay—if you see Parson Aubrey about the courtyard, beg him to come. We should have witnesses while we deal with such knaves."

CHAPTER VI

THE STORM BREAKS

WHEN the Puritan was ushered into the oriel-room above the gatehouse both Parson Aubrey and Cornet Langton were struck by the resemblance between him and his cousin, Sir Piers. Unlike though they were in dress and bearing, there was something in each face, the colour of the eyes, the tilt of the brows, the line of the jaw, that proclaimed them akin in blood.

"Kinsman," began the newcomer, in a grave but not a snuffling voice, "I am Francis Fielding, Captain in Sir William Waller's first company of foot. Your father's sister was my mother. It is written that brethren should dwell together in unity—and in the spirit of that text I have come hither."

"Kinsman," returned Sir Piers, "if I must call you so—it is much to be lamented that you and your friends did not meditate upon that text before you began this bitter strife."

"Of those matters this is not the time to talk," said Captain Fielding. "This house to me is not as the house of strangers. I would fain spare these walls—that sheltered my mother's childhood—the horrors of siege and pillage."

"Pillage!" echoed Sir Piers, bristling. "Your rascals must storm the Manor before they can pillage it."

"Bethink you, kinsman," continued the Captain, unmoved, "Westhampton is ours. Was it not in the hope of saving Westhampton that Colonel Carless—at the behest of Rupert, whom some men call Rupert the Devil—placed a garrison here? That hope has been proved vain. There would be no dishonour in yielding."

"You talk to *me* of dishonour——" began Sir Piers, and then rage choked him.

"Kinsman, there are on our side many gentlemen as strictly nurtured in the laws of honour as you are yourself. But let us to the point. I were loth that, in the evil days to come, any of my mother's kinsfolk should suffer. It has been in my power to obtain from our commanders in Kent that Aunt Lettice shall dwell quietly at White Mays: and it is in my power to use my interest with Sir William Waller so that the terms of surrender—if you will yield up the Manor—will be reasonably light."

"I am beholden to you," said Sir Piers, ironically.

"Moreover," pursued the Captain, "I am willing to bring some godly ministers of the New Light to wrestle with yonder prelatist, to the end that he may acknowledge his error and be restored to his church and his dwelling-place."

Before the indignant Parson Aubrey could answer, Sir Piers rose to his feet, almost stammering with anger.

"So," he exclaimed, "so that is the way of it! He must betray his Church and I my King. The offer is worthy of the times. Get you gone to your clattering colonels, your mumming majors, and tell them that I will not yield while I have powder in my keg, shot in my barrel, or breath in my body!"

Captain Fielding bowed gravely and said, "Farewell, kinsman. It hath not pleased the Lord Jehovah to unseal your eyes. For what must now follow you bear the blame, not I."

With these words he followed the Cornet out of the room and down the narrow stairs. In the courtyard he glanced round him and remarked in a more natural voice, "I have heard much concerning this place. There was a certain carved imp—in the porch, I think—my mother and Uncle Harry used to call it 'Don Philip.'"

"I can show you that imp," said the Cornet. "Come hither—look up. There he is, and an ugly fellow, too. The young Clavengers do not call him 'Don Philip'—they call him 'Noll Cromwell.'"

" Do they so indeed!   They are well-taught children that make mock of godly and valiant gentlemen."

And with this severe comment he took his departure.

Sir Piers expected—indeed, he almost hoped—that a shot would now be fired from one of the cannon ranged on the Green, but for a little while nothing happened.   Followed by Parson Aubrey and joined by Master Endymion, he descended to the courtyard and gathered his household and the men-at-arms of the garrison around him.   It was certain, he said, that Winford could hold out till help came, even if it should not come for a long year.   Maybe Colonel Carless would lead a flank attack upon the rebels and cut them off from their supply lines.   Prince Rupert himself might make a dash from the west and raise the siege.   The causeway was to be blown up that night, but there was a part of the moat on the side farthest from the Green where a man might wade only knee-deep. Colonel Carless had a plan with the place plainly marked, and when help came that is where it would come.   And now let them raise an honest, loyal cheer, to show those villains yonder the way of it!

The cheering which then broke out had hardly died down when another sound was heard—a sharp bang as the linstock was applied to the touch-hole of one of the Parliamentary cannon: a deep roar followed, and a crash as a cannon-ball struck the thick outer wall.   Sir Piers's hounds and Penelope's spaniels at once began to bark madly.

" They are cheering for the King," said Master Endymion, seeing that Denzil had turned pale.   " And they will cheer again after dark when Corporal Phineas blows up the causeway."

Rather to the disappointment of Sir Piers, the Cornet and the Corporal between them decided that the Manor guns should not immediately reply to the bombardment from the Green, which went on—at longish intervals and without much effect—for the best part of the day.   The Cornet, being young and impetuous, secretly agreed with Sir Piers; but he bowed to the superior knowledge of a man who had fought under Gustavus Adolphus, and agreed that the garrison had better not waste their powder and shot. Let the besiegers waste *theirs*—they could do little harm unless they shortened the range, and *then* would be the time for the Royalists to reply.

The causeway was duly blown up, and for more than a week the bombardment continued, making dints in the outer walls or splashes in the moat, splintering some of the shutters and causing some of the maidservants to scream, but doing no serious damage. The Corporal had expected that an attempt would be made to storm the Manor, and daily disposed his men accordingly; but another week passed, and then another, and finally he gave the word—which the Cornet pretended to give—that the next time the rebel cannon fired they should be answered.

" If I mistake not," said Sir Piers, peeping through the loop-hole, " they have brought their ordnance nearer by a hundred yards or more."

" Truly," agreed the Cornet, " and the Corporal says—I mean, that is why I have decided that we had better take a turn."

Then came the moment for which Sir Piers and his elder son had waited. The two pieces of ordnance trained on the Green were discharged, making a huge roar, shaking the house more than any rebel shot had done, and causing the enemy to withdraw in some haste, taking with them two dead and five wounded men.

" Now they will make an assault," said Corporal Phineas. But for once he was wrong. Days passed into weeks and the Puritans remained encamped on the Green, continued to batter the walls, and barred every road by which relief might come; but they did little more. The real fact was that Major Simpkins had no mind for anything very fierce. He was a timid fellow, placed in charge of the operations because he was a person of some importance in Westhampton and had made large contributions to the Parliamentary funds. He had none of the natural military talent possessed by many Puritans and he had not liked the results of his first close-range experiment. " If," he argued, " if I prevent the King from enjoying the use of the arms and stores yonder, and if I hold the garrison beleaguered, I am doing all that should be expected of me." And for a time it seemed as if Sir William Waller agreed with him.

Meanwhile, Francis Fielding, who had a soldier's mind if not a soldier's training, might have persuaded the Major to act with more energy; but he was summoned to Waller's camp and kept there on other duties, and the siege dragged on. The watchers in the gatehouse marked his absence, and Sir Piers went so far as to hope that he had not been among the wounded and slain. " For," said he, " he was an honest enough fellow—for a rebel." Zedekiah also had vanished. After a violent wrangle with Agag Witherspoon, he decided to betake himself to London and join one of the new religious sects there.

Life in the Manor went on pleasantly enough. The defenders took it in turns to man the loopholes, musket in hand, and the Clavenger boys regularly made the rounds, armed with their wooden swords. Humphrey was now five and had exchanged a girlish, long-skirted frock for breeches, to his great joy. Parson Aubrey ensconced himself in the bookroom, from which he seldom emerged except to conduct a service in the dining-parlour. Master Endymion, besides acting as Sir Piers's secretary, kept them all gay with his scraps of songs, his patches of plays, and his admirable mimicry of Zedekiah, Agag and Major Simpkins. He did not mock Captain Fielding, firstly because the Captain was half a Clavenger, and secondly because his quiet, unaffected bearing did not lend itself to mockery.

As summer waned into autumn the King's fortunes waned

also. Little news from the outside world reached his loyal servants besieged at Winford, and what little they got was not of a kind to cheer them. From time to time Colonel Carless was able to send a scout who, under cover of darkness, waded the moat and scrambled up the wall, bringing information and bearing messages away with him: but as months passed and the Royalist forces were pushed farther north and west, communications became more difficult and great uncertainty prevailed. The capture of Bristol by Prince Rupert had set the hearts of the King's friends singing in July, but the Parliamentarian victory at Newbury set them aching in September. Yet there was still hope. The King was still strong in the north, his cause was not yet lost in the west. All through the winter of 1643 Sir Piers and his men held out undaunted, but in the spring of 1644 they had to endure heavier, more closely pressed attacks from a commander more enterprising than Major Simpkins.

It was at the earnest urging of Captain Fielding that Colonel Radford had been sent to supplant the Major. A skilful and experienced soldier was Colonel Radford, who—like Corporal Phineas—had served under Gustavus Adolphus. The Corporal recognised him from afar, and named him to Sir Piers.

"I remember him, sir," said he, " too well I remember him. We shall have to dance to another tune now that *he* is the piper. I wish we might hope that an ammunition-train could get through to us soon."

"Why, good Corporal," returned Sir Piers in some surprise, " we have spent little powder and shot so far—and my lady tells me we are provisioned for another year at least."

" No doubt, sir—but we shall need more powder and shot soon, and we cannot charge our muskets and cannon with flitches of bacon."

In the weeks that followed the Clavenger children got used to the smell of powder and pitch, the crackle of musketry, the billowing of sour black smoke, and the necessity for bolting for cover when the bombardment grew fierce. Baby Henrietta was too young either to understand the noise or to run to shelter. The nursery now being in a perilous place, her cradle had been moved to a small room in the oldest part of the house, and there her mother would often come, white-faced and heavy-eyed, her satin gown changed for one of plain woollen stuff without lace or ribbon. Her jewels had long since been sent to Oxford, together with the family plate, to be turned into money to support the royal cause. On a certain day when Sir Piers came with her she ventured to ask him whither they should go—if the Manor *should* fall.

"Faith, Pen," he answered, trying to speak gaily, "that is a matter that we might not be permitted to decide for our-selves."

"I have been thinking," said Penelope, "what may befall. They may send you to the Tower—but if they do, surely they will let me go with you. But the children—could they find shelter with Aunt Lettice at White Mays?"

This was the name of the Kentish property that had formed the dowry of Sir Piers's mother. It was tenanted for the time being by Dame Lettice Ellershaw—the same Lettice who as a small child had recognised the air strummed on the virginals by Queen Elizabeth.

"White Mays," repeated Sir Piers. "Marry, Pen, well bethought. It is true that since she was left widowed and childless our good Aunt has seemed to incline towards the Puritan way. But she is good, she is merciful—and if Justin and old Nan could convey the children thither——"

"You remember what Francis Fielding said," hinted Penelope, with some hesitation, "he is well disposed towards her—the children would be in some sort under his protection."

"Our children—under the protection of a rebel and a renegade! God forbid! But Winford has not fallen yet. Time enough to think of such woeful matters, time enough."

But there was not as much time as the loyal Cavalier

imagined. As the spring of 1644 merged into summer even *he* had to admit that—at least for the moment—the Round-heads looked like getting the best of it both at Winford and in the country at large. Little news got through from the outside world, but that little was not good: and Colonel Radford was pressing the attack with great gallantry and determination. Breaches had been made in the outer walls: the wooden roof of the great hall had been set alight and, though what Master Endymion called " a royalist rainstorm " quenched the flames, gaping holes remained among the charred timbers. Worst of all, royalist ammunition was running low, and soon it would not be possible to open fire upon any bold fellow who should attempt to swim the moat or repair the causeway. As long as Radford remained in ignorance of the exact spot where there was a fording-place beneath the water there was still hope that fresh supplies might be got through—but it was a very faint hope, and grew fainter every day.

One hot afternoon in July—the very day upon which Cromwell's Ironsides defeated Rupert's cavaliers at Marston Moor—Master Endymion, peering through one of the splintered shutters in the dining-parlour, recognised among the buff-coated and steel-capped figures on the Green the gaunt, ungainly, steeple-crowned form of Zedekiah Miller.

" So ho," muttered Endymion, " that bird of ill omen has come to flap his black wings and crow over us! I would give something—if I possessed anything—to know what news he brings from London."

The news brought by Zedekiah was pleasing to Colonel Radford. A last desperate attempt to get ammunition to Winford had been defeated by Captain Fielding, who had cut up the company convoying the waggons and had then taken possession of both waggons and ammunition in the name of Parliament. Endymion's guess was correct. Zedekiah, scenting disaster to the Clavenger family from afar, had volunteered to be Fielding's messenger so that he might have a chance to gloat.

It was just a week later that Colonel Radford launched his supreme assault upon the Manor.   Even then he might have failed but for a suggestion made by Zedekiah, who happened to know (and to remember) just how the moat had been filled—and could be emptied again. The garrison did not fail to observe that some of the Roundheads were busy digging by the light of lanterns near the northern bank, but Corporal Phineas declared that they were merely preparing a fire-trench with earthworks, in the manner approved by Gustavus Adolphus, so no one was greatly alarmed. But when the sun rose upon July the thirtieth everyone at once perceived that the water of the moat was several feet lower than its normal level, and by sunset it had sunk so low that there was little but ooze and a matted mass of green weed in its bed.

" So," said Sir Piers, when Corporal Phineas had explained what this meant, " so—even if that convoy got through that Carless promised—it would be too late."

" Alack, sir, that convoy—if ever it started—has beyond doubt been turned back or cut up."

" Then why have the knaves not attacked where the moat is fordable ?   The leader was to have a plan upon him, showing the place.   Surely if they slew him, they must have found it ? "

" We may yet learn that they did," muttered the Cornet, anxiously.

" Well, let them come. But God have mercy on the womenfolk—and the wounded—and my babes."

" Sir," whispered Endymion, who was standing near, " if your kinsman Fielding were in command I would wager that my lady and the children would come to no hurt."

Sir Piers mused for a moment with an anxious face.

" Endymion," he said at last, " you speak truly.   There is the stuff of honour in the fellow, in spite of his cropped hair. But what matter ? He is not here.   And I have—I desire to have—no other kindred in arms against my King."

For two days more the final assault was delayed to give the drained moat time to dry up, so that it might support the weight of men, and horses, and gun-carriages. When the hour came, Lady Clavenger and the children did not see much of what happened. Sitting with old Nan and a few weeping women-servants in one of the ancient cellars, they heard the roar of the enemy cannon getting ever louder and nearer, the crackle of their muskets more menacing, and fire of the Manor guns dying down for lack of powder and shot, while the muskets of the defenders were discharged—for the same reason—at longer and longer intervals.

By noon fresh and wide gaps had been hammered in the stout old walls, and soon Radford's men were pouring through them. The garrison had little left to defend themselves with but pikes and garden tools, but with these they fought desperately to the very end. Parson Aubrey, as serene as if he were sitting in the book-room pen in hand, tended the injured and prayed with the dying. Master Endymion, in spite of his lameness, flitted hither and thither, cheering the defenders with scraps of song and patches of old plays, and flourishing one of the wooden swords which the boys had left behind when they were hurried off to shelter.

By the late afternoon it was plain that Winford Manor must surrender, even though no attack had been made by way of the moat. Cornet Langton, after a hasty consultation with Corporal Phineas, sought out Sir Piers and told him reluctantly that it had to be so. Both the Cornet and the Corporal were wounded, the older man on the shoulder, the younger on the forehead, and both had been bandaged by Parson Aubrey with strips of my lady's finest linen sheets.

" What must be the way of it? " asked Sir Piers, in a voice which he tried hard—and in vain—to keep steady.

" We must lower our flag, sir." Tattered and smoke-stained, the blue-and-gold embroidery was still waving from the flagstaff above the burnt-out hall, and Sir Piers, looking up at it with blurred eyes, cried out, " No—that we shall *not* do.   Let those dogs do it, if done it must be.   I will appear before the gatehouse unarmed—that shall be the signal."

Both the Cornet and the Corporal were very doubtful as to whether such a signal would be understood or acted upon by their enemies; but nothing could shake Sir Piers's determination.   First, he must speak to his wife and children—Parson Aubrey with him—and then he would go forth alone.

" What do you think will happen? " Master Endymion asked the Cornet.

" When once they understand what is intended they will not harm him.   But what I fear is a fusillade—before they understand."

Master Endymion nodded thoughtfully.

Not long after Sir Piers crossed the courtyard and joined the Cornet in the porch of the gatehouse.   He had laid aside his sword, replacing it with a long ebony cane with a silver knob. Round his grey velvet doublet was knotted an officers' scarf of scarlet silk with long fringes, and from a silken ribbon about his neck hung an oval medallion of gold embossed with the profile of King Charles.   From all these things it was clear that he knew he was soon to be in danger of death; but he was perfectly calm, even smiling a little with one eyebrow higher than the other, and he laid his hand very kindly—though without speaking—upon Endymion's shoulder.

" I am going up to spy out the land," remarked Endymion. " There is a lull in the fighting.   It were best that Radford himself should be there when you go forth, sir."

" Very true," agreed the Cornet.   " Give us a signal when to throw open the doors."

" In three minutes from now—count them upon your watch, Langton—if I have not descended from the ramparts, do you open the doors.   Three minutes—that should suffice." He limped away and a moment later they heard him stumbling

hastily up the little stone staircase in the thickness of the wall
to the south of the gatehouse.

"I hope he will not show himself," said the Cornet, "he
was ever a mad fellow."

Even as he spoke Colonel Radford and his brother officers
were gazing up in astonishment at the gaily-clad figure
brandishing a wooden sword on the top of the wall.

"Ha, knaves, ha, dogs!" shouted Endymion. "Look upon
one that fears none of you—look upon one that scorns all of
you—

> *With his rage and his wrath*
> *And his dagger of lath*
>   *As he cries Ha, ha! to the Devil!*"

A musket barked. The figure swayed for a moment and then
toppled over backwards, shot through the heart.

In the meantime, the three minutes being past, Cornet
Langton unbarred the double doors, and Sir Piers stepped
forth. The same marksman who had picked off Endymion
raised his musket again, but Colonel Radford stopped him.

"Hold your fire," he commanded, "that is Sir Piers
Clavenger. He is unarmed. They are not closing the doors
behind him. Let the trumpets sound. Great is Jehovah, and
we are the people of His pasture and the sheep of His hand!
Winford Manor is ours."

So speaking, he dismounted and strode hastily as far as the
centre of the causeway where was still the gap blown up by
Corporal Phineas.

"You yield?" he called to Sir Piers.

"I can no other. But I pray that the women and the
children and the wounded men may be dealt with mercifully."

Paying no heed to this appeal, Colonel Radford gave orders
that planks were to be thrown across the gap, and while this
was being done he informed Sir Piers that he was his prisoner,
but that if he wished his wife and children to be brought out

of the Manor before the sack began he would send one of his men to fetch them.

"I do most earnestly wish it," said Sir Piers.

"Corporal Grumgudgeon, do you look to it. Bring the women and the children to the house of the worshipful Master Agag Witherspoon till orders have been received concerning them."

Muttering that such clemency was ill-bestowed, Corporal

THE SAME MARKSMAN . . . RAISED HIS MUSKET AGAIN

Grumgudgeon, accompanied by half a dozen pikemen, stumped across the plank-bridge and into the Manor, where reigned a deathly silence broken only by the moans of the wounded.

"For your own safety you had best leave your house and come hither," said Colonel Radford. "You can see for yourself what my men are about."

As he came slowly across the echoing planks Sir Piers saw

that many of the soldiers were kindling long-handled torches which they swung to and fro to make them blaze. He turned back in terror towards the house, fearing that Penelope and the children might be trapped there and burnt to death; but Colonel Radford sternly bade him halt.

"Said I not that thy womenkind and thy young ones should be brought hither? Has not the godly Corporal gone to fetch them?"

And a few moments later the Corporal and his men re-appeared, ushering—not very gently—Lady Clavenger, carrying Henrietta in her arms, and the three other children all clinging closely to her skirts. Old Justin and old Nan brought up the rear. Some of the soldiers twitched at Penelope's sleeves as she passed, or grinned in her face, or puffed tobacco-smoke at her from their short clay pipes, but with their Colonel's eye upon them they dared do nothing worse.

"You are not hurt, my dear love?" was Penelope's first question when she joined her husband on the Green.

"Nay, sweet Pen. By some strange chance—a lucky chance for me—something diverted their attention when I first came forth."

"It was Endymion," said Lady Clavenger, softly. "He gave his life for you, Piers—yes, his life—I saw him lying dead at the foot of the wall."

"Come, Amalekite," grunted Corporal Grumgudgeon, using one of the scriptural nicknames which the Puritans loved to hurl at the Cavaliers. "Come—unless you would fain be choked with the smoke of destruction." With these words he hustled the Clavenger family across the Green, through rejoicing groups of buff-clad, steel-capped soldiers, and so into the vicarage, whither Colonel Radford had preceded them.

"What of Parson Aubrey?" asked Sir Piers in a low voice as they passed through the changed and now neglected garden.

" He would not quit the wounded," Penelope whispered back.

Hardly had they reached the door of the house when loud cries from within the Manor and climbing columns of blue-black smoke told only too plainly what was happening there.

" Take heed of the flitches of bacon—let the barrels of ale not be consumed! " yelled Zedekiah Miller, his voice rising above the crackle of the flames and the crash of splintered glass. Some of the soldiers were thrusting their torches against the woodwork of the great hall, others were driving their pikes through the painted windows. Soon the brave little blue-and-gold flag blazed up, only to drift to the earth in a tuft of pale grey ash.

" O my brethren," cried Zedekiah, emerging from one of the storerooms with a half-side of bacon clasped lovingly in his arms. " O my brethren, this is indeed a pouring forth of mercies! "

Meanwhile Sir Piers and his family and his two faithful servants were gathered together in the room that had been Parson Aubrey's study. The bookshelves were empty now— Agag Witherspoon was no scholar—but the comfortable chair that Sir Piers had given in happier days was still there, its green velvet cushion deeply dinted by the bony form of the Puritan. Colonel Radford deepened the dint by plumping his far from bony form upon it. As he did not suggest that Penelope should be seated, Sir Piers drew forward a little stool for her. " Let Nan take the babe," he whispered; but the babe's mother would not let her go.

" Piers Clavenger," began the Colonel, abruptly, " the Lord hath delivered thee and thine into the hands of His servants. I await a messenger who will bring me the commands of Sir William Waller as to the disposal of captives and the division of the spoil. Till he comes, ye will abide in this dwelling-place, within barred doors."

" Have we your leave to be alone together for a little space, my husband and I?" asked Penelope, before Sir Piers could speak.

The Colonel shook his head, upon which his high-crowned hat was still firmly planted.

"It may not be. One of my men must abide in the room lest ye contrive mischief between you, children of Belial that ye be. As for your sons and daughters—till orders be given for their better bestowing and nurture—they can be removed to another part of this dwelling, where the godly Agag Witherspoon may strive to bring light to the spiritual darkness of such of them as are of years of understanding."

Only Lucasta and Denzil understood the drift of these words, but when they burst into tears and clung to Penelope, Humphrey burst into tears also and clung to Sir Piers.

"Sir," began the Cavalier, in a voice which mingled anger and despair made hoarse and unsteady, "I pray you—for the little time that may remain——"

Before Radford could answer an interruption occurred in the person of Corporal Grumgudgeon, who clanked into the room and muttered gruffly in his officer's ear, ducking under the broad brim of his hat to do so. The Colonel seemed more vexed than content at the purport of the message, and snapped out, "Let him enter, let him enter," in no very eager tone.

Almost before the words were out of his mouth Captain Francis Fielding appeared, dusty and dishevelled with hard riding and looking much less stiff and stern than on the occasion of his visit to the Manor. On seeing Penelope, he plucked his hat from his head.

Radford, like the rest of his persuasion, was never slow to find a text from scripture, and he welcomed Fielding with a verse from the thirty-seventh Psalm.

"Such," he said, "as are blessed of God shall possess the land; and they that are cursed of Him shall be rooted out."

He expected to be answered in the same manner, but the Captain gave him merely a hasty nod before he turned to

Sir Piers, saying breathlessly, "Kinsman, I have done for you what I could. You are to be sent to the Tower—but not to Tower Hill. Your wife will be permitted to go with you and to remain with you for the term of your captivity."

It was Penelope who answered, for Sir Piers found no words.

"God reward you," she said. "But—oh, kinsman—what of our babes? They talk of taking them from us——"

"The Tower is no place for babes, even at the best," returned the Captain, pleased by the word "kinsman." "We will speak further—we will speak alone. Colonel, is there some other room whither we may repair? I will be answerable for the prisoners—great and small."

The Colonel glared; but remembering how high the young man stood in the favour of Sir William Waller—and of personages even more powerful than Sir William—he had no choice but to give way.

"Ye can abide here," he grunted, "I have other things to do than to hearken to a Captain of Jehovah's host parleying with Amalekites."

So saying he rose and marched out of the room, to be seen a moment later passing the window on his way back to the Manor.

Francis Fielding's first action was to lead Penelope to the chair just vacated by the Colonel. The children were still weeping softly, but when once the alarming person in the high-crowned hat had departed they felt less afraid, and ceased to cling to their parents.

"Kinsman Piers," the Puritan began, "it is right that I should tell you—before we speak further—that it was I who cut off and destroyed the last of Colonel Carless's convoys bringing supplies to the Manor."

Sir Piers stiffened a little as he answered.

"It was you, therefore, who delivered the home of my fathers up to destruction. Had that convoy reached us——"

then he paused, for he himself was not certain that the arrival of the convoy would have meant final victory for the besieged garrison, and added rather wearily—" But why do we talk of these things now? "

" Bethink you," said the Puritan, drawing nearer and dropping his voice, " bethink you what might have befallen—if Colonel Radford had had in his hands the plan showing the place where the moat is fordable."

" Ha—that plan! I have marvelled a dozen times about that plan—but I thought—but I did not think——"

" You shall hear the truth. I found that plan in the pocket of the officer commanding the convoy."

" You *found* it—and yet——"

" I saw at once that if the Manor were assailed from two sides—from the Winford side and from the east—there would be no time for surrender—the whole garrison would be put to the sword, and you and yours would perish with them."

" Better so, maybe—better so. But since—since you did this with good intent—for what my thanks are worth, they are yours."

" I ask—I desire—no thanks. I would pray only that henceforth you will be ready to believe that a man may be a man of honour without being either a prelatist or a Cavalier."

" We do believe it, kinsman," interposed Penelope, " and now—concerning our children——"

" They cannot go with you to the Tower."

Penelope shook her head sadly.

" And must not. Yet what can we do? That man— Colonel—as he calls himself—Radford—he spoke of taking them away—of setting Witherspoon to teach them——"

" Colonel Radford's part is not to decide such matters. I have spoken to Sir William Waller. If you are willing to send your children to White Mays, to the care of Aunt Lettice— nothing worse need befall them."

" White Mays! I had thought of White Mays. If Aunt Lettice——" Penelope paused, afraid to voice her doubts as to whether four young children would be welcome invaders in the house of an old widowed lady.

The Captain read her mind.

" Have no fear," said he, " the care she gives to her doves and her ducks will gladly be shared with these sons and daughters of her race."

" Do you hear that, my darlings? " asked Penelope, turning to Denzil and Lucasta. " There are doves and ducks where you are going."

" But, Mam, we want to go with *you*! " cried Denzil, beginning to weep again.

" That cannot be, my son. But have patience—we shall all be together again some day. Justin and old Nan will be with you. And your great-aunt Lettice—who used to live——" Penelope would have added " at Winford," but the remembrance of what had befallen that beloved place checked the words in her throat. She tried to hide her face against the white mantle of baby Henrietta—and it was then that she saw with some surprise that baby Henrietta was holding out two friendly fat paws to Captain Fielding.

" Here is one who bears no malice," remarked the Captain, patting her head with an awkward hand.

" Let us learn of her, Piers," hinted Penelope; but Sir Piers was still too stunned and too unhappy to do more than mutter a few words of halting thanks to his kinsman. It was not until Captain Fielding was about to quit the room that he roused himself sufficiently to say, " If the stables have not perished in the fire—my horse, Bevis—he lacks exercise— he has long lacked fodder—but 'tis a brave beast—yours, if you will have him."

" He shall not perish if there is yet time," cried the Captain. " I will go myself, but he shall not call *me* master while *you* live."

And with these words he dashed away, and hurried towards the now smoke-shrouded Manor.

There was no small indignation when it became known among Colonel Radford's men that the Amalekites were to be treated with all honour and respect, the elders escorted to London by Captain Fielding in person, Sir Piers riding on his own Flemish steed; and the children allowed to journey to Kent in the charge of their own servants. There was also some disappointment because neither gold nor jewels could be discovered in the vaults under the gutted Manor. Corporal Phineas died of his wounds towards sunset on the day that the siege ended, Parson Aubrey praying beside him to the last. After that, in the smoke, confusion and hubbub, the Parson seemed to vanish as if he had been made of smoke himself: and the body of Cornet Langton was not among the dead. Rumour declared later that the Parson and the Cornet had escaped together, and had found a hazardous refuge in the deserted house at Brackenden. It is certain that when King Charles the Second was restored to the throne of England he appointed the Reverend Edmund Aubrey one of his chaplains; and the Colonel Langton who fought with great gallantry under Marshal Turenne in the Thirty Years War was probably our old friend and no other.

One very surprising result of the lenience with which the Clavengers were treated was a brief truce between Zedekiah Miller and Agag Witherspoon, who heartily agreed that it was iniquitous that Sir Piers and his wife should be released from the Tower after an imprisonment of only seven months. It is true that Sir Piers had to pay an enormous fine for having borne arms against Parliament, and that he had to choose between leaving England and swearing never to draw the sword again for " the man Charles Stuart "; but these measures did not satisfy the two indignant preachers.

The Cavalier and his lady went to The Hague, where they found many exiled royalists as faithful as themselves—and as poor. There they lived for some years, comforted after 1648 by the presence of their children, whom Parliament allowed to join their parents upon the death of Aunt Lettice at the end of that year. Long before then Agag and Zedekiah had fallen out, not over politics but over the interpretation of some knotty text in the Book of the Prophet Micah. Feeling his talents wasted in the country, Agag presently made up his mind to return to London, and Zedekiah settled down in Winford, where his small band of narrow and noisy followers continued to harass the next occupant of the pulpit—an ex-cobbler from Haverley. And then came the marvellous year, 1660, in which " the King enjoyed his own again ": but many more years were to pass before the descendants of Piers and Penelope returned to Winford St. Mary.

CHAPTER VII

A NEW HOUSE WITH AN OLD NAME

" To think that by next holiday time White Mays will be ours no more! "

George Clavenger, thirteen-year-old Etonian and eldest son of Sir Robert of that name, heaved a sigh so deep that it made the gilt buttons of his white silk waistcoat rise and fall: John, his brother, shook his head sadly, causing his black silk hair-tie to wag to and fro; but their eldest sister Caroline neither sighed nor shook her head.

" For my part," she said primly, " I shall like living in a fine new house, and I am glad that Grandpapa made such a lot of money out of the Bubble."

" Why, sister, how could one make money out of a Bubble? " asked six-year-old Amelia, who was usually relegated to the nursery with the younger children, but had followed John—her favourite brother—into the large, low-ceilinged playroom which the elders regarded as their own domain.

" You are too young to understand," retorted Caroline with scorn.

Amelia said no more, in case she should be banished from that honourable society; but she privately resolved to ask John to explain about this mysterious Bubble which she had heard mentioned before. She had not forgotten that one day when Mamma took her and Caro with her on a shopping expedition to the city, they had passed a big, dull-looking house in Leadenhall Street, near the Royal Exchange, and Mamma had said that it was the house to which people went running after the South Sea Bubble. Amelia had never seen the sea; but she had an idea that it was very large and very blue, and she supposed a Sea Bubble would be very large and very blue also—such a beautiful thing that it was no wonder that people went running to see it. She kept this idea to herself, however, in case Caro should laugh at her.

More than thirty years had passed since a wild wave of speculation had swept England and fortunes had been made and lost by people gambling in the stocks and shares of

SOUTH SEA HOUSE, WHERE "PEOPLE WENT RUNNING AFTER THE BUBBLE"

the South Sea Company, which supplied negro slaves and other commodities to the Spanish colonies in Central and South America. Well was it called the South Sea Bubble, for it glittered with dazzling colours and swelled to a huge size before it shared the fate of all bubbles—and burst. Among the lucky investors who sold out before that happened was Sir Charles Clavenger, the grandfather of the four young people seated in the playroom at White Mays one day in the early spring of the year 1745. He was the son of that Denzil Clavenger who, as a small boy, had been sent there with his brothers and sisters after the Manor of Winford St. Mary had been besieged, stormed and sacked during the Civil War. Though the Royalist Parliament summoned at the Restoration voted a sum of money to Sir Piers Clavenger by way of compensation for the losses inflicted on him and the fine exacted from him by the "rebels," the Clavengers remained too poor to bear the heavy expense of rebuilding the Manor, and they were glad to make their home on the Kentish estate brought into the family by the wife of the first Baronet. King Charles the Second, with the best will in the world to be agreeable to the impoverished supporters of King Charles the First, could do nothing more for Sir Piers than stand godfather to his eldest grandchild, Denzil's son. Very gravely His Majesty renounced in the baby's name "the devil and all his works and the vain pomp and glory of the world"; very graciously, with a charming smile on his dark, ugly face, did he hand a silver-gilt christening-cup to Denzil's shy young wife, the baby's mother; and very proud was the nurse to receive the gift of a golden guinea from the royal hand.

It was in a Kentish meadow and not in his native soil of Hampshire that Sir Piers planted the red clover seeds given to him by another exiled Cavalier, Sir Richard Weston. They had both marked the sleekness of the cattle in the Low Countries, and Sir Richard, concluding that it was due to the clover on which they grazed, resolved on his return to England to set about planting it there—where it had never been known before. Three generations of Clavengers lived and died at White Mays, a place well-beloved by Denzil's children, grandchildren and great-grandchildren. Particularly did they love its dovecot and its duck-pond, its cherry orchard, its copse rich in filberts, blackberries and hazels. None of them knew any other home; and though they had all heard about Winford, it seemed to them like a house in a fairy-tale—marvellous, almost magical, but not quite real. Sir Charles, as a small boy, had delighted in hearing stories of the famous siege from his father, Sir Denzil; and he nursed a secret wish that he might some day return to the Manor, pull down the tottering ruins, and build on the historic site a new habitation in a more elegant, classical style. When he grew up, he entered Parliament as Member for a small Kentish borough and was so fortunate as to win the good will of Sir Robert Walpole, the Prime Minister of the period. They were both passionate fox-hunters, and Sir Charles used to be honoured with week-end invitations to Walpole's hunting-lodge in Richmond Park, where they thought and spoke less of politics and Parliament than of horses and hounds.

It was to this love of sport that Charles Clavenger owed his chance to invest in South Sea stock when the " Bubble " was swelling and glittering and to sell out just before it broke into a thousand fragments. Walpole gave him the hint at the right moment, Sir Charles acted upon it, and in a short time the Clavengers entered into possession of a London house, one of the new ones near the Green Park. It was a high, narrow house of red brick with a fanlight of clear glass and fine leaden tracery over the door; it had its own oil lamp in an iron bracket and two cone-shaped extinguishers in which the link-boys escorting sedan chairs could quench their torches. Presently Sir Charles went on a jaunt into Hampshire, taking with him his eldest son Robert (named after the statesman), and together they contemplated all that remained of their ancestral home—the grassy mounds, the jagged fragments of brickwork, the heaps of carved stone, marking the place where the ancient, beautiful and strong-walled Manor of Winford St. Mary had once stood. The villagers gazed in curiosity at the highly varnished travelling-coach painted with the Clavenger arms, and the vicar, the Rev. Theophilus Matcham, came bustling forward to offer cider and plum-cake. When word went round that Sir Charles had a mind to rebuild the Manor and transport his family from Kent to Hampshire there was general satisfaction. The villagers and the farmers had long been paying rent to a distant and unknown landlord, and it was hoped that when once he was in their midst their complaints might receive more sympathetic attention than they ever gained from his bailiff on the spot.

Mr. Matcham, wearing his cleanest bands and the finer of his two grey wigs, entertained father and son hospitably in his vicarage and warmly applauded Sir Charles's intention to make Winford St. Mary his home. No doubt the church would then be re-roofed, the Royal Arms over the communion-table re-painted, and a new pulpit set up? As Sir Charles would see, all these things were very necessary. Mrs. Matcham, a faded woman in a striped chintz morning-gown, glanced anxiously at her husband as if to implore him to put in a word for the vicarage, which needed re-roofing as badly as the church; but Matcham was clever enough to realise that he would make a better impression if he left his own interests last, and that Sir Charles would hardly be likely to restore the sacred building and leave the vicar's dwelling in bad repair.

Meanwhile, the three daughters of the house, Temperance, aged sixteen, Prudence, aged eighteen, and Patience, aged twenty, were hastily removing the curl-papers which had adorned their hair ever since they heard that Sir Charles and his son were coming, putting knots of fresh ribbon on their mob-caps, and sprucing themselves up generally. Sir Charles also had three daughters, all older than his only son, but they were married by now, being pretty and well-dowered— unlike the unfortunate Misses Matcham. The baronet commented uncharitably upon their lack of beauty as the travelling-coach bore him and Robert back to London.

"Very true, sir," assented Robert, "but that was a monstrous fine girl we passed just now—a dark-eyed girl in a green habit, riding a chestnut mare. Did you observe her, sir?"

"I observed the mare," rejoined Sir Charles. "There is sure to be some pretty horseflesh down here, with two good packs in the neighbourhood——"

" Another reason to return to the cradle of our race," said the young man, as a violent jolt over a deep rut cut short his father's remarks.

The next time Sir Charles visited Winford he brought with him Mr. Flitcroft, the fashionable architect who was about that time drawing plans for a new church on the site of a ruinous old one at St. Giles'-in-the-Fields. Nobody would have guessed from his fine clothes and jaunty manner that he had begun life in quite a humble way as a carpenter's apprentice, and had owed all his later success to the circumstance that he accidentally broke his leg when working upon Lord Burlington's new mansion in Piccadilly. The mishap had attracted his lordship's notice to young Flitcroft, who soon demonstrated to his noble patron that he could prepare architectural plans even better than he could carry them out: and it was not long before his fortune was made.

Sir Charles found his condescending manners a little trying, but all his friends assured him that he could make no better choice of an architect for the new Manor of Winford.

" Do you propose to use any of these materials, Mr. Flitcroft? " he enquired, as they stood among the ruins. " I fear the cottagers on the estate have come to regard this place as a free quarry—and, of course, local stone will not be used for the mansion itself—but there is—ahem—there is a good amount of the old stuff still."

" Old stuff indeed, sir, barbarous Gothic," retorted the other, spurning with his buckled shoe some fragments of the ancient porch. " My lord of Burlington would not have allowed me to use it even out of sight in his wine-cellars. But the masons can be instructed to cart some of the larger portions away and deposit them in some remote part of the grounds. Then if your barns or kennels should one day need repair——" and Mr. Flitcroft changed the subject with an air of disgust.

The carved stone imp that had been dubbed in turn " Mahound," " Don Philip " and " Noll Cromwell," lay nameless on the earth; but he grinned up at Mr. Flitcroft as cheerfully as he had grinned down at Lionel of Antwerp and Queen Elizabeth, and just as if he knew that the last word had not been spoken yet.

Young Robert, now twenty-one years old and studying law in London, had been very anxious to accompany his father on this second visit to Winford, but Sir Charles decided that it would be unwise to interrupt his studies again. Robert brooded a little at first; but he was completely consoled in a very short time. At a ridotto, one of the gay dancing parties then fashionable, he saw and was introduced to the same dark-eyed girl whom he had seen riding a chestnut mare on the Haverley road and whom to meet again had been his chief object in wanting to return to Winford. She danced as well as she rode; she was as pretty in a hooped dress of daffodil yellow silk as she had been in a severe green riding-habit; and her name was Lady Sophia Fenworth.

Good Dame Clavenger of Queen Elizabeth's time would, indeed, have been amazed and indignant if she could have seen how " those upstart Fenworths " had drawn level with the ancient family of Clavenger and finally left it behind in the race for worldly glory. The eighteenth-century descendant of the sixteenth-century merchant was an Earl, and his dark-eyed daughter was Maid of Honour to the Princess of Wales, Caroline of Anspach.

Very grateful was young Robert that his father had serenely accepted the House of Hanover when Queen Anne died and the choice had to be made between the Elector George and Prince James as the next occupant of the English throne. The Brackenden Clavengers were Catholics and Jacobites, of course: the head of that branch had followed James II to France and had died fighting for him at the battle of the Boyne ; but the present representative of the family, Mr. Alban Clavenger, was living quietly enough at the little manor-house deep in the woods. He had been brought up by a childless aunt and uncle who, never having meddled in politics, were not regarded with suspicion by the Government.

Long before Mr. Flitcroft's plans were ready Robert Clavenger was married to Sophia Fenworth: they were the parents of the children who sat in the nursery at White Mays, on that spring day in the year 1745, lamenting that they must leave their Kentish home for ever. As for Winford Manor, it seemed as if it would never be finished and ready for occupation. Sir Charles and Mr. Flitcroft constantly quarrelled over designs and materials: there were delays in obtaining the kind of stone desired, and in carting it from Whitby in Yorkshire. There was plenty of good stone in Surrey and Hampshire, but the lord of the manor insisted that his new house should be built of exactly the same fabric as Sir Robert Walpole's great palace in Norfolk. Then when the walls were reared and the roof was on—that is to say, seven years after Sir Charles' first visit to the old site—much time was wasted over the columns for the colonnade and the stone mouldings for the pediment—the triangular space topping the colonnade. Poor Sir Charles did not live to see even the outside of the house completed: he died of a sharp attack of gout in 1737, and it was left to his heir, Sir Robert, to tackle the question of interior decoration.

From their babyhood the children of Robert and Sophia had heard their elders talking about Winford ; but they could hardly think of it as their future home, for the day when they should move there seemed always to recede instead of drawing nearer. Even now, when White Mays had been sold to Colonel Falkner of His Majesty's Foot Guards, and he was coming in another week or two to take possession, the idea of Winford seemed as far-off as ever, for they were not to go there for good until the following year.

"For my part," said George, "I am glad that it is the Colonel who is to own this place. He is a gallant soldier—one of Marlborough's men. I wonder if he will have a trophy of swords and muskets in the hall—and his own picture in his red coat—like great-uncle Lionel has in *his* house."

"Are our pictures to go with us to London?" asked Amelia. "I hope the one of great-grandfather Denzil and great-granduncle Humphrey is to go—because of the pretty little dogs."

"That is a Van Dyck," said Caroline. "Of course it will not be left behind."

"Van Dyck," whispered John to Amelia. "He was a famous painter—he painted Sir Piers and his wife, Penelope, too—you know—the picture hangs in the breakfast-parlour in Clarges Street."

The small girl thanked him with a grateful glance. How good John was—how she would miss him when he went to sea next year on Uncle Maurice's ship!

Their father had made the acquaintance of Colonel Falkner in the hunting-field, and, hearing that the elderly warrior wanted to settle down in Kent, proposed that he should purchase White Mays when the Clavenger family returned to their ancestral domains in Hampshire.

"Hampshire, egad," the Colonel had then said. "There should be some ancestral domains of *mine* in Hampshire. We came from somewhere near Westhampton, I believe. But all that goes back a devilish long way—devilish long."

Colonel Falkner was an honest man. He really did believe that the Hampshire property, of which his father, Alderman Sir Edward Falkner, had vaguely told him, was a manorial estate similar to that of Winford St. Mary: and he would have been surprised, though not in the least put out, if he had known that his ancestors had been yeoman-tenants of the Clavengers, and quite humble folk beside the lord of the manor.

"I shall hate spending my holidays in London," grumbled George. "It will be another hundred years before we go down to Winford—and *then* it won't be a jolly, homely place like White Mays."

"I think it will please *me*," said Caro, smoothing down her sprigged muslin frock. "*I* have no objection to polished marble pavements and panels of Chinese brocade; and I have no doubt that everything will be highly genteel."

Her brothers burst out laughing at her solemn air, and Amelia laughed with them in sympathy, though in her heart of hearts she thought that Caro was probably right and that Winford would be a marvellously beautiful place.

"The dogs will simply loathe it at first," said George, when the laughter had died down. "They are to be sent down there with Stockbridge when we leave here, you know. I heard Papa say so."

"I wish we could be sent down with Stockbridge, too," sighed John, "instead of being mewed up in Clarges Street.

"What, and sleep in kennels, and eat out of troughs?" asked his brother in mock horror.

"Yes—even *that*! Rather than have no home but in London."

Stockbridge was the head kennelman and a great friend of both the boys. As a Kentishman he viewed with horror the prospect of "going to the shires," that strange, unknown country where he had never thought to go; but he faced the adventurous journey with courage for the sake of the hounds. Each of the two boys had some reason to regret White Mays. With George it was his delight in shooting and hunting over country he had known all his life; with John it was his love of the place itself and his friendship with Joe Mackery, the head gamekeeper's son. There was nothing that Joe did not know about the haunts and habits of wild beasts and birds, there was no flower, tree or herb that he could not name; yet on learning that Master John was to go to sea as a midshipman under his uncle, Captain the Honourable Maurice Fenworth, he resolved that he would go too, instead of taking service under his father. Mackery, unlike Stockbridge, had jibbed at " going to the shires," and was glad to remain as head keeper to the Colonel.

Joe was devoted to John just as Wat had been to Piers four hundred years before, and asked nothing better than to serve and follow him ; but the framework of society was stiffer in the 1740's than it had been in the 1350's, and Mackery was constantly reminding his son to knuckle his forehead when either of the young gentlemen drew near, and to be sure to " speak respectful to quality."

Amelia also had struck up a friendship with Joe, who used to make furniture of twigs and acorns and plaited straw for her dolls and could tell wonderful tales about squirrels and badgers and foxes. She was sorry he was not coming to Winford, but glad he was to go to sea with John. While her elder brothers were talking, the little girl was silently wondering if there would be a dovecot and a duck-pond at Winford, and whether they would be made of silver and gold instead of squared grey stones and overlapping red-brown tiles. She had already obtained a promise from Mrs. Chittenden, the housekeeper, that her baby-house and its wax-faced inhabitants should not be left behind at White Mays, but should go with the rest of the nursery baggage to London. Nothing else mattered very much from Amelia's point of view.

A few weeks later the whole family had bidden farewell to White Mays—where Colonel Falkner was already directing the arrangement of trophies of glittering weapons on the staircase walls—and were on their way to London.

Rumours were flying to and fro that young Prince Charles Edward, the son of the Stuart claimant to the British throne, would shortly attempt to land somewhere in Britain, push little, podgy, red-faced King George the Second off the throne, and set up in his stead the dark, depressed-looking elderly gentleman whom the Jacobites called King James the Third

and the anti-Jacobites the "Old Pretender."[1]   It had seemed
as if something of the sort were going to happen in the
previous year, when the King of France had thought it a good
move to attempt to invade England
with fifteen thousand troops,
headed by Prince Charles, but
actually commanded by a more
experienced soldier, Marshal Saxe.
Then the French naval squadron
which was to have convoyed the
troopships fled as the British fleet
hove in sight, and the troopships
themselves were scattered by a
sudden storm. After that France
lost interest in the Stuart cause,
and Louis XV decided that Marshal
Saxe would be more usefully employed fighting England and Austria
on the Continent, where the War
of the Austrian Succession was
raging.

Sir Robert and his lady were
discussing these matters in their
great travelling-coach as they rattled
and jingled on their way to London.
The three eldest children were with
them, but Amelia, Frederick and

JACOBITE WINE-GLASS WITH
HEAD OF PRINCE CHARLES

Maria followed with their nursemaids in a smaller and less
comfortable carriage.

"La, Sir Robert," said Lady Sophia, fanning herself,
"you do not apprehend further danger in that quarter, do
you? Without French aid, what can the foolish young man
obtain?"

"Nothing, madam, nothing—but he *is* a foolish young man,

[1] The Old Claimant, *not* the Old Impostor.

and he may embarrass us by some crackbrained adventure. Recollect, madam, that things are not going too well for us abroad: we have now no Marlborough to command our armies."

" Fie, fie, sir—I vow we shall do very well. And have we not a royal Hercules in young William of Cumberland ? I shall be vastly surprised if he does not cut all the seven heads off this Gorgon."

" Hydra, madam, hydra—unless you mean Perseus, not Hercules. It was the hydra, not the Gorgon—— "

" 'Tis of no consequence, Sir Robert—you know I never could abide mythology. Might I trouble you to unbuckle that case ? I have a fancy for some chocolate."

The case was a sort of casket of embossed leather in which nestled a silver flask of the fashionable beverage and a small silver beaker bearing the Clavenger crest. It was no easy matter to take a sip between each lurch of the coach, but Lady Sophia managed it very cleverly. No doubt she was right in declaring that none of the children could do the same without drenching themselves, though each one of them secretly disagreed.

" Oh, by the by," said her ladyship, when the case had been strapped up again, " I forgot to tell you. Papa, in the letter which I received yesterday, mentions that they say down yonder that Alban Clavenger has quitted Brackenden."

" Quitted Brackenden, madam ? Do you mean that he has given the place up for good ? "

" Nay, Sir Robert. It seems that he has been absent for some weeks and that no one knows where he has gone."

" On some Popish pilgrimage, no doubt—unless—stay—I had not thought of that. Unless there *is* some Jacobite mischief afoot and he has gone to meddle in it."

" Papa seems to be of your mind. Poor kinsman Alban—such a pity he was bred a Papist—he is such an elegant-looking man, and has such a fine seat on a horse. It must be seven

years or more since we last met, but I remember him
well."

"For my part," said Sir Robert, "I wish he had remained
at Brackenden: that would have been the best surety for his
good behaviour."

"'Twas rumoured at one time that he had a mind to be
a monk," mused Lady Sophia.

"Pity that such a straight rider to hounds should be cooped
up in a cloister," said Sir Robert, feelingly, "and yet"—he
added—"and yet—that might be the better way."

"Better than *what*, Sir Robert?"

"Better, madam, than a headsman's axe on Tower Hill."

The children were listening to this conversation with more
interest than they usually paid to the remarks of their elders.
Though they had never seen their mysterious kinsman or been
anywhere near Brackenden, they had heard vague rumours of
spying and plotting, of midnight journeys and secret ciphers,
and treasonable trafficking with the old gentleman in Rome
who so foolishly maintained that he was the King of England.
These "goings on" were a frequent subject of conversation in
the housekeeper's room, and when George, John and Caro
were privileged to eat Mrs. Chittenden's quince preserve off
her very own blue-and-white plates they often heard her and
Bulstrode the butler talking with bated breath of "that
Jacobite gentleman." The housekeeper was a Hampshire
woman, bred on the Haverley abbey estate, and she prided
herself on knowing all about the gossip (only she did not call it
"gossip") of three counties—Hampshire, Middlesex and
Kent. She was particularly interested in news from her native
county, and corresponded regularly with her sister, who was
personal maid to old Lady Fenworth, now over seventy and
past riding to hounds, though not past enjoying a pinch of
snuff, a dish of tea, and a game of cards.

A few weeks after the Clavengers were established in their
London house intelligence reached England that the young,

herculean Duke of Cumberland—the same in whom Lady Sophia felt such confidence—had been defeated by Marshal Saxe at the battle of Fontenoy. King Louis had been right in thinking that the Marshal would be more useful to France on the Continent; yet the battle might have been a " draw " but for the brilliant part played by the Irish Brigade, a body of Jacobites from Ireland serving under the French flag.

George wrote indignantly from Eton to ask Papa's assurance that the news was false. John swore that if Fontenoy had been a sea-fight the end would have been different: and Sir Robert remarked darkly that if that Boy (as he always called Prince Charles) had a mind to risk a throw, now was his time.

The Boy *had* a mind ; and the next piece of information to set London buzzing was that he had landed on the little island of Eriskay in the Outer Hebrides, with no more support from France than the loan of a French frigate in which to make the journey. Some accounts said he had seventy companions— some, completely wild, said seven hundred: in plain truth he had but seven. Less than a month later he had raised his father's standard in Glenfinnan and many Highland chieftans marched to join him, followed by their clansmen, who were armed with ancient daggers, swords and round shields and cheered by the shrill notes of the bagpipes as they came.

London in the late summer was hot, dusty and uncomfortable, and the young Clavengers sighed for White Mays, all except Caro, who persisted in sighing for Winford instead. With such strange tidings coming from Scotland many people were in much doubt as to whether it would be wiser to stay in the capital or flee to the country. George wished passionately that he were two years older and therefore able to take up his commission as Ensign in the 38th or Duke of Marlborough's Regiment of Foot. John was equally anxious to join his sailor uncle afloat: even four-year-old Frederick stamped about the nursery with a small toy pistol and said he was killing " Tots." Sir Robert, who at first had listened with more amusement than alarm to tales of what was happening in Scotland, presently began to wonder whether Mr. Clavenger of Brackenden would put in a word for his Protestant kinsfolk with King James the Third—if the unlikely should occur and the House of Hanover were driven from the English throne.

As for Lady Sophia, she vowed she did not know what to make of it all, but it was vastly provoking. If these dreadful savages from the Scottish mountains had captured Edinburgh, what was to prevent them doing the same to London?

"Permit me, madam, to point out," said Sir Robert, with some annoyance, "that they have not captured the whole of Edinburgh. The English garrison still holds out on the Castle Rock."

"It would be more to the purpose if they came down from the Castle Rock and drove the rascals out of the city," retorted his wife. "Who knows what may befall? They say that Scottish ladies of the first fashion pelted the Prince with white roses."

"What is more grave, madam, is that Scottish gentlemen of the first consequence are wearing the white cockade to show that they are Jacobites."

"White roses," mused Lady Sophia, laying down the tambour-frame upon which she was embroidering a new waistcoat for Sir Robert, "white roses—there was a prodigious fine white rose-bush in the rosery at White Mays, but I suppose nothing has been laid out properly at Winford yet. As for cockades, I might drive down to the City to-morrow and buy some dozens of yards of ribbon; but there is a vast quantity of quilled white ribbon on the curtains and coverlet of Maria's cradle, and Mimms could very well flatten it out."

"Madam," exclaimed Sir Robert, clutching with both hands at his crisply-curled and freshly-powdered wig, "you speak as if all were already lost! All is *not* lost——"

"Lud, Sir Robert, how can you be sure of that?"

rejoined his lady, holding her frame at arms' length to admire the effect of her handiwork.

It was indeed very difficult to be sure of anything as the year waned; and when news came that the good-looking young Prince with the red-gold hair had crossed the Border at Carlisle and was marching south with more than six thousand men, many nervous people rushed to withdraw their money from the Bank of England, while shopkeepers were afraid to take down their shutters in the morning lest before evening a horde of naked-kneed Highlanders should burst in and plunder the shops. Those terrible fellows had defeated the English under Sir John Cope at Prestonpans, near Edinburgh: would it be possible to drive them back to Scotland again—and the Young Pretender back to France? Or would the English people be chained in Popish chains?

One day Sir Robert met Mr. Horace Walpole, son of the great statesman then recently dead, and reported their conversation to his lady.

"Horry does not know what to be at. He is at one moment in a flutter about the rebellion and at the next in a flutter about an ancient Roman eagle which he has just added to his collection. But I agree with him that the good people of England have at last rubbed their eyes and looked about them, and that this is no time for what he calls wet-brown-paperness."

Cumberland, smarting from his defeat at the hands of Marshal Saxe, undertook with alacrity the task of clearing Great Britain of the "rebels." There had been little or no enthusiasm for the rising among the English Jacobites, most of whom were far away in the West Country, and even in Scotland the Lowlands were almost solid for the House of Hanover while the Highlands were not completely solid for the House of Stuart. Every day after the mixed Anglo-Hanoverian army set out on its northward march there was less and less "wet-brown-paperness" in England. It is true that Mimms, Lady Sophia's maid, gave a loud scream and fainted away when she heard that the Young Pretender and his kilted barbarians had reached Derby; but Mrs. Chittenden revived her by holding burning feathers to her nose and told her roundly that she was a silly wench.

When George and John came home for the Christmas holidays it was known that the Scottish army was in retreat, and the year 1746 was ushered in by joybells celebrating the surrender of Carlisle to Cumberland. The quilled ribbon was allowed to remain on Maria's cradle, and the gardener directing the planting of the rose-garden at Winford received no instructions to cultivate white roses with particular care.

Mr. Horace Walpole came to dine in Clarges Street, and said " Pho! " at the very idea of a Jacobite victory. He asked if he might see George and John, and learn from them how they fared at his old school. Did the clock still strike with the same cracked sound? How often were they " in a bill " for laughing in chapel? Was their dame very severe? Did the boys still bowl hoops and keep pet linnets as they did in *his* Eton days?

The boys answered all these eager questions politely, interested in the questioner because they knew he was the son of the great Sir Robert Walpole, their grandfather's friend. But this spindle-shanked, pale-faced gentleman did not look as if *he* were a keen fox-hunter. Caro, who was also present, appreciated the elegant bow with which he offered her some comfits from an enamelled box suddenly produced from a pocket in his long-skirted lavender-coloured coat. She noticed that he wore his hair as her brothers did theirs, unpowdered and tied behind with a drooping black bow. Papa, however, had changed his full-bottomed brown wig for a white tie-wig some years before.

It had been arranged that John was to join his uncle's ship, the *Intractable,* in February, when she was due to set sail for the West Indies, where the English were endeavouring to inter-

cept French convoys on their way to the trading settlements of
the French East India Company in Madras. As the move to
Winford would not be made until March it seemed as if a
year—or more—might elapse before he could hope to see his
new home, though he passed within twelve miles of it on his
way to Portsmouth. Mrs. Chittenden, affectionately known
as " Old Chitty," rejoiced that Master John should be the
first of the young gentlemen to breathe " the good Hampshire
air "—for he was as great a favourite with her as he was with
Amelia.

Amelia, herself was inconsolable when her second brother
departed, but a few weeks later she was enchanted to receive
a letter from him, written in round, chubby characters, easy
for a seven-year-old to read. He painted a cheerful picture
of his life at sea, with joking remarks about sleeping in a
hammock well below the water-line and eating iron-hard salt
beef and stony biscuits from which weevils were wont to
creep: he did not add that the cabin of the midshipmen com-
pared very unfavourably with the kennels that housed Sir
Robert's pointers, or that those intelligent animals would
undoubtedly have turned away from the food which the
hungry young gentlemen were glad enough to gulp down.

The blue-and-white naval uniform was not introduced for
another year, so the officers dressed as they pleased and the men
as they could. Amelia was much amused to hear about the
seamen with their flapping canvas trousers, bright kerchiefs,
brass ear-rings and long pigtails stiff with tar. The figure-head
of the *Intractable*, declared John, only needed a pleated white
mob-cap with a grey silk bow to be a perfect likeness of " Old
Chitty." What he did not tell his sister—nor, indeed, anybody—was that he had been desperately seasick at first and
was often homesick still. Their uncle, the Captain, wisely
refrained from showing him too much favour in case the other
midshipmen should grow jealous; but what was harder for
John was the discovery that his friend Joe would not be

allowed to wait on him, as they had both hoped he might. Captain Fenworth warned his nephew—quite kindly—that if he were to single Joe out for marks of good will he would merely make the boy's life miserable among the rough lads of the lower deck. When Joe resolved to follow Master John to sea little did he guess that he would get only brief and far-off glimpses of him: yet both boys took kindly enough to their new way of life when once its newness began to wear off.

At John's earnest request George, during the Easter holidays, wrote a full account of their Hampshire home. A prodigious fine house, he pronounced it to be, mighty fine outside, with pillars, and a portico, and sashed windows like those in Clarges Street, not barbarous casements as at White Mays. Inside he had to confess that it was rather bleak and bare: the Chinese panels were not yet in place, the various curtains, Genoa velvet, glazed chintz, striped cotton, had not all been hung, and except in the great bedchamber not a carpet had been laid. The library was mighty fine, with mahogany shelves enclosed in glass doors, but Papa's books had not yet been unpacked. There were alcoves in the corners, painted pale green, in which Mamma intended to set forth some of her Chinese porcelain.

" Old Chitty," George reported, was beside herself with joy to be in Hampshire again, and the dogs seemed to be settling down well enough, but Stockbridge had not ceased to sigh for Kent. Later, when the weather improved and the roads dried up, there would be formal visits to be paid to Grandmamma Fenworth at Haverley Abbey—did John remember her, her lap-dog and her snuff?—and to Uncle and Aunt Fenworth and some small cousins; but for the present Mamma was too busy and the roads were too muddy. As to the park, it would no doubt be uncommon fine in time, but some of the trees were still very young and small, and had to be held up by stakes larger than themselves. The garden, too, would be even better than the one at White Mays, though as yet the orchard was too newly-planted to be worth attention. A duck-pond had been promised, and later there might be a lake, and an artificial island, and a bridge in the Chinese fashion: "but," added George, gloomily, "I doubt if we shall be allowed to play Robinson Crusoe on that island." Then came the most exciting part of his letter:

"Brother, there is a better place for such sport. Beyond the park, where no one ever goes, there is a sort of thicket with winding paths, all overgrown with high bushes: in the midst is a clearing, and a heap of old stones, some of them carved with monstrous strange faces. Shall we not play Crusoe there when you come home? You can be Man Friday. Caro would serve for the parrot: she talks enough, and she has got a new green gown; but the governess, Miss Pipps, or Fipps, or some such name, is coming after the summer holidays and we shall be less plagued with Madam Caro then."

"We went to church on Sunday. Our pew has red curtains like the one in St. James's, Piccadilly, but the church here is not near so elegant. One part of it is full of old tombs of Clavengers, knights in armour and ladies with monstrous strange headdresses, and scarcely a nose or a finger among them. The Vicar bowed low to Papa before he began his sermon: it was a prodigious long sermon. He took for his text—"I have heard of thee with the hearing of the ear and now mine eye seeth thee," and every time he said it he bowed to Papa. Mamma speaks of starting a dame's school for the children in the village, but there is no old dame hereabouts that can tell A from B except an aged one who lives in a thatched hut on the Westhampton road and is said to be a witch. She has three black cats. They are named after the Vicar's three ugly daughters, Patience, Temperance and Prudence."

Shortly after this letter was dispatched news came from the north that William Augustus, Duke of Cumberland, and his well-equipped, war-hardened army of English and German soldiers had met and defeated " the Boy " and his devoted, undisciplined Highlanders on the lonely moor of Culloden, near Inverness.   Experience and artillery proved more than a match for wild valour imperfectly armed with old-fashioned weapons.   It was all over in little more than two hours, and Charles Edward escaped to the mountains.   The English Government promptly offered £30,000 to anyone who should deliver him up, alive or dead; and, knowing how desperately poor were the humble folk upon whose aid he would depend, they confidently expected that someone would soon betray him and claim the handsome reward.

Three of his most important followers, the Earls of Cromartie and Kilmarnock and Lord Balmerino, were brought to London and tried upon a charge of high treason in Westminster Hall—draped with scarlet cloth for the occasion.   Sir Robert decided to return to London to witness the trial, and Lady Sophia accompanied him, for she was beginning to find the echoing, carpetless Manor a little depressing and the younger children were quite safe there with Nurse and Old Chitty.   Also, she did not want to miss the fireworks in Hyde Park—a gorgeous display in honour of Cumberland's victory. Her ladyship was inclined to be sorry for Lord Kilmarnock when she learned that he was young, good-looking and wore his hair very elegantly dressed and tied; but Sir Robert's sympathy was all for Lord Balmerino, who was past middle age and yet remained cheerful and unconcerned up to his last moments upon the scaffold on Tower Hill.

Many of the Clavengers' friends went to see the execution of the two " rebel " lords—Cromartie was pardoned, and so ceased to be interesting—and though Sir Robert did not himself care much for spectacles of that sort, he remained in London until the event was over, and listened with interest to the accounts of those who were present. Kilmarnock died bravely enough, though he had pleaded with undignified earnestness for his life, but Balmerino, who had refused to beg for pardon, trod the scaffold with the air of a victorious general, declared that if he had a thousand lives he would lay them all down in the same cause, pulled a nightcap of tartan on to his head, and gave the signal to the executioner by tossing up his arm as if he were giving the signal for battle.

Mr. Walpole was nearly in tears over the heroic conduct of " brave old Balmerino " when he came to drink a dish of tea with Lady Sophia on the morrow of the execution; but this did not prevent him from reading to her the rough draft of some lines which he was busy composing in honour of the Duke of Cumberland.

> " *What youth is he with comeliest conquest crowned,*
> *His war-like brow with full-blown laurels bound?* "

Lady Sophia repeated the words with enthusiasm: vastly elegant, she assured Mr. Walpole, and richly deserved.

Meanwhile, the people of London, though quite ready to gape at fireworks and rejoice at their delivery from " Popish chains," had heard something of the ruthless brutality with which Cumberland was treating the vanquished Scots and they had bestowed upon him the nickname of " the Butcher," by which he will always be known. Presently the whole of England learned of his deeds: and in the nursery of Winford Manor Frederick Clavenger put away his toy pistol with the comment " Tots all dead now."

CHAPTER VIII

"KINSMAN CRUSOE"

GEORGE had hoped and expected that when Eton broke up for the summer holidays he would be allowed to join his parents in Clarges Street: his disappointment was great when he was packed off to Hampshire instead. Lady Sophia was very fond of her eldest son, but she felt that he would be vastly in the way in London without John to bear him company. George, she pointed out to Sir Robert, was just at that awkward age when you could not dismiss him to the nursery and yet did not want him in the drawing-room. Sir Robert agreed; adding that the boy would do very well at Winford, where he could shoot over the coverts with the new gamekeeper and go riding with the head groom. Was not his own mare installed down there in waiting for him? And his dog, Growler?

Caro, Amelia and Frederick welcomed their brother with joy, but it must be confessed that for the first three weeks they did not find him very cheerful company. Then something wonderful happened—nothing less than the arrival of a coach from Portsmouth with a rather yellow-faced and hollow-eyed midshipman sitting inside—Midshipman John Clavenger, on special sick-leave after a bad bout of fever in Barbados.

The ship's doctor of the *Intractable* had bled and blistered and physicked the Captain's nephew with anxious energy, but John remained so weak that his uncle became alarmed. " I would rather," barked Captain Fenworth, " face all the guns in the mounseers' navy all at once than face sister Sophia if a son of hers had died aboard my ship." His next step was to approach the Admiral in command of the West Indies Fleet for permission to send the invalid home on a fast frigate then due

GENTLEMAN'S COSTUME, FIRST HALF OF EIGHTEENTH CENTURY

to sail.   The Admiral happened to be in a good humour after
a glass of choice Curaçoa and a particularly juicy pineapple:
permission was granted, and the next morning John found

himself in one of the *Intractable's* boats being rowed towards the frigate *Nereid*. One of the two rowers was Joe Mackery, for whom John had called in his delirium, and who had been allowed to nurse him when the fever was at its height. Regardless of what the effect might be on the feelings of the other rower, the midshipman put his hand on his friend's shoulder and said in a rather unsteady voice. " I wish you were coming with me, Joe."

Not a word did Joe answer as he sat resting on his oars and watching John prepare to climb up the rope-ladder swaying against the side of the *Nereid*; but each boy knew perfectly well what was passing in the mind of the other. An hour later John took a last look at his own ship from the deck of the frigate. Very beautiful the *Intractable* looked, her bunched-up, tawny-white sails leaving the fine lines of her masts and rigging etched against the purple-blue sky, and her figure-head dipping and rising gently with the motion of the lazy little waves.

" To think," mused the midshipman, " to think that four months ago I knew the right names of none of those ropes— and now I know them all! "

When he reached Winford he had among his baggage, in addition to his sea-chest, a wooden case full of gifts from Captain Fenworth to his sister—a jar of ginger, a length of India muslin as thin as gauze and as soft as silk, and a marvellous fringed shawl woven in many gay colours. On his knee the midshipman held a brass cage containing a small and lively green parrot which never ceased to scream, " Bring me my rum, you lubbers—bring me my rum! " Amelia jumped with joy when she made the acquaintance of Quanko—as the parrot was named—and half forgot her disappointment that Joe Mackery had not returned with brother John. She had hoped that Joe would, not only because she liked him but also because she needed some new furniture for her baby-house. All the Clavenger children were excited by John's arrival, but none of them more so than Mrs. Chittenden and Nurse, who almost came to blows in their eagerness to coddle the convalescent. Nurse dosed him with tar-water, which tasted, he said, as if it had been stirred with a sailor's pigtail, and would fain have kept him in bed, or, at least, indoors all day: " Chitty," whose ideas were quite different, cheered him with treacle possets and spiced warm ale, and rebuked her rival for trying to deny to him the benefits of " the good Hampshire air." Each good soul took all the credit when— in a very few days—he began to look more robust; and each vowed that *she* would have him all to rights again by the time that Sir Robert and her ladyship came down to Winford at the end of the month.

" Now we shall not need Caro when we play Robinson Crusoe," whispered George to John, as they fed the parrot with hard-boiled egg. Both boys were longing for an after-noon so fine and dry and yet so temperate that they would be allowed to go out and explore the wilderness beyond the park. Chitty urged that they should take George's dog, Growler, with them: for she had heard that poachers and vagabonds sometimes used that wild piece of ground as a hiding-place. There was one particularly bad character whom she hoped they would not meet—who was, she trusted, in jail again—an old ruffian called Abel Miller, who, when tipsy, would tell a crazy story that his forefathers had once been prosperous farmers in the parish. The story, though it sounded crazy, was true: while the descendants of William Falconer had risen in the world, the last remaining descendant of Nick the Miller, the great-grandson of the Puritan Zedekiah, had sunk as low as the mud.

At last the desired day came, dappled with high clouds but without any threat of rain. Leaving Caro—to her great indignation—to play with Frederick, and Amelia under the eye of Nurse, the two elder boys hurried off in the direction of what they intended to claim as their own domain. Growler went with them, but they decided to leave Quanko, the parrot, at home until they had built Robinson Crusoe's hut.

It was indeed a fascinating playground, this wilderness that had sprung up where once Queen Elizabeth had sauntered along sanded paths edged with trimly clipped hornbeam and yew. Twenty years had passed since Mr. Flitcroft's masons had dumped a quantity of broken stones in its depths, and briars and creeping ivy had obliterated their tracks almost entirely. Only here and there could faint traces be seen of the original pathways, and the old hedges had grown up so high that the undergrowth was always in shadow. To the left— as you went in—the trees thinned a little and the tangled vegetation merged into a tract of rough ground where Mr. Flitcroft had made preparations to lay out the stables until checked by Grandpapa Charles, who wished to have them nearer the house. Growler immediately started a rabbit in that direction, and the boys did not trouble to whistle him back.

" Where are the old carved stones ? " demanded John, as he and George struggled forward.

" Bear to the right—there is a little clearing beyond that tall clump of yew. Let me go ahead."

And George plunged on, only to halt with an exclamation of surprise:

" Someone has been here since last I came! "

" What makes you think that ? " demanded John, hurrying after him.

" Look—yonder—the undergrowth has been broken—and the track has been made plainer on the ground."

" Perhaps a badger has an earth somewhere yonder."

" A badger! Has sea-water washed away all your wit that you do not remember that the path to a badger's earth is always strewn with sticks and pebbles and feathers and bones ? "

" To be sure, brother, it is. What a pity that the ground is too dry to take the print of a foot. Are you certain that these things were not thus when you came before ? "

"I swear they were not. I took particular heed because I wanted to find my way back to the old stones."

"Maybe it is the vagabond Chitty told us of—one Mill or Miller, or some such name."

"Well," retorted George stoutly, "even if it be, we are two to one, and Growler will come if we whistle. But more likely it is one of the keepers, or some gipsy after rabbits."

"I thought you said nobody ever came here."

"No matter what I said, somebody *has* come here. And I should like to know who. Look, there are the stones—but——"

George halted as before, with a puzzled face—"but they have been shifted—that block was on its side that now stands upright. Brother, anyone would think that Robinson Crusoe himself had been here and had begun to build him a hut."

John peered about on every side, lamenting that he had left his spy-glass with his sword and sextant on the *Intractable*.

"Whoever it is has come from the farther end of the thicket," said he. "Do you know what lies beyond on that side?"

"Marshland—with some strips of willow and thorn among the rushes."

John raised a seaman's eye towards the place where a silvery blur behind the clouds showed the position of the sun.

"It must be close on half-past five, and we promised we would return no later. Let us be content for now; and to-morrow we will come again. Perhaps we will find Mr. Crusoe sitting under his goat-skin umbrella."

George agreed with regret, muttering that after Papa and Mamma arrived they would have fewer chances to slip away and amuse themselves.

Unluckily the next day was wet and stormy, and the day after *that* Grandmamma Fenworth drove over from Haverley to visit the children and to see for herself how John was faring. He was still rather pale under his sunburn, and the old lady pronounced him to be as yellow as a guinea; but as she gave him one, "to match his face" she said, he did not mind the comparison. There then remained only a single day before Papa and Mamma were expected, and to the horror of both boys Chitty and Nurse took it into their heads to watch them carefully in case they should get into any mischief, or over-exert themselves, with bad effects upon John's health: "for," declared Chitty, "I wish her ladyship to see how the dear

SIR ROBERT AND LADY SOPHIA ADMIRING THEIR NEW HOUSE

young gentleman has thriven in my care"; "for," said Nurse, "I want dear Master John to do his old nurse credit."

When Lady Sophia *did* arrive she was rather shocked at the altered looks of her second son, who was taller and thinner as well as more sallow than she had imagined that he would be: but in her excitement at the presents he brought from Uncle Maurice she soon forgot about it. Sir Robert added a guinea to that bestowed by old Lady Fenworth, asked a few questions about his brother-in-law and his ship, and then hurried out to inspect the stables and the kennels, and to give orders that the coach-horses should be harnessed betimes next morning to take him into Westhampton, to an emergency meeting of Justices of the Peace.

All up and down England people were on the look-out for Jacobite plotters, Jacobite fugitives, Jacobite sympathisers, and though the decisive victory on Culloden Moor was held to have ended their hopes for ever, the Government in London was anxious to round up all the notorious rebels, and, by fines and banishment when execution seemed too severe a penalty, to stamp out the last smouldering embers of the " rebellion." It was known that there were one or two Catholic (and therefore presumably Jacobite) families in the neighbourhood, and the Justices had decided to meet in order to discuss the best methods of getting them under lock and key.

" I only hope," said Sir Robert at breakfast next day, " that it may not be my painful duty to sign a warrant for the apprehension of my kinsman, Alban Clavenger of Bracken-den."

" He is the last of that line, is he not? " asked Lady Sophia, sipping her China tea from a lovely little cup without a handle.

" The very last—and if one could be sure that he would in good sooth turn monk, and so have no sons to carry on that Popish strain, I would almost be inclined to wish him safely overseas."

With these words Sir Robert took a pinch of snuff, flicked his lace ruffle with a fine cambric handkerchief embroidered with the Clavenger crest, bowed slightly to Lady Sophia, and departed.

His departure gave his two impatient sons the opportunity for which they had been longing. Would Mamma allow them, please, to go and play in the park? They would be very careful not to tear their clothes or to get too hot. Lady Sophia, who was promising herself a pleasant morning with

Chitty examining patterns of stamped velvet for the new dining-room chairs and inspecting store-cupboards and linen-chests, gave a ready assent. Might they take some Naples biscuits with them? To be sure—she had brought some specially for John from the Italian shop at the sign of the Pineapple in Berkeley Square: and Mrs. Chittenden would give them an orange apiece.

Their pockets well stuffed, George and John hurried off—this time without Growler, for it had occurred to them that he might frighten away the mysterious person whom they were so anxious to discover.

They followed the same path that they had taken before, and when they reached the clump of yew they both uttered cries of surprise. In the distance they could see a rough sort of cabin made of odd blocks of stone and roofed with brushwood. Leading to it from the farther edge of the thicket were the tracks of a pair of feet, some going, some coming, but always the same feet, shod with shoes that were certainly not a tramp's, for they had the rather high heels and angular toes that the shoes of gentlemen had at that period.

"Brother, we were right!" breathed George, almost speechless. "Look at those footmarks—you can see them well enough after all that rain. Look at that hut——"

"I do, and I am going to look inside."

With these bold words John stepped forward and peered under the low timber screen that formed the roof.

"Come hither," he called to George, "come hither quickly."

He pointed into the hut, which was about eight feet long, five feet wide, and not quite five feet high, and George saw that on the earthern floor there was a heap of bracken over which was spread a cloak of dark blue cloth lined with crimson. On the top of the cloak was a small book bound in black leather, and beside that lay a crumpled handkerchief of fine cambric smeared with the brown stain of dried blood.

For a moment the two boys stood gazing at all these things in the narrow patch of light that shone through the entrance to the rough structure.

"What's to be done?" asked George, perplexed; "ought we to go and tell someone—perhaps Papa?"

"Wait a little," urged John, "I have a notion—we shall soon see if it is a mad one or no. First I must anchor alongside and look closer at that book and that handkerchief."

Already his life at sea had made him more resolute and audacious than his brother, who watched him in alarm mixed with admiration as he picked up the slender volume and turned over the leaves.

"Latin, it is Latin—*Pater noster—credo—Dominus vobiscum*—it must be a Popish prayer book. So—I will put it just where it was—it has made itself a little hollow—and now for the handkerchief—ah!"

He held it out for George's inspection so that the light fell upon the corner, embroidered—as Sir Robert's handkerchiefs were always embroidered—with the Clavenger key.

"I thought so," said John.

"These things belong to our kinsman who lives at Brackenden," muttered George, like one in a dream, "then he—then this——"

"Yes," nodded John, "we have discovered his hiding-place. And I wish we had not."

"So do I," agreed George, after a moment's reflection; "he is a rebel and a Papist, to be sure—and we ought not to be sorry for him. Yet I am. What shall we do?"

"Leave him an orange and some of our biscuits—and come back—if we can—later in the day."

Another idea struck George.

"How," said he, "how if the man Mill—or Miller—should have murdered our kinsman and stolen these things?"

John meditated a little and then shook his head.

"Nay," he remarked wisely, "vagabonds steal money—

and silver plate—and watches, not prayer books and handker-chiefs. Let us go home and say nothing. When he finds the orange and the biscuits he will know that he has been discovered—but he will know that we are friends."

"*Are* we friends?" protested George. "*Ought* we to be friends? He is a rebel, brother—a rebel, and a Papist. Yet Papa *did* say that he was a straight rider to hounds. Do you remember? That day in the coach, coming from White Mays."

"Well," said John, "we can decide that when we have seen him—I am determined to see him. I wonder where he is *now*?"

"There are some ashes outside the hut," cried George, "and there are some bones—birds' bones. Maybe he has been catching birds on the marshes and cooking them."

"You are right," agreed John; "that means he must intend to lodge here for a time—that, and his book, and his bed of bracken. Let us go home. When Papa returns we shall hear what the Justices of the Peace are about. But say nothing. This is *our* secret, brother."

"This is our secret," repeated the elder solemnly.

When her brothers reappeared, Caro, who was an in-quisitive child, at once wanted to know where they had been, why their clothes were all muddy and torn, and what they were looking so important about.

"When Miss Phipps comes," retorted George, "I hope the first sampler she sets you a-sewing will be *Curiosity killed the Cat*."

"Sampler!" echoed Caro. "I have sewn enough samplers, I promise you. I hope Miss Phipps will teach me feather-work and stitchery with spangles."

Her attention had been successfully distracted, and after a scornful remark about the pleasure which boys seemed to take in making themselves dirty, she returned to *The Little Pretty Pocket Book* which said that it was designed " to make Tommy a good boy and Polly a good girl," but was not as dull as it sounded.

In spite of their honest intentions, George and John *had* torn their clothes, and they soon realised with alarm that a return trip to the wilderness would be out of the question that evening. Nurse hustled them into fresh clothes—their best, of blue velvet braided with lighter blue; with these suits their

BOYS' COSTUME, FIRST HALF OF EIGHTEENTH CENTURY

finest lace ruffles were worn, their white silk stockings and their black buckled shoes. It appeared that Lady Sophia had given the word that they were to dine with her and Sir Robert—the dinner-hour being six o'clock. George was inconsolable, but John whispered in his ear that they might hear some news. "Tack about, brother," urged John; "run up other colours, or they will think you are about some unlawful business and send a shot across your bows."

This naval language was unfamiliar to George, but he understood the gist of it well enough and did his best to smooth the anxious frown from his forehead before they descended the wide, nobly-curving staircase and joined their parents in the white-panelled dining-room.

It was not long before Sir Robert began to speak of what had passed at the Justices' meeting in Westhampton. Two Catholic families had been closely questioned, but had succeeded in persuading their questioners that they had taken no part in " the late rebellion ": there remained Mr. Clavenger of Brackenden, who was now known to have journeyed stealthily to Scotland in the month of August, 1745, and to have joined the Young Pretender in Edinburgh. It was clear that if the Jacobites had overrun England and had reached the south coast his local knowledge would have been of great service to them. He was believed to have taken all the family jewels with him, and others which he had obtained in exchange for the family plate: and the more sensational rumours said that he was the bearer of treasonable correspondence from certain English Jacobites with whom he had been in touch for some time past.

" I am bound to confess," remarked Sir Robert, setting down his long-stemmed wine-glass, " I am bound to confess that things look mighty black against him. To-morrow a company of dragoons will ride over from Westhampton to search Brackenden—and to interrogate him, if they find him there."

" And what, pray, if he is not to be found? " asked Lady Sophia.

" A warrant will then be issued for his apprehension, and search-parties will be sent out."

" La, how foolish—when for all you know he may be hiding in the Scottish hills with the Young Pretender—or he may even have escaped overseas."

" Nay, not so foolish, madam, not so foolish. He was

seen—he was recognised—less than a week ago—near the little fishing hamlet of Swanford."

" By whom was he seen, pray ? "

" By a vagabond whom we have just clapped into jail—the worst rogue in the country, I am told—what is his name ? Ay, Miller, Abel Miller."

Lady Sophia suggested that the man might be lying to gain his own ends, but Sir Robert seemed to think that there must be something in what he said. He had known Mr. Clavenger for many years: he even claimed that before the gentleman came to man's estate he had taught him how to snare birds on the marshes: and he had added, with some tipsy tears, that he was sorry to betray him now, but that he was a poor man and —as an afterthought—a loyal subject of King George.

The boys listened with cocked ears to this part of the conversation. Snaring birds—why, that was the very thing that they had guessed the mysterious stranger had been doing that afternoon! The pieces of the puzzle were fitting themselves together. Impatiently they waited for the moment when Bulstrode, at a sign from Sir Robert, would pour out for each of them a small wineglass of Oporto wine. After that Papa always bade them drink to the King: and after *that* they were always dismissed to bed.

The moment, which usually came all too soon, seemed a long time in coming ; but it came at last, and the two conspirators were able to discuss their plans in the privacy of the big bedroom which they shared. It was a statelier room than the one they had occupied at White Mays, but their familiar tent-bed with its festooned curtains of green-and-white striped chintz had been transported from their old home. The two little girls had the room opposite, and Frederick and Maria had cot-beds beside Nurse's four-poster next door; so the elder boys thought it prudent to whisper.

"Listen," breathed John, " I have an idea. Let us wake very early—I can wake myself at what hour I please—put on our oldest clothes—and creep out by the kitchen door. Whoever finds it unbolted will think one of the servants did it. Then we can run quickly to the wilderness—and catch him still asleep."

"Catch him?" repeated George, surprised. "What, are you going to arrest him in the King's name? What if he resists? What if he is armed? Do you mean to try to seize him?"

"I'll run up no such colours," returned John. "What I want is to see him and speak with him. Then we can decide what course to steer."

George, after some further argument, agreed to this scheme; and soon they had donned their nightcaps and nightshirts, and were climbing sleepily into the white softness of the feather-bed.

So early were they astir the next morning not even the youngest kitchenmaid had left her pallet in the attic and descended to light the kitchen fire. On tiptoe, carrying their shoes, they crept along the uncarpeted corridors and down the polished stairs. Quanko half heard them, poked his yellow head out from under his green wing, and meditated calling for his rum ; but he was too lazy to make the effort, and soon tucked his head in again.

The most difficult part of the adventure was drawing back the heavy bolts and chains of the kitchen door without making enough noise to rouse the household. One of the footmen slept in the small room next the pantry, and though he could not have prevented them from going out, he might have mentioned to Bulstrode that they had gone—with results that they preferred to avoid. George was still worried as to what should be done after the encounter with " Kinsman Crusoe," but John insisted that all that must be decided later.

Their next difficulty was to make their way to the hut without much crackling and snapping of boughs. Luckily their previous journeys had left a fairly clear way through the undergrowth, and when they emerged in the little clearing they were rewarded—for the first thing they saw was the empty skin of an orange lying on the ground. They looked at each other, their eyes bright with excitement: then John, gently thrusting his brother aside, tiptoed towards the hut and peered in.

After a moment he beckoned George to join him, which—forgetting his annoyance at not being allowed to go first—George hastened to do.

It was not yet broad day and the shadows were deep under the brushwood roof; but as their eyes became accustomed to the gloom they could make out the figure of a tall man lying asleep on the bracken with the blue cloak—the cloak they had seen before—closely gathered round him. But for its rise and fall as he breathed he might have been dead instead of sleeping, so white and hollow was his face. A half-healed scar on the right temple showed that he had been wounded or injured recently. His right hand loosely clasped a silver-mounted pistol, his left was tucked under his cheek: near his head was a black three-cornered hat with one of its flaps hanging loose, and in the farthest corner of the cabin lay—crumpled and stained—the white cockade that had once adorned it, flanked by a coil of knotted string such as poachers use to snare small birds.

Mute and rigid, the two boys gazed at all these things, but not for long. Fugitives sleep lightly, and with what seemed like one movement the stranger opened his eyes, heaved himself up on to one knee, and levelled the pistol at the intruders. All three remained motionless for what the boys thought was a long time, though it was in truth only a matter of seconds. Then Alban Clavenger threw the pistol down, scrambled to his feet and emerged from his hiding-place.

"Your servant, gentlemen," he said, in a pleasant, rather unEnglish voice, "and, if I mistake not, your prisoner also."

He bowed gravely to his young kinsmen, who were too

bewildered to do anything but gaze. This, then, was the rebel, Papist, traitor, about whom they had heard so much! He did not look sly or wicked, only ill and tired. Though not an old, or even an elderly man, his uncombed, tangled locks were well streaked with white. A razor as well as a comb had evidently been lacking lately, for his cheeks and his peaked chin—the Clavenger chin—were filmed with a stubble of sprouting hair. His dress was simple; a grey suit much stained with moss, mud and rain, ruffles of plain lawn, riding-boots of black leather with rather high, square heels, and a small sword with a silver hilt.

" Well, gentlemen? " he prompted, as neither boy spoke, " You should be Clavengers, by your faces and by your presence here. Let me introduce myself. Your kinsman, Alban Clavenger——" and he bowed again.

" Mr. Clavenger," said George, flushing to the roots of his hair, " we did think, my brother and I—when we found this hut, with your cloak and your book——" he faltered, and turned to John for help.

" Sir," said John, politely, " it is as my brother says. We read those signals aright. But what to do we were not sure— until we had seen you."

" You see me now, kinsman. Are you still in doubt? "

George and John glanced at each other, and then John blurted out, " We are willing to go away and tell no one— but it would not be safe for you to stay here."

" Generously said; but—supposing—after I have gone—it came to be known that you had seen me—would you not be punished, and that severely? "

" We are willing to risk that," said George stoutly.

" Papa was saying only yesterday," added John, " that he would wish you safely overseas if——"

He broke off, remembering exactly *what* Papa had said.

" If," echoed Alban Clavenger, interested. " Will you not tell me what followed that ' if ' ? "

" Tell," prompted George.

" If he could be sure that—that you would turn monk, and so have no sons—to—to carry on the Popish line," John mumbled, awkwardly.

Instead of being offended Mr. Clavenger seemed, for some reason, to be relieved.

" So! " said he. "Why, the Saints are kind to me, and my dream may yet come true. Kinsmen, I am going to ask a grace of you. Return to your home—get speech with your father where no man may overhear—and pray him to come hither instantly—*alone*—except that you can come with him to show the way."

" Yes, sir—but how if Papa will not come ? " hinted George.

" Tell him the truth. He will not tarry when he hears it."

" Is there nothing else we can do ? " asked John, whose sympathy for the Jacobite was growing every minute.

" Yes—I have been cut off from all news this ten days past. Have you heard anything about my Prince ? "

" The Young Pretender, sir ? " queried John.

Mr. Clavenger's tired eyes flashed.

" I said *my Prince*, young man—and if justice were done he would be the Prince of every honest Englishman. But, if you are so particular—how could you be otherwise, being bred to call the Elector of Hanover ' King '?—Prince Charles. Have the English caught him yet ? "

" We have heard nothing of that, sir," said John, a little uneasily, feeling that he was listening to treason.

Mr. Clavenger took a deep breath and his lips moved as if he were saying a brief prayer.

" I thank you," said he, " not only for your courtesy to-day, but for the orange and the Naples biscuits that I found yesterday and supposed that Robin Goodfellow had put here. And now—will you not do my errand ? Time presses. I will wait in the hut for your return."

And without more words he ducked his head, plunged into

the shadow, and, seating himself cross-legged on the blue
cloak, pulled the little black book from his pocket and began
to read.

Feeling that they must certainly be in the midst of an
extraordinarily vivid dream, George and John started to retrace
their steps through the wilderness. Not until they were clear
of it and out in the open park-land did either of them speak.
Then George said almost crossly, " I wish he had not sent us
to fetch Papa. I had liefer he had got away."

" And I. But maybe Papa will let him go. He seemed to
think he might."

" It is a pity he is a Jacobite and a Papist," said George.
" There is something about him—I cannot tell what—but I
cannot mislike him, even if I try."

" Nor I. But let us hurry. Papa will be sitting down to
breakfast. We must put our clothes to rights and tie up our
hair before he sees us."

The absence of the two young gentlemen had been duly
noted by the household, but no one had yet mentioned it to
Sir Robert, so they were able to make themselves reasonably
neat before they entered his stately presence. They found him
in the breakfast-parlour, pouring a second cup of tea from a
white china pot adorned with blue leaves: and, quailing a
little at their own daring, they said almost in one voice:
" Pray, sir, can we speak with you? "

Sir Robert set down the teapot and looked sternly from
one of his sons to the other. As he was wearing a sort of
turban of tawny-coloured silk—his usual headgear before he
donned his freshly-powdered tie-wig—his appearance was less
majestic than it might have been at a later hour; but it was
awe-inspiring enough even so.

" Why, what mischief have you been at *now*? " he demanded.

" No mischief, Papa—truly—none. But—John, do you
tell Papa."

Sir Robert perceived from the suppressed excitement in each young face that this was no question of some foolish prank.

"Tell on, son John," he urged. "Stop shuffling your feet and tell on."

"Sir," blurted forth John, "we have found Mr. Clavenger."

"You have—*what*? Speak up! *You have found Mr. Clavenger?*"

"Yes, sir."

"In heaven's name, *where*?" asked Sir Robert, gazing wildly round him as if Mr. Clavenger might possibly be lurking behind the Chinese lacquer screen or under the mahogany sideboard.

"In the wilderness, beyond the park. He is waiting there—he prays you to go there, Papa—alone—except for George and me to show you the way."

Sir Robert rose to his feet in no small agitation, uttering a hasty wish that his kinsman were in the moon rather than where he was: then, regardless of his anxious sons, he took one or two turns up and down the room, muttering to himself and frowning in perplexity.

"You have told no one of this? " he asked.

"No, Papa—no one."

"Did Mr. Clavenger appear to be wounded? The vagrant who saw him said he had a kerchief tied round his head."

"There is a mark, sir, as if he *had* been hurt—but he is not wearing the kerchief now."

Sir Robert continued his restless pacing.

"Is he armed? " he asked, after a short interval.

"He has a sword and a pistol. He threw the pistol down when he saw us clearly. And he said he supposed he was our prisoner."

"Ha! " said Sir Robert, coming to a halt.

"Indeed, Papa, if you would—if you were——" John's voice trailed into silence.

"Well," said Sir Robert, "if it must be so, it must. Wait for me by the old oak tree at the entrance to the park—and say nothing to anyone."

He strode away to his dressing-room, calling for his valet, and his sons made their way as quietly as possible to the appointed place. Luckily Lady Sophia was breakfasting in bed, as she often did, and Caro was practising on the harpsichord, and Frederick, Amelia and Maria were in the nursery. Growler wanted to join the expedition, but was driven off.

After what seemed a very long time Sir Robert appeared, wearing a long cloak, his gold-laced hat pulled over his brows, and his whole bearing at once irritable and unhappy. As his sons walked beside him in the direction of the wilderness he questioned them closely, but said nothing to show whether he was pleased with what they had done—or otherwise. Presently they reached their destination and arrived at the clearing, where Mr. Clavenger was standing bareheaded, his sword and pistol lying on the turf at his feet.

The two gentlemen looked at each other gravely, both a little embarrassed but Sir Robert the more ill at ease of the two. They bowed, but Papa did not remove his hat.

"I am sorry, sir," he said, at last, "to find you in this—this plight."

"Not more sorry than I am to be found in it," returned Mr. Clavenger, with a faint smile. "And I am more especially sorry that the necessities of my position forced me to seek a refuge upon your domain."

"To-day," said Sir Robert, as if he hated saying it, "a warrant will be out for your apprehension—when the dragoons who are going to search Brackenden bring word that you are not there."

"Brackenden—no, they have drawn a blank, those bold dragoons. Nothing for their pains but some heaps of fine ash in my library fireplace."

"I understand you, sir. You burned all treasonable correspondence before you fled—and thus destroyed the evidence against yourself."

"The papers I burned would have endangered others besides myself, sir. They can harm nobody—and help nobody—now. But they might have been interesting to the Elector of Hanover."

"To King George the Second," corrected Sir Robert, firmly. Mr. Clavenger allowed the correction to pass.

"Well, sir," he said, "as you see, I am unarmed. If you call upon me to go with you and be handed over to the military, I neither can nor shall resist."

Sir Robert took a few worried steps up and down the little clearing.

"Come, sir," he jerked out, "forswear your allegiance to the Stuarts—their cause is lost beyond repair—and I will undertake to make your peace with King George. You, I doubt not, would have done the same for me with King James—if things had fallen out differently."

"Indeed, sir—and gladly. But—though I fear their cause *is* lost—I cannot deny my master and his son. What I had proposed to do—if I had escaped from England—was to renounce—not my loyalty—but the world itself. I had hoped to end my days in a monastery in France."

For some reason this revelation seemed to please Sir Robert.

"Egad," he said, "you could not work much against King George *there*. But how were you going to *get* there?"

"You must pardon me if I tell you only this—that I have a humble friend in Swanford—and that a fishing vessel will wait for me at the outgoing of the tide to-night."

"Sir, I will ask no more. But I wish," exclaimed Sir Robert, abruptly exchanging his formal tone for one of unaffected bewilderment, "I wish I knew what the devil I ought to do. I am a loyal subject of King George—no one knows better how the laws against treason run; but, damme, you are my kinsman—we used to ride to hounds together when we were lads. Think again. Is there no other way?"

"There is none—in honour—for me. But content you, sir. Whether they behead me as they beheaded my lords Kilmarnock and Balmerino—or whether I pass beyond the sea and change my cocked hat for a cowl—there will be no child of mine at Brackenden. The line will end with me."

"Egad," exclaimed Sir Robert, "that sounds monstrous melancholy—upon my word it does. No fox-hunting in the cloisters—and you were once ever first in the field. Yet —if that is how things are—upon my word, it solves our difficulty."

All this time the two boys had been standing very still, hoping that their presence had been forgotten—as, indeed, it had till then. But Sir Robert's last remark made Mr. Clavenger remember it. With a half sad, half kindly glance towards them he said, "No, kinsman—it shall never be my happiness—as it is yours—to say of such promising scions of our race, 'these are my sons.'"

If Sir Robert was touched by this compliment he did not show it. Turning sharply, he bade George and John give him their word of honour that to nobody in the world would they reveal the events of that morning: then he swung round to Mr. Clavenger.

"Sir, after what has passed I feel that I cannot—that loyalty does not compel me—in short, I wish you well out of England, and damme if I will do anything to hinder you!"

"I thank you," said his kinsman. "The prayers of a Papist you may think not worth having, but you will at least accept my thanks. Before to-morrow dawns I hope to be in France. Whither I am going I may take neither pistol nor sword. Have I your good leave to give these to your sons? The crest on the pistol is ours—no one need ever guess the giver."

Sir Robert hesitated for a moment, in spite of imploring

glances from the two boys. There was a brief silence, broken only by the sound of the old clock in the church tower of Winford St. Mary striking the quarter. Then Mr. Clavenger spoke again.

" Bethink you, sir; if there had been a price upon my worthless head—as there might well have been, for I confess I have done some small disservice to the Elector of Hanover——"

" King George the Second," corrected Sir Robert, almost mechanically.

" I chose my words amiss," said Mr. Clavenger, with a faint smile. " Let me say rather that I have done some poor service to Prince Charles, and this same worthless head is therefore ripe for the block—on Tower Hill, I trust, kinsman; as *your* humble kinsman I feel that I should be considered not unworthy to die on Tower Hill?"

" Needn't die anywhere unless you want to," mumbled Sir Robert, somewhat out of his depth.

" Well, then, sir—if these young gentlemen had chosen to send me thither——"

" If," cried out Sir Robert, forgetting all about his loyalty to King George and his hatred of the Pope, " if any son of mine were to betray a kinsman—egad, I would thrash the rascal more heartily than ever at Eton my old master thrashed *me*! "

Neither George nor John dared interrupt to protest that it was the last thing either of them wished to do; but Mr. Clavenger shot a kindly look at them which seemed to show that he understood this very well.

" Then, sir, do they not merit some small reward for their prudent conduct? "

" Oh, their conduct was prudent, was it? " said their surprised parent. " It was for the first time in their lives, then."

" Surely, sir, they told no one but yourself of their discovery—thus leaving *you* to decide what had best be done about it."

"Egad, that's true. That's very true. There might have been the devil to pay if they had gone blabbing to someone else: that I will grant ye."

"And so, sir—by your leave"—he bent down as he spoke and gathered up the two weapons from the ground.

"As you will, sir—as you will."

"Gentlemen," said Mr. Clavenger, turning with the utmost seriousness to the two boys, "I beg your acceptance of these trifling tokens of my regard."

Blushing and stammering, George received the sword and John the pistol: it would have been difficult to say which of them was the more delighted—or the more abashed.

"And now," said Sir Robert, feeling that all these civilities were likely to turn the two youthful heads, "and now, sir, the best grace I can do you is to leave you. Some provisions for your journey I would gladly send—and some salve—my housekeeper compounds a sovereign salve for cracked skulls; but I dread to draw attention to your presence here."

"No need, but I thank you none the less. Farewell, Sir Robert. Farewell, my young kinsmen, whose very names I do not know."

After a moment's hesitation Sir Robert removed his hat and held out his hand, but he said no word. The two men shook hands in silence: then Alban Clavenger dived back into his hut and Sir Robert, gruffly bidding his sons lead the way, began the difficult homeward walk through the dense boughs. George was clutching the sword and John the pistol; and when they were out of the wood and half across the park their father said, "Hide those things under your coats when you enter the house. George, put the sword in the wardrobe in your room—John can stow the pistol in his sea-chest. If anyone should ask you where you got them—you can say, egad, you can say that they are old family pieces."

The warrant for the arrest of Alban Clavenger Esquire of Brackenden was duly signed before the day was out, but not by Sir Robert Clavenger. He sent word to Westhampton that an attack of gout would prevent him attending the meeting of the Justices of the Peace, and before they met again (to discuss the mysterious disappearance of the wanted man) he was back in London, George was back at Eton, and John had sailed aboard a frigate to rejoin the *Intractable* in the West Indies.

As for Caro and Amelia, the reign of Miss Euphemia Phipps had begun and the playroom—now the schoolroom—was cumbered with sheaves of feathers, and skeins of silk, and rolls of canvas waiting to be embroidered upon by their small fingers. There were also a few books, but not many: little girls were not expected to learn a lot of things, or much about any of them. Only for baby Maria was life more or less the same as it had been before that eventful summer; for Frederick had been sent to a boarding-school at Hackney. His grandmamma, Lady Fenworth, feared that the little pupils were sadly coddled there, for each had a bed to himself.

CHAPTER IX

UNDER THE SHADOW OF "BONEY"

On a certain fine morning in the year 1812 a boy was sitting on the top of the same little Hampshire hill where his ancestor, Piers Clavenger, had sat in the year 1357—four hundred and fifty-five years before. The landscape spread out below had altered in many ways, and Piers might have had some difficulty in recognising it. Only the square tower of the ancient church and its dark grove of yews remained the same. Where the Manor had stood, moated and fortified, with the great hall in the midst of it, there was now a mansion of a kind of architecture never even dreamed of in Plantagenet England, very dignified, with its pillars and its long, glittering windows, and its severe, well-balanced lines. Grassy park-lands as smooth as green velvet, tufted with clumps of oak and beech, surrounded the house, and high iron gates wrought with the crest of the hand holding the key stood at the entrance to the curving carriage-drive half a mile in length. The village of Winford St. Mary was also changed. None of the flimsy wattle-and-mud huts remained, though a number of the Tudor cottages, with their overhanging upper storeys faced with pale pink plaster and silver-brown oak beams, still stood. Many houses had been built since the return of the Clavengers in 1745 had brought renewed prosperity, and most of these were of snug red brick or milk-white stucco. Some of the most recently built had bow-windows and gaily painted green or blue front doors with winking brass knockers. The old Tudor vicarage had been pulled down to make way for a new one as prim and as trim as a needlework house on a sampler. No longer were the fields divided into narrow strips with baulks of turf between. Neatly-cut hedges separated them into squares, and within those squares, in addition to oats, corn and barley, there grew some crops unknown in the days of Edward the Third—turnips, mangold-wurzels, potatoes and hops.

Where Piers would have seen only a rough, uneven track, muddy in wet weather and dusty in dry, his descendant could follow with his eyes the line of a smooth (though occasionally dusty) high road upon which coaches rattled to and fro between Westhampton and London to the merry sound made by the guard's long copper horn.

The dress worn by Master William Clavenger, second son of Sir Augustus, seventh baronet of that name, also marked the contrast between Plantagenet and Georgian days. The blue jacket with its double row of brass buttons was so short that it made the long white nankeen trousers look rather comically long. The broad turned-down collar was edged with a narrow frill. On his head William wore a flat-topped cap with a stiff peak shading the eyes and a tassel hanging from the centre of the crown.

Though he had climbed that little hill especially to have a good view he was not paying any attention to the village, or the park, or even to the high road where the London mail-coach was at that moment travelling at a brisk pace, gleaming scarlet through the white dust raised by its four horses. With a shining brass spy-glass fixed to his right eye, William was scanning the distant sea and committing to memory the first five ships that crossed the field of vision.

"A four-masted East Indiaman," murmured he, "that is *one*. Next—oh, those are two fishing-boats, single-masted—that is *three*. Next—no, there is nothing yet. I do hope there will be a man o' war soon."

He continued to rake the horizon with his glass, secretly pretending that he was on board ship and starting on his first voyage—which he expected to do in about eighteen months' time: for the Clavengers had kept up the habit started by Sir

Robert that in each generation the first-born son should enter the Army and his brother next in age the Navy. Younger sons of younger sons had more than once done the same thing.

Sir Augustus, William's father, had served with distinction under Sir Arthur Wellesley[1] in India and in the Peninsula, and his grandfather, Sir George, had been on General Wolfe's staff at the capture of Quebec; his Uncle Edward had fought under Lord Howe in the great sea-fight off Ushant on the "Glorious First of June," 1794; and two of the sons of Great-Uncle Frederick—the same Frederick who had played at killing "Tots" in 1745—had been present at the even greater and more glorious battle of Trafalgar, the elder, Fenworth, as an officer in the *Agamemnon* and the younger, Joshua, as a midshipman in the *Victory*. William had never seen either Fenworth or Joshua Clavenger; but he liked Uncle Edward, who had a mahogany-coloured face, a rolling walk and a jolly quarter-deck voice. Most of all he liked Great-Uncle John whom he was to be taken to visit at his house at Brackenden that very afternoon. Seventy-nine years of age was Great-Uncle John, a trifle deaf in one ear and exceedingly lame in one leg, but still alert and cheerful. He had fought at Quiberon Bay; he had been one of Rodney's captains on the Leeward Islands station in 1762 when the islands of Martinique, St. Lucia and Grenada were captured; but it was his constant regret that he had not been born late enough to serve under St. Vincent and Nelson, whose exploits he used to read aloud to anyone who cared to listen and whose portraits he had hanging beside those of Hood, Rodney and Howe on the white panelled wall of his breakfast-parlour. Even his parrot—a younger and gayer bird than Quanko—learned to exclaim, "Great fellow, St. Vincent, great fellow, Nelson," in an admiring tone. Quanko was still alive, and at the Manor, but he was growing old and bald.

The spy-glass with which William was scanning the

---

[1] Afterwards Duke of Wellington.

English Channel was a real naval spy-glass and had been given to him by Great-Uncle John, who would also give him, every time he visited Brackenden, five shillings—one to each ship— if he could name correctly the first five ships he had seen the last time he had used it. William was an honest boy and he knew that he was on his honour about those ships; but even if he had wanted to cheat, he would not have risked being detected by the keen dark eyes under the shaggy white eyebrows.

"I don't believe," sighed William, "that there are any more ships afloat this morning."

It was a depressing thought, for he knew that it would soon be time for him to descend from his hill-top and go with his younger brother, Adolphus, to the vicarage for their daily two-hours' lessons. His elder brother, Denzil, was at Winchester, whither Adolphus was to follow him in due course, but it was not considered necessary to send the future sailor to a public school.

William sighed again; then he cheered up.

"A barque—that makes *four*—in ballast, I think. And—oh, glory—five *is* a man o' war—a ship of the line—a 74, by the looks of her—beating up-channel to Portsmouth."

When he called the ship "a 74" he meant that she carried seventy-four guns: not a very big ship—Nelson's *Victory* carried a hundred, and the Spanish *Santissima Trinidad* had carried a hundred and twenty-six—yet a "ship of the line." William had often heard Great-Uncle John declare that it was English warships that would break France's land armies in the end, and he never forgot those words. Delighted that his list included at least one naval item, he tucked his spy-glass under his arm and began to run, gaining speed and momentum as he ran and finally arriving with a rush at the stile which barred the path at the bottom of the slope.

It was a fine May morning, full of comfortable sounds. The jackdaws called to each other as they wheeled round the belfry, a murmur of young voices chanting "C, A, T, cat, B, A, T, bat " came through the half-open door of the Dame's school; a clip-clop of hoofs announced that a blue-painted farm-cart with red wheels was on its way to the Manor barn; milk-pails jingled and clanked as Patty the milkmaid ap-

" A 74, BY THE LOOKS OF HER "

proached with a wooden yoke across her strong shoulders and a brimming pail hanging from each tip.

William called out a hasty " Good day " to Patty and to the man trudging beside the cart: when he reached the vicarage he found the vicar, the Reverend Septimus Smith, doing a little weeding in his well-kept patch of garden.

" Good morning, sir," said William, " I am on my way to fetch Dolly."

The Reverend Septimus straightened his stooping back and peered benevolently at the boy through his thick-lensed spectacles.

"Good morning, William. You had better make haste. It has just chimed half-past eight."

Taking the hint, William quickened his pace, but when he reached the Manor and went to look for his brother that young person was not to be found. Betty, the neat housemaid with pink ribbons in her starched mob-cap and a flapping feather-broom in her hand, volunteered that she had seen Master Dolly run out into the flower-garden with Miss Charlotte, and thither William scampered in quest of them, followed with delighted barks by Duff—short for Plum Duff— the spotted Dalmatian.

The flower-garden had been planned and planted by the children's great-grandmother, Lady Sophia. Owing to her affection for statues—in lead and in stone—there had at one time been little space left for flower-beds or shaven turf; but the present Lady Clavenger's ideas of garden planning were different. She had many of the statues, shepherds and shepherdesses, nymphs and fauns, removed to remote parts of the park, where they posed for the admiration of the fallow deer. Though her children had found these objects rather amusing, there were moments when they were also rather frightening, especially to Charlotte, who was a timid little girl; it was without much regret that she, at least, saw them carted away. Denzil and William, it is true, laughed at Charlotte's fancy that they might suddenly come to life and step down from their pedestals and run after one; but Dolly thought there might be something in it.

When William reached the flower-garden he saw at once that interesting things were happening. A cart stood on the broad gravel path, the horse nibbling at the grassy border, and from this cart two under-gardeners, directed by the head-gardener and earnestly watched by Dolly and Charlotte, were lifting odd fragments of shaped and carved stone.

Dolly was dressed exactly like William except that his short jacket was green instead of blue; Charlotte had a high-waisted frock of crisp white dimity beneath which appeared a pair of frilled pantalettes reaching to her ankles. She was hatless; and her light brown hair was cut short like a boy's.

"Oh, William, do come and look," she exclaimed, when she saw her second brother; "we are going to have a real ruin!"

"With ivy," added Dolly, "and moss, lots of moss."

"Ay," grumbled the head-gardener, half under his breath: "me, that has spent the best part o' my days rootin' out and cuttin' down and scrapin' off them pests, now I've got to *cultivate* 'em."

"When the ruin has been built," continued Charlotte, with enthusiasm, "there will be a weeping willow drooping over one side."

"Ay," grumbled the head-gardener. "My orders is as the willow is to hang over poetical. Poetical!"

William was inspecting the lumps of masonry as the men unloaded them. Presently they laid at his feet a grinning mask of stone—the very imp that Piers had dubbed "Mahound," the very imp that had received in turn the nicknames of "Don Philip" and "Noll Cromwell," but had lain nameless and forgotten for many years.

"Why, here's an ugly fellow," cried William; "what's to be done with *him*, Crockett?"

The head-gardener glanced disdainfully at the fragment.

"Happen he'd do for the keystone," he grunted. "Her ladyship did say as she wanted the ruin to be in the form of a h'arch."

"He reminds me of somebody," mused William, "somebody very wicked-looking, with a big nose and two big eyes. *I* know! Boney!"

Charlotte and Dolly crowded up to see.

CARTOON OF NAPOLEON

"Yes," said Charlotte, "he *is* like that funny picture of Boney that Papa brought from London."

"Boney, Boney," chanted Dolly, dancing round the carved imp, "Boney, Boney, *I*'m not afraid of *you*!"

"Oh, Dolly," said Charlotte, "you know what Nurse says —that he'll come and fetch us if we're naughty. I *am* afraid of him. I wake up sometimes in the night and think he is coming."

"Great-Uncle John says Nurse ought not to say so," announced William. "He says Boney would dearly like to cross the Channel but the British Navy won't let him. So you mustn't be afraid, Char."

"You don't think he could *fly*, do you?" asked Charlotte, only half comforted.

"Angels can fly," announced Dolly to no one in particular.

"That there Boney he sure ain't no angel, Master 'dolphus," grinned the young gardener nearest to him.

For as long as any of the Clavenger children could remember their elders had been thinking and talking a great deal about "Boney"—otherwise Napoleon Bonaparte, self-created Emperor of the French. William, now thirteen years old, had been six when the huge army gathered at Bologne for the invasion of England had suddenly been withdrawn from the French coast and marched off inland to fight the Austrians instead, but Denzil had been eight, quite old enough to remember Great-Uncle John showing him the swift English frigates tacking up and down the Channel on the look-out for the French invasion rafts. Many things had happened since then. Boney had made peace with the Emperor of Austria, who had been forced to give him his daughter, the Archduchess Marie Louise, as his wife; the New Order was being relentlessly imposed on the greater part of Europe; and the question in everybody's mind was: what would that terrible man do next?

Sir Augustus had a sharp disagreement with Lady Clavenger's only brother, Mr. Warren Arkwright, over the wisest course for Britain to pursue in the face of this growing menace on the Continent. Mr. Arkwright was a banker, and, like most people interested in commerce and finance, he was alarmed at the damage done to British trade by the "Continental system," invented and put into operation by Napoleon Bonaparte as a retort to the British blockade of his far-stretched dominions. Surely the most prudent policy would be to come to terms with the Emperor! Several English statesmen shared that cautious view; but Sir Augustus was heart and soul on the side of the Prime Minister, Mr. Perceval, who didn't, and who was in favour of giving blow for blow, and going on hitting wherever it would hurt most, until the Corsican bully was knocked out or driven from the ring.

The news that Boney had declared war upon Russia—his former ally—startled the world in April, 1812. Sir Augustus rubbed his hands gleefully together and vowed that this was a blunder that would cost the Corsican dear. But Mr. Arkwright clutched at his hair, and said that there was now *no* hope of standing up to such a powerful opponent, and that the sooner we recognised this fact the better it would be for everyone. Then Sir Augustus called him a poor-spirited, short-sighted, weak-kneed money-grubber; then Mr. Arkwright threatened to challenge Sir Augustus to a duel; and then Lady Clavenger fainted so often and wept so passionately between the faints, and appealed so frantically to her husband

and her brother not to break her heart by shedding each other's blood, that the two gentlemen had no choice but to shake hands, though each secretly adhered to his former opinion.

At the moment Sir Augustus was not in very good trim for fighting duels. He had been serving with the Third Division, the famous "Fighting Third," in the Peninsular campaign and, after being severely wounded at the battle of Ciudad Rodrigo, he had been invalided home—greatly to his own indignation. Now, five months after the battle, he loudly declared that he was fit to rejoin his regiment, only to be assured by three grave medical men, each tapping a gold-headed cane on the carpet to emphasise his words, that he *must* wait until the broken ribs had joined again which by his impatience he had twice prevented from joining perfectly before.

This delay, which infuriated Sir Augustus, delighted his family. Though a strict disciplinarian he was also a very companionable parent, and the joy of Charlotte, William and Dolly knew no bounds when they heard that he proposed to take them himself to Brackenden to visit Great-Uncle John. Mamma preferred to remain at home, for she found it difficult—if not impossible—to get on with Great-Aunt Caro who was on a visit to that house. After being worldly and unbelieving for most of her long life, Miss Caroline Clavenger had suddenly joined a dissenting community known as the Countess of Huntingdon's Connexion, and she never wearied of trying to persuade others to follow her example. Conversion had not made her less disagreeable; it had merely made her disagreeable in a new way.

Brackenden—but *this* Brackenden was not the same mouldering old mansion deep in the Wiltshire woods where the Popish Clavengers had had their home. How did a non-Popish member of the family come to possess the estate? And who was it who built a neat white villa on the highest part of it, with a view across the blue estuary where ships sailed in and out in all weathers, all day?

CHARLOTTE GOES WITH PAPA IN THE TILBURY (*see page* 221)

COUSIN FENWORTH DRAWS A PLAN OF THE ACTION OFF
CAPE ST. VINCENT (*see page* 231)

After Alban Clavenger had escaped to France and entered the Carthusian monastery at Grenoble, his possessions were declared forfeited to the Crown, and for nearly thirty years the old house was tenanted and the land leased by a farmer, who neglected the one and failed to raise good crops from the other. Then along came Captain John Clavenger, with enough prize-money in his pockets to buy the property if the Crown were willing to sell. The Crown was quite willing: the shiftless tenant was bundled out; and the Captain proceeded to build himself a house according to his own fancy, retiring there when he quitted the Service in 1778.

Two generations of young Clavengers had found Brackenden Lodge a place of enchantment; first the Captain's nephews and nieces and then their children, his great-nephews and nieces. He had never married—because, he used jokingly to say, he had been kept too busy fighting and seafaring to look for a wife until he was too old and battered and ugly to have any hopes of finding one. But his younger sister Amelia came to keep house for him—poor little Amelia, whose betrothed, the nephew of Colonel Falkner [1] of White Mays, had been killed at the storming of Havana in 1762.

Meanwhile Caro, their sister, had grown up a prodigious beauty, but so pert, cross-tempered and unamiable that no one was bold—or foolish—enough to ask her hand in marriage. As it was not considered correct for spinster ladies to live by themselves, she made various members of her family uncomfortable by quartering herself upon them, with her maid and her lap-dog, both of whom were as disagreeable as their mistress. Then, about the year 1791, when the French Revolution had made many people feel restless and independent, Miss Caroline Clavenger astonished London by taking a neat little house in Curzon Street and settling down to the steady enjoyment of card-games, gossip and snuff—to which was added later the reading of lurid sermons promising eternal

[1] See Chapter VII.

torments to everyone who did not agree with her. Though she regarded her brother John and her sister Amelia as hopeless heathens, she none the less accepted with regularity the invitation to visit them which they sent every summer.

William and Dolly often found some difficulty in paying attention to their lessons on the days when they were to go to visit Great-Uncle John. Sir Augustus had requested Mr. Smith to try to improve Dolly's very shaky arithmetic, as his third son was destined for the banking house of Arkwright, and mathematics filled the first place in William's curriculum.

There seemed to be something in the air of Winford Vicarage which made almost every vicar an ardent gardener. Father Oswald had been one, and Parson Aubrey; Parson Matcham, with a wife and three spinster daughters to feed, had given his mind mainly to vegetables, and his successor, the Reverend Spencer Prittlewell, had concentrated on herbaceous borders; but now for the first time the vicar was a scientific botanist. He was also a very conscientious little man, and anxious to please his patron—yet somehow his pet hobby had a way of popping up oftener than Sir Augustus might have approved—had he known. A lesson that began with history, geography or Latin frequently wandered off into botany, and albums of pale, brittle specimens took the place of atlas and grammar-book. Dolly, who was lazy, did not mind this at all; but William was apt to yawn and fidget while Mr. Smith droned away about the different orders of flowers, sprinkling his discourse with botanical terms and often forgetting about everything else until it was too late in the day to pick up the dropped thread.

As the two boys, with regretful backward glances at the future ruin, made their way by a short cut across the park to the vicarage, Dolly confided to his elder brother that he hoped their tutor *would* wander off into the names of flowers *that* morning, for he had not prepared his sums the night before or committed his grammar lesson to memory.

The hope was fulfilled. A friend happened to have sent Mr. Smith some dried specimens of alpine plants, and in his excitement he spent the best part of the morning showing these to his pupils and discoursing happily about edelweiss and gentian. By the time that he recollected Dolly's sums the church clock was striking eleven and William was able to remark that as they were going to Brackenden that day, he was afraid they could not stay longer.

When the two boys reached home they found that Mamma and Papa were out in the park inspecting the proposed ruin. Sir Augustus had little taste for art, and the romantic craze then so fiercely fashionable left him unaffected; but he was rather proud of having a wife so full of sensibility and he stood by without impatience while she pointed with her long-handled, deep-fringed green parasol at the place where the Gothic arch was soon to rise.

Lady Clavenger was fashionable in her dress as well as in her hobbies. Her India muslin gown was high-waisted, short-sleeved and narrow-skirted in the most approved classical fashion; over it she wore a little pelissette of blue silk piped with pale yellow. Under her turban-shaped hat of blue straw with a dangling yellow feather her light brown hair was arranged in a Greek knot with three long curls upon the nape of her neck. Beside her tall husband in his blue coat, crisp white stock, buckskin breeches and brightly polished top-boots, she looked like an elegant little figure of porcelain.

As the boys drew near they saw that Charlotte was there, too, standing close to Papa and holding his hand. They were all looking at the carved imp which one of the under-gardeners was holding up for their inspection.

" He's like Boney, isn't he, Papa? " asked William, and he was delighted when Sir Augustus, after gazing through his eyeglass, admitted that the imp *had* " a look of the demmed fella."

The eyeglass was a square one rimmed with gold and

mounted on a long handle attached to a black ribbon passing round the wearer's neck.

The elder children lunched with their parents, though not on the same fare. Soup and bread-and-milk were considered more suitable than cold chicken and tongue, but the boys had each a glass of mild ale and Charlotte a glass of wine-and-water. They then were dismissed to the care of Nurse, who set about making them clean and tidy with a waspish vigour that drew faint squeals from Charlotte and loud protests from William and Dolly.

"Ouch, Nurse, you are pulling out my hair," cried William, "I shall be as bald as Quanko."

"If you could be trusted to comb your *own* hair, Master William," retorted Nurse, briskly, "I should not have the trouble and worrit of doing it for you."

Quanko the parrot, now very old but still quite lively, stirred on his perch when he heard his name, and demanded that his rum should be brought. Nurse, who disapproved of rum (having had a brother who drank it too freely), had tried in vain to teach the bird to say, "Bring me my milk," instead; but all that he consented to pick up from *her* was, "Were there ever such naughty children born!" The real fact was that Nurse was one of those people who prefer very small children to the no-longer-very-small. The three little ones in the nursery, Arthur, Sophy and Matilda, found her as indulgent as the elders found her severe.

At last the longed-for moment came, and preparations for the departure were nearly completed. Sir Augustus was going to drive his own tilbury, a smart two-wheeled vehicle made fashionable by the Prince Regent, while the head-groom drove the hooded phaeton, the three young Clavengers being divided between the two.

"My little Char will come with me in the tilbury," proclaimed Sir Augustus. Charlotte looked timidly at the high wheels and at the spirited cob which was dancing with im-

patience and almost wrenching the reins out of the hands of the
stable-boy who was holding it.   Far more willingly would she
have squeezed into the phaeton which, having four wheels,
did not bounce and sway, and was, moreover, drawn by one
of the most staid horses in the Manor stables.   But it was a
great honour to be allowed to sit beside Papa, and when he
bent down from the driving-seat and lifted her up as easily
as if she had weighed no more than the largest of her own dolls
pride got the better of timidity.

"What message shall I take from you to Great-Aunt Caro ? "
called out Sir Augustus to his wife, who was watching their
departure from the top of the fine flight of stone steps that Sir
George had added to the west front of the Manor.

" My best compliments, if you will be so good," Lady
Clavenger called back.

" What, not your *dear love* ? " asked Sir Augustus, laughing.

" My dear love to Great-Aunt Amelia—and to Great-Uncle
John," retorted his lady, waving her parasol, " but not—but
never—to Great-Aunt Caro ! "

Sir Augustus laughed again, louder than before, raised his
grey beaver hat, cracked his whip, and bowled away down the
drive, followed by the phaeton, Plum Duff scampering near.

At first the rush of air through her best bonnet, the speed
with which trees and hedges flew past, and the rapid beat of the
cob's hooves seemed to daze Charlotte; but she soon became
accustomed to these things and began to enjoy herself.   It was
a delightful day, not too hot; Papa smiled down at her kindly
from time to time; and she knew that the boys were envying
her with all their might.   As they emerged from the high iron
gates of the park they turned to the right, leaving the old
church on their left.   Char liked going to that old church far
better than going to St. James', Piccadilly, where they went
when in London.   The sermons were equally long and prosy
at both churches, but at Winford you could peep between the
crimson curtains of the family pew and get glimpses of fascin-

ating monuments, some of them lying down as if asleep, some kneeling, some standing majestically upright. There was a noseless lady with a butterfly-shaped head-dress; there was a fingerless gentleman in armour that looked like the over-lapping shell of a lobster; and—best of all—there was a lady in ruff and farthingale with three little girls kneeling behind her—Katherine, Judith and Joan, according to the faded lettering on a black slate slab at the back of the tomb.

HORACE WALPOLE'S " PLAYTHING HOUSE " AT STRAWBERRY HILL

Though Charlotte did not know it, she had the merest chance to thank for the presence of all those ancient carvings. In the time of Sir Robert Clavenger nobody valued such pieces of antiquity at all—we heard what Mr. Flitcroft said about that sort of thing—and there was every chance that Sir Thomas and Dame Eleanor, proud Dame Alice, valiant Sir Lionel and far-wandering Sir Piers might have been carted away to make room for the fine new organ, with as little regard for their dignity as the Cromwellians had shown to Sir Denzil and

Dame Philippa and their seven daughters when they tore up their brass effigies and melted them down to make ammunition. But just about the time when plans were being made for the installation of the organ who should come on a visit to Winford but Mr. Horace Walpole! To the very great astonishment of Sir Robert and Lady Sophia he screamed with delight when he saw the ancestral chapel of the Clavengers, and offered with enthusiasm to remove Sir Lionel and Dame Eleanor to his garden at Strawberry Hill. He had built himself a Gothic house, full of tracery and pinnacles, and now he wanted to ornament the grounds with relics of the Middle Ages. Would his dear friends permit him to add these two admirable examples to his collection? Most politely his dear friends regretted that they could not consent: for Lady Sophia had suddenly decided that if "Horry" prized them and wanted to have them, then she and Sir Robert also prized them and wanted to keep them. Mr. Walpole returned to Strawberry Hill much disappointed; and a place was found for the organ in another part of the church.

Now the old square tower and the shaggy dark yews were left behind and the tilbury and the phaeton were rattling up the village street, Sir Augustus acknowledging the salutations of the passers-by by raising his whip. When Miss Melissa and Miss Clarissa Prittlewell came out of their neat, rose-covered cottage the Squire raised his hat instead of his whip, and Charlotte waved her hand. The two elderly ladies were the daughters of the late Vicar of Winford, spending the evening of their days near the church where he had ministered —always described by them as "that venerable dome." At least once a year the young Clavengers went to tea with the Misses Prittlewell, whose house was full of wonderful needlework pictures (worked by themselves) and whose apple jelly was reputed to be the best in the county of Hampshire. Very large were the turbans worn by the sisters (both indoors and out), very tight and narrow were their skirts, very small and flat their sandal-shoes. Though they dressed exactly alike, they did not always agree. Some years earlier they had disagreed about the two leading statesmen of the time—Mr. Pitt and Mr. Fox. Miss Melissa wore a cameo of Mr. Pitt on a black ribbon round her wrist; Miss Clarissa hung a print of Mr. Fox over her bed. Miss Melissa was seen to wag her head scornfully at the large ungainly figure and the heavy, black-browed face of Mr. Fox: Miss Clarissa retorted by sniffing every time her sister gazed sentimentally at the sharply peaked profile of Mr. Pitt. Rumour said that their quarrel rose to such a height that each lady had plucked the turban from the brows of the other; but that was all over now; both the portly Mr. Fox and the sharp-nosed Mr. Pitt were dead, and there was complete agreement over the wickedness of Boney and the elegance of the Prince Regent's manners.

The twenty-mile drive to Brackenden occupied the best part of three hours, for a long stretch of the road sloped uphill and Sir Augustus never overstrained his horses. Plum Duff, who belonged to a breed trained on purpose to run beside carriages, kept pace easily with the tilbury, but at the half-way corner he was taken up to sit at Charlotte's feet, which he did with a grin on his face and his tongue flapping. It was about half-past three when the two vehicles turned into a green-painted double gate and began to ascend the neatly-gravelled drive leading to Brackenden Lodge.

Many of the ancient trees which had grown decayed and dangerous had been felled when Captain John Clavenger bought the property, but groves of little oak-saplings were springing up where the Captain, with an eye to the future needs of the Royal Navy, had systematically sown acorns.

A capable farmer, Noah Stockbridge by name, lived in the house that had once been the Manor and cultivated the estate—not without frequent interference from the proprietor who, like most retired sailors, imagined that he knew as much about farming as any country gentleman. No longer mossy and mouldering, the home of the Popish Clavengers was now a pleasant farmhouse, covered with climbing roses. The peaked gables and the mullioned windows remained, but the priests' holes had been filled up and the sliding panels closed with strong nails. Mrs. Stockbridge said that this was to discourage rats and mice, but there were also tales of ghosts, and even the sturdiest of her red-cheeked maidservants turned pale at the thought of those mysterious hollow places.

The drive made a loop half round the quaint old house and Mrs. Stockbridge herself came out to curtsy to the visitors, smiling up at them under her broad-brimmed straw hat and smoothing down her crisp white apron. Then it was not long before Sir Augustus pulled up before the bright blue front-door of his uncle's house.

This house stood on high ground, and faced south-west to the sea. It was flanked by a lofty flagstaff from which the Union Jack fluttered gaily, and beside the flagstaff was a large telescope on a three-legged stand. Charlotte noticed with surprise that the face of a little girl was peering from the bow-window to the left of the door—she had not expected to find any other children at Brackenden. Before she had time to wonder who this could be the face had disappeared, and the head-groom, having tied the phaeton horse to a white post with a ring, hurried to hold the still frisky cob while Sir Augustus climbed down. At the same moment the front door opened and an old man came hopping out on a peg-leg, peering eagerly at them out of one very bright eye—the other being hidden by a black patch which also covered half his forehead and was fastened with a brilliant spotted handkerchief, scarlet, yellow and blue. What little could be seen of his hair was iron-grey, and hung in neatly combed locks, twisted into a pigtail on the nape of his neck. He wore a trim suit of black, a striped waistcoat, and a very stiff cambric frill, presenting a curious appearance, half-manservant, half Jack Tar. His withered, sunbrowned face was crinkled in a welcoming smile as he hobbled forward, and he greeted Sir Augustus with a smart naval salute.

" Well, Joe," said Sir Augustus, " how is my uncle? And how are *you*? "

" Cap'en and me is wonderful, Sir Augustus, sir—old timbers are tough, you know, sir: salt preserves, salt do. Will Miss Charlotte let Joe Mackery lift her down? "

" Oh, yes, please, Joe," said Charlotte, holding out her arms. All the Clavenger children knew Joe Mackery who had gone to sea as a boy when Great-Uncle John went, and had served under him all through his naval career; and they all knew that Joe had saved his captain's life at St. Lucia. Never was a more gay old cripple than Joe; for he had been granted the wish of his heart, denied to him for many hard years, and that was to serve " Master John," if not afloat, why, then, ashore.

" Rare pleased, Cap'en'll be," said Joe, setting Charlotte gently down and turning to salute the two boys only a little less ceremoniously than he had saluted their father. They both crowded up to him demanding to know how he did, when they might have a peep through the telescope, and whether his wooden leg was sprouting yet. That was one of Joe's most successful jokes, the story that some day his wooden leg would put forth green buds like a young tree.

" Not yet, young gentlemen—not as *I* can see. But some fine morning when I jump out of my hammock I'll see five green leafs where my five toes ought to be. I ask your pardon, Sir Augustus, sir. Cap'en's in the drawing-room, if you'll please to come in. Plum Duff he can lie here in the shade till I fetch him into the kitchen for a bite and sup."

This Plum Duff seemed very willing to do.

" We've got other visitors besides Miss Clavenger, Sir Augustus, sir," whispered Joe mysteriously, as he removed that gentleman's many-caped driving-coat of fawn cloth. A jerk of Sir Augustus's eyebrow indicated to the old man that he might speak further.

" Mr. Fenworth Clavenger is here, sir—come over from Portsmouth where his ship is laid up to refit: the *Menelaus*, ninety guns. And little Miss Lydia—you remember, Sir Augustus, sir ? "

The eyebrow jerked still higher, but Sir Augustus said no more, and a minute later Joe was announcing in his cracked but still powerful voice, " Sir Augustus Clavenger, Miss Charlotte Clavenger, Master William Clavenger, Master Dolly—I *should* say—Master Adolphus Clavenger."

An old gentleman in a sprucelycurled and powdered tie-wig rose with some difficulty from a vast padded arm-chair and limped two steps to meet them. His face was of the colour and texture of a dry brown leaf, his hands were striped with big grey veins and shook a little as he leaned on his ebony cane; but his dark eyes were wonderfully keen and penetrating. The big padded chair had a twin on the opposite side of the mantelpiece, and between its arms sat an old lady, bolt upright, looking like some fantastic image with her powdered hair piled high on her head and tufted with silver leaves; her long-waisted, wide-hooped silk dress, dim lavender-colour festooned with Brussels lace, was of the cut and fashion that had been worn before the French Revolution wrought such a startling change in European taste. Miss Caroline Clavenger was one of the very few ladies in all England who remained faithful to the old style: her younger sister, Miss Amelia, had abandoned wide skirts in favour of narrow ones, a long waist for a short, a high-piled head-dress for a pretty bonnet of gauffered and starched white lawn tied beneath the chin with a bow of white satin ribbon.

Miss Amelia's gown was of black bombazin, a sort of silk usually worn by people in deep mourning: she had appeared in no other fabric for more than forty years—not, indeed, since the death of her betrothed. She sat on a four-legged mahogany stool, busily netting a purse of dark green silk; but when Sir Augustus and the children were announced she jumped up with youthful eagerness and almost ran to meet them.

"Recollect yourself, Sister Amelia," said a grating voice from the second padded chair. "Will you *never* acquire decorum?"

Miss Amelia paid no heed to Miss Caroline's rebuke: she was too busy kissing Charlotte and taking off her bonnet and exclaiming how the dear child had grown.

Meanwhile Sir Augustus, after shaking hands with his uncle, gently convoyed that warrior back to his chair and re-installed him in it: then Charlotte was summoned, her head patted and her cheek kissed; and then the boys made their bows to their various relatives, including one whom everybody seemed to have forgotten, but who now came out of the shadow of the bow-window and was presented as "my nevy Fenworth—the same who had the happiness of serving under my lord Nelson at Trafalgar."

Fenworth Clavenger was a pleasant-looking fellow, with a tanned face and the very blue Clavenger eyes. He wore his own hair slightly powdered and twisted in a queue behind, and William looked with interest both at his uniform—dark blue, pure white and gleaming gold—and at his very large naval cocked hat standing on the table where the white coral and the ostrich's egg lived.

"If we had met before," said Sir Augustus, "I should have craved your kind favour for my son William here, who is shortly to enter your profession."

"Indeed it shall not be lacking when the time comes," answered Mr. Fenworth readily. "I am sorry Lady Clavenger is not with you. I had a request of the same colour to make to her—and you."

"Damme, cousin, you are too young to have a son of William's age," cried Sir Augustus, raising his glass to take another look at Fenworth, who laughed as he answered, "Assuredly, sir: but not too young to have a niece of Charlotte's age. It is for her—why, where is she?"

No one seemed to know where "she" could be, and there was a puzzled search round the room, which was full of odd corners where a child might easily hide. Then Charlotte plucked up courage to whisper in Great-Aunt Amelia's ear that she had seen a little girl peeping out of the window of the breakfast parlour.

"Such a shy little Miss it is!" said Great-Aunt Amelia. "She must have crept away when she heard the wheels. Would you believe it, nephew Augustus, she hid under one of the ormolu tables at Carlton House when she was taken to see the Prince Regent!"

"Send Char to fetch her," commanded Great-Uncle John. "Let the two little Misses make friends. Hey, nevy?"

Fenworth, the "nevy" whom he addressed, begged that Miss Charlotte would be so good; and that small person, feeling important, curious and timid all at once, trotted out of the room.

"You see, nevy Augustus," said the old warrior, beckoning Sir Augustus to come and sit beside his better ear, "the question is—what's to be done with Lydia de la Vignerie. Mother dead—father dead—Aunt Albinia going to the West Indies to join her husband—and Uncle Fenworth putting to sea again as soon as the *Menelaus* refits."

Sir Augustus shook his head sadly.

"Let me see, sir—she will be—how old precisely?"

"Frederick's second gel—Honoria—you remember her?"

"Not very well, sir. My father and his brother did not always agree, I am sorry to say, and the two families seldom met."

"To be sure—and I'll wager brother Frederick was in the wrong. Still, that's no matter now, no matter. Frederick's dead—so is your father—and poor Honoria into the bargain. Poor Honoria—it was a great mistake her taking drawing-room lessons from that frog fellow."

"I have always understood, sir, that Monsieur de la Vignerie was a person of quality in his own country before that accursed Revolution."

" So he was, nevy, so he was—a Marquis, bless ye—though I believe that a French Marquis carries less sail and fewer guns than an English one. Still, that's no matter now. He escaped the guillotine and slipped across the Channel. And what does my fine Mounseer do for a living but teach drawing? And what does my niece Honoria do but take lessons from him— and fall in love with him—and run off and marry him without a word to anyone? "

" No doubt Uncle Frederick was highly displeased, sir."

" Displeased? He would have served for a figurehead to the frigate *Furious*! But then poor Honoria died—and Albinia, having no infants of her own, took charge of Lydia."

" What happened to de la Vignerie, sir? I know very little of all these matters."

" Bless ye, what does my fine Mounseer do but slip back across the Channel and mix himself up in a crazy plot to get rid of Bonaparte and hoist the Bourbons on to the French throne again! *Plots* will never get rid of Bonaparte, nevy Augustus. My lord Nelson beat him at sea—let him be as soundly beaten by land, and no *plots* will be needed to sink him."

" But de la Vignerie, sir——"

" The guillotine got him in the end, nevy. He cheated her in 1794—but she got him ten years later."

CHAPTER X

LAURELS FOR VICTORY

WHILE Captain Clavenger and Sir Augustus were having this interesting conversation Cousin Fenworth was good-naturedly entertaining the two boys with anecdotes of his life at sea. They listened wide-eyed to the story of Cape St. Vincent, where a fleet of fifteen English ships defeated twenty-seven much larger and heavier Spanish men-o'-war, and thereby prevented them from joining hands with their French allies. He produced a pencil and on the back of his tailor's bill traced a plan of the battle, showing how the third ship from the rear of the English line—the *Captain*, under Commodore Horatio Nelson—had flung herself across the path of six Spanish vessels and held them engaged until Captain Troubridge in the *Culloden* joined in the fray. Foremost among the towering Spaniards was the *Santissima Trinidad*, the largest vessel then afloat, painted bright scarlet and pure white, and carrying an armament of a hundred and twenty-six guns—the *Captain*, explained Cousin Fenworth, carried only seventy-four. He himself was a midshipman in the *Excellent* under Captain Collingwood, and he well remembered the roar of delight that went up from her crew when Admiral Sir John Jervis ("now my lord St. Vincent") signalled to the ship to go to Nelson's aid.

Presently the Spaniards turned tail; and then the *Captain* deliberately fouled one of them, the *San Nicolas*, in order to check her flight. Cousin Fenworth's voice thrilled as he told how, after boarding and capturing her, Nelson led his tars straight across her deck on to the deck of her sister-ship the *San José* and captured that as well.

" Where were *you*, sir? " William ventured to ask.

"Not where I should have liked to be, my boy. The rigging of my ship was all shot away and we could not pursue the *Santissima Trinidad*—she would have struck her colours had we pursued."

"And Lord Nelson, sir—did you ever see him, quite close to? He wore a patch over his eye like Joe Mackery's, didn't he?"

"A patch, yes—but not a coloured kerchief like Joe's. To be sure I saw Lord Nelson—as close as I am to you. A little fellow he was—as flimsy as a night-moth—you felt as if you could have caught him between your finger and thumb. But there has been no greater man born in these thousand years. Mark that well, young William."

William nodded, much impressed; and then, encouraged by Cousin Fenworth's friendly air, he ventured another question.

"You were at Trafalgar, too, weren't you, sir? Were you in the *Victory*?"

The sailor shook his head.

"No, my boy: it was my younger brother, Joshua. I was in the *Agamemnon*. Josh can tell you more about Lord Nelson than I can. All the midshipmen worshipped him. Why, when Josh first went to sea and his lordship spied him standing solitary and woebegone on deck, he challenged him to race to the mainmast."

The boys listened in amazement: the great Admiral, the famous Nelson, racing against a little midshipman along the deck of his own flagship!

"But it was not only the middies who cried their eyes out when the signal went round that Lord Nelson was dead," continued Fenworth. "Great grim fellows sat blubbering like girls—and no shame to 'em."

"What happened to the scarlet-and-white ship, the very big one, sir? Was she in the battle?" asked Dolly.

"The *Santissima Trinidad*? Yes, she was at Trafalgar, too—and we thought to have made a prize of her and towed her into Portsmouth, but a storm sprang up, and she foundered in Cadiz Bay."

This seemed a tame ending to the story; and, except for the wonderful vision of Nelson challenging young Joshua to a race, both William and Dolly secretly thought that Uncle Edward's tale of the " Glorious First of June " was almost as exciting. During that engagement the figurehead of the *Brunswick* had its wooden cocked hat shot away, and the boys never wearied of hearing how the crew begged the Captain to let them have one of his own cocked hats with which to replace it; and how he gave them the best he had, and the ship's carpenter, swinging himself under the jib-boom, nailed it to the wooden skull of the figure while the battle was at its height.

Great-Uncle John now called to William to come and tell him whether he could name the first five ships that had crossed his field of sight when last he scanned the English Channel through his spy-glass. If he *could*—well, he knew what his reward would be. William took a deep breath, clasped his hands behind him, shut his eyes tight, and said:

"First, an East Indiaman—four masts—all sails spread— outward bound: then two fishing-smacks, single-masted, running for harbour: then a barque——"

"How did ye know she was a barque?" interrupted Great-Uncle John.

"Because her mizzen-mast was rigged fore and aft, sir, not square-rigged. I think she was in ballast: she was high out of the water."

"Good. That makes four."

"Then a man-o'-war, sir—a 74 by the looks of her; anyway, a ship of the line."

"Good lad——" said the old warrior, "we'll make a seaman of ye yet." And he fished from the pocket of his white knee-breeches the round, shining five-shilling piece which he had had all ready for the purpose.

Cousin Fenworth took this opportunity of drawing Sir Augustus aside and returning to the subject of Lydia. She had been made too much of a pet and a heroine: her mother having been a lady in waiting to one of the princesses, she had been taken to see Queen Charlotte at Buckingham House and the Prince Regent at Carlton House, and all the good-natured royals had been kind to the little orphan whose Papa had been a French nobleman and had lost his life in an effort to overthrow Bonaparte the Monster. Fortunately, she was a shy and timid child, otherwise she would have been hopelessly spoiled. Did Sir Augustus think——? Sir Augustus, understanding the half-uttered question, said that he would be happy to mention the matter to Lady Clavenger.

Meanwhile Charlotte had gone softly over to the breakfast parlour where she found Lydia kneeling on the chintz-covered window-seat and gazing out with interest at Plum Duff.

" Do you like dogs? " asked Charlotte, by way of opening the conversation.

Lydia turned with a start, but when she saw that the speaker was a little girl of her own age, she seemed reassured.

" Indeed, I do; but I have never had one of my own."

Oddly enough, the dresses of the two children were much alike. India muslin sewn with bands of white satin ribbon— but whereas Charlotte's hair was cropped in the fashionable manner, Lydia's hung in long, chestnut-brown curls to her waist.

They looked at each other in friendly silence for a moment, their eyes travelling up and down, and then Charlotte said:

" I am very rude. I was counting the rows of ribbon on your gown."

" And *I* was counting the rows on *yours*," confessed Lydia. " You have ten and I have only seven. Are you Charlotte? Great-Uncle John told me of you."

" Yes, I am Charlotte. Do you like staying here? "

Lydia hesitated.

" Yes, I do. I am rather frightened of Great-Aunt Caro—but I do love Great-Aunt Amelia, and Great-Uncle John, and Joe Mackery. Only—only I do wish sometimes I had someone to play with. There was no one at Aunt Albinia's—and there is no one here. *You* have brothers and sisters, haven't you? "

" Four brothers and two sisters—but my sisters are babies, not old enough to play with me. Boys always want to play at battles. Do you do lessons? "

Lydia sighed.

" Yes. A governess used to come every day to teach me. Are you good at spelling, Charlotte? Do you understand the use of the globes? "

It was Charlotte's turn to sigh.

" I have a governess too. She doesn't come every day—she lives with us always, but now she is spending a fortnight with her Mamma at Tunbridge Wells. I am afraid I am *not* good at spelling."

" And the globes? "

" I can find my way round the world," said Charlotte, proudly. " I can find all the places where Papa and Grandpapa and Great-Uncle John have been; but I am very stupid with the *other* globe—the one which shows the sky and the stars. Miss Thimbleton gets quite cross with me sometimes."

" Joe Mackery knows all about the stars *without* a globe," confided Lydia. " One night I had toothache and I could not sleep—and Great-Aunt Amelia put some drops on the tooth—but still I couldn't sleep. So she brought me downstairs—it was dark, Charlotte—it was after eight o'clock—and Joe Mackery said ' would I like to look at the stars with old Joe.' "

" And did you? "

" Oh, yes. He wrapped me in a big Indian shawl and took me to the window upstairs which has the best view. And he told me the names of the stars, and showed me the lovely patterns they make on the sky."

"Has Great-Aunt Amelia shown you the dolls' furniture that Joe made for her when she was a little girl? It is in the corner cabinet in the drawing-room."

Lydia nodded.

"Yes: but she wouldn't let me touch it—she said it was so old and frail that it would fall to pieces if I breathed on it. Some day she is going to tell me who these people are"— Lydia pointed vaguely to the prints and portraits hanging round the breakfast-parlour—"I don't mean the ones that aren't coloured—Joe Mackery named them to me—and their names are printed on their pictures, too—I mean the gentleman in the flowered brocade coat—and the one in the scarlet coat and the cocked hat—and the sad-looking one in grey."

"*I* can tell you," said Charlotte, taking her new friend by the hand. "Look. The first one is Great-Grandpapa Robert —he lived at Winford Manor, where we live. Grandpapa George is the one in the scarlet coat. He was a soldier, you know. Do you like his wig? Great-Uncle John thinks every one ought to wear a wig. Boney doesn't, and he is very wicked. But Papa doesn't either—not *now*—and *he* is very good."

Lydia had no comment to offer on the great question of wigs or no wigs, though she knew that Uncle Julian—Aunt Albinia's husband—had recently stopped wearing his, and that Great-Uncle John had declared that if this sort of thing spread, the British Constitution would fall to pieces. Lydia was not quite sure what the British Constitution might be—but the notion that it might fall to pieces seemed to upset Great-Uncle John very much.

"The one in grey," continued Charlotte, "was Alban Clavenger—a sort of cousin of ours. Brackenden belonged to him once, long ago. He lived in the old house that is the farmhouse now. One of the pistols on the staircase wall was his. But——" she dropped her voice to a horrified whisper, "he was a Papist."

The effect of the whisper was curious. Lydia flushed scarlet, hung her head, twisted her bands of ribbon between her fingers, and then blurted out, " My Papa—my Papa was a Papist, too."

Charlotte absorbed this startling confession in silence; then she said anxiously, " But *you* are not, are you? "

" Oh, *no*."

" And your Papa is dead? "

" Yes. Boney had him put to death."

" Oh, well," said Charlotte, cheerfully dismissing the late Marquis de la Vignerie, " then I do not think it is of any consequence. Would you like to come out and make friends with Duff, our plum-pudding dog? "

A few moments later Cousin Fenworth, looking from the bow-window of the drawing-room, saw the two little girls walk out sedately hand-in-hand and cross the close-cropped turf in the direction of the place where Plum Duff lay snoozing after his drive.

" Lydia," said Charlotte, as they stooped to pat the sleeper, " is it true that you have seen the Prince Regent? "

Lydia nodded.

" Is he a very beautiful man, Lydia? Miss Clarissa and Miss Melissa—they are two old ladies who live in Winford Village —they say that the Prince Regent is the most beautiful man in the world—and has the most beautiful manners."

Lydia looked slightly surprised.

" He is very fat," she said, " you can't *think* how fat he is. And *he* wears a wig—I heard Uncle Fenworth say it was a wig— but it is not a white one—it is brown and curly, like real hair."

" Oh, I don't think he *can* be beautiful if he is so fat. How shocked Miss Clarissa and Miss Melissa would be! How was he dressed? "

" He had a dark-coloured coat—braided a great deal—with a high fur collar; there was a lovely star sewn on one side of the coat."

"Did he talk to you? Really talk to you?"

"It was dreadful," confessed Lydia. "I got so frightened while we were waiting that I crawled under a table—and when he came into the room Aunt Albinia was trying to pull me out by my legs!"

"Oh, Lydia—what did he say?"

"He laughed; and when I stood up he patted my head—his hand smelt of lavender-water. And he said 'Sister Sophy' had told him about me and that I must see Charlotte—*Princess* Charlotte," added Lydia, firmly, in case there should be any confusion.

"And *did* you?"

"Yes. I was taken up a staircase with dark green marble pillars—and then to a large room with a blue sky and white clouds painted on the ceiling. And the Princess was there—with a thin, dark lady called Miss Knight. And the Princess asked me if I would like to see her dolls."

"Does she still play with dolls? I thought she was nearly grown-up."

"Aunt Albinia told me she is fifteen. She is very tall—and she stands with her feet apart and her hands behind her back—like boys stand sometimes. And she talks loud. Sometimes she talks like this—'my b-b-baby d-d-doll.'"

"That is what is called 'stammering,'" said Charlotte wisely. "Is she pretty? Princesses ought to be pretty."

"Not very," confessed Lydia, after a moment's thought. "Her eyes are a very pale blue, and they stick out a little, and she has no eyebrows; but she has beautiful hair, yellow hair. And she was so kind when she saw that I was shy. Just think, Charlotte—her big doll has a bed covered with purple velvet—and it has a little doll of its own. I was not shy a bit when she was showing me her dolls; but it was *dreadful* going to see the Queen."

"Oh, do tell me, Lydia. Why was it dreadful? She

doesn't cut off people's heads.   Was she wearing a big golden crown?"

"No, only a sort of brown gauze bonnet with a feather, and an ugly gown of brown silk.   Her face was brown, too, and she had black eyes.   I'll tell you what she looked like; the wolf in the story of Red Riding Hood—when it put on the Grandmother's nightcap.   She was kind, too—but she had such a funny voice: like this—*Ach, so—grumph*."

Charlotte gazed in admiration at her new friend.

"How clever you are, Lydia, to be able to do that—*Ach, so—grumph*.   Is that right?"

"Nearly right.   Try again.   *Ach, so*—then, *grumph*—that was when she took snuff."

"Great-Aunt Caro doesn't say *grumph* when she takes snuff. I wish I could say it like you do; *Ach, so—grumph*—oh, it makes me choke!   Was anyone there besides the Queen?"

"Oh, yes—two of the Princesses.   A fat one—nearly as fat as the Prince Regent—with three yellow feathers in her hair— they called her ' Eliza '; and a little tiny one with big, big blue eyes: they called her ' Sophy.'   The fat one was sitting at a table painting; it was a picture of a little girl, with a bundle of sticks on her head, walking in the snow—she called me to look at it."

"I should be very proud if I had been to see such great folk," said Charlotte, not enviously but with a touch of wistfulness. "Aren't *you* proud, Lydia?"

"Oh, no.   Aunt Albinia says they only want to see me because Boney was unkind to my Papa."

Charlotte hardly heard this last remark: another idea had struck her.

"I wish I were a Princess," she said, "then I should not have to practise the pianoforte—or learn the use of the globes. How happy I should be!"

"But they are grown-up, Charlotte—of course they don't have to learn the use of the globes any more.   As for being

happy—I didn't think any of them looked happy, only the
Queen looked unhappy and cross, and the Princesses looked
unhappy and kind."

Charlotte was doing some counting in her head.

"You have seen a Queen," she remarked, "and three
Princesses and a Prince: and I haven't seen *one*."

"I'd rather have some brothers and sisters than see a
thousand million Queens," returned Lydia.

At this moment they heard the clumping of Joe Mackery's
wooden leg as he came hopping towards them.

"Now then, little ladies," said he, "what are you a-doing
with no spread of sail on your mizzen-masts, and the sun a-
beating down?"

Charlotte, who had heard this joke before, explained to
Lydia that what Joe meant was why were they not wearing
their bonnets, but when they obediently offered to go and
fetch them the old man said there was no need, for the collation was ready and he had been sent to bring them in.

A marvellous collation it was that had been spread in the
breakfast-parlour—lobster patties, green peas, cucumber,
apricot jellies, pineapples and cream, all lovely to behold, and
all—as well the children knew—the very things that they were
not supposed to eat. If the nurse from Winford had been
there, she would have hustled her charges out of the room with
croaks of dismay, predicting all sorts of pains and promising
various horrible medicines to cure them; but luckily she was
not there and—even more luckily—by some miracle not one
of the children suffered any bad effects from the banquet.
Great-Aunt Caro was heard to remark that bread-and-milk
would be a more suitable diet for young persons and that
gluttony was a very serious sin, but Great-Uncle John and
Great-Aunt Amelia paid no attention to her, and Sir Augustus
was too busy discussing Boney's latest move with Cousin
Fenworth to notice how much his sons and daughter were
eating. Plum Duff, meanwhile, was in the kitchen, enjoying

himself in *his* way as much as his young human friends were in *theirs*.

All good things and all happy times come to an end. The bright May afternoon waned, Sir Augustus decreed that the tilbury and the phaeton should be reharnessed and preparations made for the return journey. William was to sit with him in the tilbury and Charlotte between Dolly and the groom in the phaeton—a plan which pleased both children very much.

When the moment came to say good-bye the two boys were clinging to Joe Mackery, begging him to carve them more whistles—he was an amazingly skilful carver with nothing but a penknife as a tool, but whistles being small were easily lost—and the little girls were discovered perched side-by-side on the oak settle in the hall.

" Your Papa looks kind," Lydia was saying just before Great-Aunt Amelia found them. " Is he ever cross ? "

" Not often—only when we cry because the bath-water is cold—or when Arthur won't drink his milk. He once came with a hunting-crop to make Arthur drink his milk."

Lydia listened wide-eyed to these revelations: that was not *her* idea of a kind Papa: yet when Sir Augustus took her hand to bid her good-bye he smiled down at her with such a comical jerk of one eyebrow that she felt reassured and smiled back again. Then she ran to the phaeton to take leave of Charlotte, who leaned down and called out merrily to her, " *Ach, so—grumph !* "

Lydia laughed so much she could hardly call " *Ach, so—grumph !* " in reply: Great-Uncle John and Great-Aunt Caro, sitting in their two big padded chairs, heard her laughing. " Never knew little Miss so gay," remarked Great-Uncle John, approvingly.

" Let him who laughs beware lest he weep," returned Great-Aunt Caro, taking snuff with a peevish twist of her nose.

" Methody nonsense, Methody nonsense," muttered her

brother under his breath: he would have said it aloud but for the fact that Miss Clavenger was his guest.

"Before the child retires to rest to-night," continued the old lady, plunging her mittened hand into a large quilted silk bag which rustled as she did so, "I will give her a tract to read. I have several here. *Dreadful Death of a Little Boy who Laughed*, or *Sudden End of Thoughtless Susan* might serve."

"Indeed, sister," cried Miss Amelia, "you shall not frighten her so cruelly. You will give her bad dreams."

"If those lobster patties do not give her bad dreams, a little serious reading won't do it," retorted Miss Caroline, bristling.

"Amelia's word is final, Sister Caro," interposed Great-Uncle John, rapping on the ground with his ebony stick. "Lydia is in her care for the moment, not yours."

So Lydia was spared the horrors of Great-Aunt Caroline's tracts.

Meanwhile, Sir Augustus and his children were well on their way home, William fingering the five-shilling piece in his breeches pocket and Charlotte practising *Ach, so—grumph* under her breath to the astonishment of Dolly and the groom.

During the days that followed Charlotte wished more than ever that she had a sister near her own age whom she could tell about Lydia, and Lydia's wonderful descriptions of the great folk she had seen, and Lydia's laughter-making mimicry of the strange grunts uttered by the old Queen. The boys (including five-year-old Arthur) were too full of interest in Cousin Fenworth's tales of the sea to pay any attention to anything less warlike and stirring, and Sophy and Matilda were only eighteen months and three years old respectively, so it was no use trying to interest *them*. On the third morning Mamma came up to the nursery, looking lovely in a blue muslin gown with a little short-sleeved white jacket over it. She called Nurse aside, and though Charlotte did not try to overhear what was being said she could not help catching a word here and there—"To-morrow afternoon—a little tent-bed in Miss

Charlotte's room—a well-behaved child—she will give no trouble." What could it mean? To question Nurse would have been foolish: she had a strong objection to being questioned; so all that the impatient Charlotte could do was to wait as best she might until the following day.

It was about three o'clock on that day when a smart two-wheeled gig turned up the long drive and came bowling merrily towards the pillared west front of the Manor. In it sat a small figure in a pink pelisse and a white straw bonnet, and roped on behind was a trunk covered with black horsehair and studded with brass nails. The driver was Sam Widgeon, Great-Uncle John's groom, another old Tar and another old shipmate from the days of the *Intractable*. A few moments later Charlotte was summoned to the drawing-room and there—to her delight—she found Lydia, bonnet in hand, standing shyly between Sir Augustus and his lady and looking as if she would have liked to crawl under the nearest elegant satinwood table.

Lady Clavenger explained that Lydia was coming to live with them, at least while Aunt Albinia was abroad, and she added sentimentally that she trusted her Charlotte would ever be ready to cherish the lonely orphan in her heart. Charlotte asked nothing better. She was speechless with joy, but her face spoke for her when she took Lydia by the hand. Their elders, well content to see both children look so pleased, dismissed them to the nursery and fell to discussing the plans for the approaching departure of Sir Augustus—a subject which Lady Clavenger found it almost impossible to consider without the aid of a bottle of smelling-salts, or even a glass of hartshorn-and-water.

When William and Dolly learned that the newcomer was to remain at Winford they were surprised but not altogether dissatisfied. Now, they supposed, Sister Char would not be for ever trying to mingle in their more manly pastimes, nor would they be constantly pestered to join in dolls' tea-parties and other girlish games.

The delight of having a playmate of her own age had not lost its first novelty when the sad moment came to bid Papa good-bye: for the ribs had mended at last, the medical gentlemen, being unable to shake their heads, had nodded them; and Sir Augustus Clavenger's burning desire to return to duty was fulfilled. Lady Clavenger went up to Clarges Street to take leave of him, but the children remained at Winford.

"I am glad," remarked William on the morrow of their parents' departure for London, "I am glad that there has only been one big battle in Spain while Papa has been at home. He does not like missing battles."

"Was it a *very* big battle?" asked Lydia, who had won William's heart by her willingness to be instructed.

"Oh, *enormously* big. It was at a Spanish city called Badajoz. The British had been besieging it for two whole months and then they took it by storm. They put ladders up against the walls, and climbed up, and didn't turn back however hard the people inside shot off their guns at them."

"Was Boney there?" asked Lydia.

"Of course not, silly. Boney is in Russia. He couldn't be in Spain and in Russia at the same time, could he?"

"No, I suppose not," agreed Lydia; but she did not seem to be too sure about it.

Even in the nurseries of England the doings of Napoleon were a subject of conversation during that eventful summer of 1812. Sir Augustus left to rejoin his regiment just before the Emperor of the French invaded Russia, towards the end of June; but William and Dolly gathered many scraps of war news from their tutor. For Mr. Smith subscribed to *The Times* newspaper, being (in the absence of the Squire) the only person in Winford to do so. Each copy cost sixpence-half-penny and was brought from London by the Westhampton coach just one day late. When Sir Augustus was at home one of the grooms was sent down to the cross-roads to collect the

Manor-house newspapers, tossed to him from the top of the coach by the guard. A fine sight was the guard, in his many-caped coat, his hat laced with gold braid and often a posy in his button-hole; and disdainfully did he glance at the Reverend Septimus Smith when his was the only packet to fling down. Mr. Smith came himself to fetch it, sometimes on foot, some-times in his rusty, rattling old gig drawn—very slowly—by his hungry-looking mare, Berenice; sometimes he came alone, sometimes, especially in the summer, William and Dolly came with him. Always he was so impatient to read the news that he started unfolding the paper at once, standing stock still in the middle of the road if he were not driving, sitting spell-bound with the reins loose on Berenice's back if he were. After that, *The Times* went the round of the village, going first to the doctor, then to the schoolmaster, then to the Misses Prittlewell, and finally to the sexton. Just as one copy finished its journeys in a very tattered condition the next one started off still smelling of printers' ink.

Though dispatches took many days—even weeks—to arrive, important military and naval intelligence was con-veyed with what then seemed almost magical rapidity by means of the semaphore signalling system introduced seven-teen years before. As there was a signalling tower at West-hampton visible through the telescope on Great-Uncle John's terrace Joe Mackery was sometimes able to see—and to read—the messages it was sending out. It was thus that he had picked up and hastily carried to his master the glorious tidings of Trafalgar and the sorrowful news of Nelson's death.

Another person who took a lively interest in the war news was Miss Letitia Thimbleton, governess to Charlotte and Arthur Clavenger and now also to their kinswoman, Lydia de la Vignerie. Miss Thimbleton was quite as eager to acquire knowledge as to impart it, and during that summer of 1812 she had gradually formed a habit of asking the vicar for information about the plants and flowers characteristic of

Russia and Spain so that *her* pupils might enjoy the same botanical advantages as *his*. Nothing loth, the worthy Septimus wrote lists, mostly in Latin, full of pomegranates, lemons, oleanders, olives and cacti diversified by the dwarf willow, the Siberian moss, and the snow pine. Miss Thimbleton then explained that " being only a female " she feared that she might not pronounce the Latin terms correctly; and Septimus went through the lists with her word by word while the children amused themselves with his albums of specimens. She would fain have persuaded Captain John Clavenger to explain the nature of coral and the habits of the ostrich so that she could use some of the curiosities in the cabinets at Brackenden as a medium of instruction; but the old warrior said, " Bless ye, my good young 'ooman, Joe Mackery knows as much about it as I do; ask Joe "; which for some reason or other Miss Thimbleton never remembered to do.

When news came that Napoleon, at the head of a strangely mixed force of some six hundred thousand Frenchmen, Italians, Germans, Swiss, Dutchmen and Poles, had crossed the river Niemen and was marching through Poland into Russia, Miss Letitia Thimbleton had been staying with her widowed Mamma at Tunbridge Wells. There, as the elder lady subscribed to the lending library on the Pantiles, they were both able to snatch eager daily glimpses of official *Gazettes* and London papers only two or three days old; but when her duties called her back to Winford the governess realised with a sigh that her appetite for military dispatches would be sadly thwarted, for no newspapers came to the Manor when Sir Augustus was away, and Lady Clavenger subscribed only to *La Belle Assemblée* and *The Lady's Monthly Museum or Polite Repository*, which contained little but sentimental verse and prettily-coloured fashion pictures. Then a happy thought struck her. If their Mamma had no objection—and surely she would have none—might not the two little girls and Arthur, escorted, of course, by Miss Thimbleton, go with William

SUMMER FASHIONS, 1812

From Mamma's favourite magazine, *The Lady's Monthly Museum*

and Dolly on a fine evening to see the coach pass? They all loved to see the coach pass: and the vicar would no doubt impart suitable items of intelligence from his *Times* if he felt that for once there was someone eager and thankful to listen. The plan worked to perfection. All the children, from thirteen-year-old William to five-year-old Arthur, enjoyed the walk to the cross-roads in the cool of the summer evening; and good, shy, solitary Mr. Smith found it very agreeable to read snatches from his newspaper to the attentive little lady in the dove-coloured dress, with the faded face that perhaps had once been a pretty one. Presently, as they made their way back to the Manor (the vicar leading Berenice if he had come in the gig), it became the custom for him to invite Miss Thimbleton and her charges to come in to the vicarage and rest for a little while, and hear the remainder of the news. The poor man and his house were much neglected by his housekeeper, Mrs. Ramping, a sour-faced widow-woman, sister to the sexton, and it made Miss Thimbleton quite sad to contemplate the undusted table, the unburnished brass candlesticks, and—most sad of all—the frayed elbows and knees of Mr. Septimus Smith's shabby black coat and knee-breeches.

Sometimes the vicar wondered if he dared suggest adding Miss Thimbleton's name to the list of those with whom he shared *The Times*: then he reflected that Lady Clavenger might disapprove; so he read aloud instead—a much better plan, for she loved to listen, and it prolonged those visits to the dim little library—visits that were fast becoming a bright patch in his otherwise colourless day. How much he would miss those visits when autumn and winter put a stop to them he could hardly bear to think. Then he would have to go and return all by himself, carrying a lantern, and groping his way along the dark street with a stick.

Being a most conscientious and correct person, Letitia Thimbleton informed Lady Clavenger that the vicar was so good as to invite her and the children to repose and refresh themselves on their return from their evening walk. She hoped—did her ladyship approve? Her ladyship not only approved; she invited the vicar to come and drink tea with her and the governess after dinner—a thing she had never thought of doing before.

Dinner was at six; the tea-board, with all the elegant apparatus for making tea, was brought into the drawing-room about a quarter to eight. Mr. Smith arrived punctually, wearing his neatest suit of black, and the less shabby of his two grey wigs (most clergymen clung to their wigs as Great-Uncle John considered all Englishmen should), and blinking happily through his strong spectacles. Though he was always invited to dine at the Manor twice a year, when Sir Augustus was at home, there was something infinitely more agreeable in drinking tea there in this friendly, informal fashion. Lady Clavenger made the tea, with graceful flourishes of the hand and bends of the wrist; then she invited Miss Thimbleton to play upon the high golden harp that stood in the corner by the tulip-wood bureau; and then she suggested that her guest and her governess should sit down to a game of cribbage while she herself finished reading the latest number of *La Belle Assemblée*.

In the next of her weekly letters to Sir Augustus her ladyship related what she had done. " You will laugh at me, my dear Augustus," she wrote, " but I vow I caught the gleam of one of Cupid's gilded arrows and heard the flutter of his rosy wings; " and she added in a less romantic tone: " We have often agreed that married clergymen are more useful to their poor parishioners than bachelors can be. If anything comes of all this I shall be certain that the soup and flannel we send for the poorer mothers and their infants really reach them, and are not seized by that Ramping person."

On the very day that that letter was written—on July 22— Wellington fought what he was always to regard as the most brilliant of all his battles—the battle of Salamanca, which opened the way for the capture of Madrid and sealed the loss of Southern Spain to the enemy.   William and Dolly liked to imagine the English Commander in a scarlet coat, his cocked hat sprouting white plumes, a golden-hilted sword in his right hand and a prancing steed beneath him; but Great-Uncle John told them that, according to their Papa, Wellington's usual dress in the field was " a plain grey frock-coat buttoned close to the chin, a cocked hat without plumes and covered with black oilskin, grey pantaloons with boots buckled at the side, and a steel-mounted light sabre."   Also he frequently drove about in a sort of hooded gig instead of riding on horseback.   Worst of all in the eyes of Great-Uncle John, he wore no wig, and did not even powder his own hair or twist it into a queue.   Yet as the news of his victories in the Peninsula continued to arrive, briefly and quickly by semaphore, slowly and at great length in letters and dispatches, Quanko's younger fellow-parrot at Brackenden added a new saying to his list—" Great man, Wellington, great man! "

Bonfires were lit all over England at the news of the victory of Salamanca, and the people on the Winford estate asked Lady Clavenger's permission to build one in the park; but she begged them to wait until she had heard from Spain whether Sir Augustus was safe; by that time Master Denzil would be home from Winchester for the summer vacation, and *he* would kindle the bonfire—if all was well.   The villagers did not have to wait, and *their* bonfire blazed gaily as soon as the official announcement was made.   The bells, too, rang a merry peal, for it had not occurred to the Reverend Septimus that the great news should be celebrated only if the Lord of the Manor had come safely through the battle.   Lady Clavenger spoke quite sharply to the poor man about it, and was only partly soothed when he pleaded that Haverley and Little Bunstead and Churp had *all* rung their bells and that he was sure that neither Sir Augustus nor her ladyship would wish Winford to be lacking in loyalty to the King and thankfulness to God.

For more than a fortnight the vicar was not invited to drink tea with her ladyship and Miss Thimbleton, and a bleak and anxious fortnight it was for him. Then dispatches arrived, with lists of the killed and wounded, and Sir Augustus was not named; and then more dispatches arrived, with mention of officers who had distinguished themselves, and there Sir Augustus *did* appear. So the bonfire was commanded, and Mr. Smith was bidden to drink tea again at the Manor, and—at her ladyship's suggestion—the Winford bells rang a *second* peal of joy, thereby scoring a point over Haverley, and Little Bunstead and Churp.

Then something happened which from the point of view of Mr. Smith and Miss Thimbleton was almost as sad as her ladyship's momentary annoyance. When Denzil came home he persuaded his mother to have *The Times* sent down from London as it was when Sir Augustus was at the Manor. This meant that one of the grooms would go down to fetch it, and even if the governess and her charges did still take an evening walk sometimes to see the coach pass, there would now be no excuse for her to beg the vicar to impart the latest news from Russia and Spain, or for him to read aloud to her during the brief halt at the vicarage.

Denzil was particularly interested in the news from Russia. He remembered what his father had said about the invasion of that country being a huge blunder on the part of Napoleon, and his imagination was so stirred by the accounts of the Russian peasants burning their crops rather than let them fall into enemy hands that he wrote a piece of poetry beginning:

> The love of Freedom glowing in the mind
> Adorns the story of the Russian hind.

Never before had any Clavenger written poetry: seldom, indeed, had any Clavenger cared much about reading it. But Denzil took after his Mamma; he was romantic, he was musical. In his dormitory at Winchester he practised (beneath the bed-clothes) on a small flute, until the other boys threatened to smother him with his own pillow; nor did he intend to give up his flute, as Wellington had given up his fiddle, when he became a soldier. In fact, his secret ambition was to imitate the Elder Pitt, Earl of Chatham, and turn from soldiering to politics—or perhaps diplomacy.

Not without some blushes he showed his Russian poem to Charlotte, who declared that it was a thousand times finer than Mr. Walter Scott's *Marmion*—the highest praise she knew how to give. She persuaded him to show it to Miss Thimbleton, who begged leave to communicate it to Mr. Smith, who vowed that Lady Clavenger must see it. It was a pity, her ladyship considered, that Denzil had not chosen to write about the campaign in the Peninsula. Papa did not care greatly for such things, to be sure, but he might have been gratified. The youthful poet then confessed that it had been his intention to write about the battle of Badajoz, but the ideas would not come.

Though secretly inclined to agree with Charlotte about the merits of *Russia: An Ode*, Mamma did not contemplate doing anything with it except to put it away in her tulip-wood bureau with Denzil's first shoe and a lock of his infant hair; but Mr. Smith earnestly craved permission to send a copy to the Editor of *The Gentleman's Magazine*. He would not, of course, divulge the name of the author, but state merely that this was the work of " a young gentleman only fifteen years of age." After some demur, and anxious protestations that " Sir Augustus must never know," Lady Clavenger agreed; and great was the delight at the Manor (and only a little less great at the vicarage) when the *Ode* was printed in full, with an editorial note commending the noble sentiments of " this promising young votary of the Muses." Lady Clavenger was so pleased that she tipped the young votary a guinea, which he expended upon a copy of Mr. Robert Southey's poetical narrative, *The Curse of Kehama*.

After Salamanca there was a lull in Spain, and all eyes were focused upon Russia. Mr. Septimus Smith, abandoning all pretence of a regular course of study and forgetting that such a science as botany existed, gave William and Dolly long dictations from the war news every day and set them conning the map of the south-eastern part of the Tsar's vast dominions. Denzil went back to school just after the desperate battle of Borodino—which left the French victors more weakened and shaken than it did the Russians whom they forced to withdraw; so Lady Clavenger cancelled the order for a daily copy of *The Times* to be sent from London, and once more the vicar was able to share the contents of his own copy with the delighted Miss Thimbleton. Together they shook their heads sadly over the burning of the ancient and historic city of Moscow: in unison they raised their hands and eyes with thankfulness when the news came that the French armies were in full retreat.

It was not only to Napoleon Bonaparte that the waning of the summer of 1812 brought sadness: the Reverend Septimus heaved many a sigh when dusk began to fall so early that Miss Thimbleton and her cheerful young charges could no longer take the evening stroll which had been resumed when Denzil returned to Winchester. But, unlike Napoleon, good Septimus had a source of consolation: Lady Clavenger now invited him to drink tea at the Manor twice a week instead of only once as formerly: and at her suggestion Great-Uncle John begged the pleasure of his company upon the last occasion that the children drove over to Brackenden before the winter set in. Then her Ladyship herself would not have to go; for, though Miss Caroline Clavenger had returned to London, a visit to Uncle John and Aunt Amelia was still rather an ordeal to the lady, and she knew very well that it was the young people whom they really desired to see.

All the children looked forward to that expedition. The elder boys were chiefly interested in getting more whistles from Joe Mackery and begging peeps through the telescope, but William was in the highest glee because of the five ships he had seen that morning through his spy-glass no less than three had been naval vessels: Charlotte and Lydia were hoping that Great-Aunt Amelia would unlock the corner-cabinet and show them some of the pretty and wonderful things kept there: Arthur was excited because it was the first time he had been considered old enough to join the party: but who shall measure the delight of the Reverend Septimus when he was told that Miss Thimbleton and the youngest visitor would make the journey in his gig? He groomed Berenice with his own hands—much to her surprise—and he saw to it that she had a good feed of oats—of which the sexton often stinted her without her master's knowledge. He also polished up his shoe-buckles, his knee-buckles and his spectacles in honour of the event.

There had been one cloud, and one only, on the pleasure of the young Clavengers. When Mamma came too she never troubled to restrain their enjoyment of the delicious foods which their ancient relatives always set before them; but Miss Thimbleton sometimes had an anxious, watchful eye and a firm hand. They need not have feared, however; for on this occasion she was entirely absorbed in listening while Great-Uncle John expounded to the respectful vicar how Boney was undoubtedly done-for this time—scuttled—sunk; and also how, whatever anybody might think or say, it was in reality the British Navy that had sunk him.

Three years later—it is a June evening in the year 1815. At the cross-roads a small but anxious group of people has gathered to wait for the mail-coach. It is known that somewhere in the Low Countries—somewhere near Brussels—Wellington, at the head of the Allied armies, will soon meet—perhaps has already met—Napoleon and his army of French veterans. Upon the result of that meeting the whole future

THE MAIL-COACH ON ITS WAY FROM LONDON WITH NEWS OF VICTORY

of Europe will depend. When the mail-coach comes in sight it will be easy to guess the latest news: if the driver and guard look just as usual, nothing decisive has yet occurred; if they are garlanded with laurel, there has been a British victory; if with laurel and crape (as after Trafalgar) the price has been the death in battle of the victor.

Most of the waiting people are Winford villagers—the blacksmith is there, the grocer, the innkeeper and the butcher; they are soon joined by some farm labourers coming home from work.

" Happen old Nosey's got 'un *this* time," they say hopefully to each other—" Old Nosey " being Field-Marshal the Duke of Wellington and " 'un " the Emperor of the French. Presently there is a stir and the crowd divides, with a general raising of hats and knuckling of forelocks, to make room for a little company of " quality " approaching on foot from the direction of the Manor.

" Master William he do sure be grown a fine young gen'leman since he went for a sailor," is the comment of one admiring onlooker. For the tall youth in naval uniform is William Clavenger, now sixteen years of age, on leave from his ship, H.M.S. *Cocytto*, by permission of her captain, Cousin Fenworth; and the graceful young ladies on either arm, very elegant in chip straw bonnets, trimmed one with mignonette and the other with marguerites, carrying fringed parasols and wearing gowns of sprigged muslin, they are Charlotte Clavenger and Lydia de la Vignerie. Dolly is not there—he is at Winchester now—but eight-year-old Arthur keeps as close as he can to his sailor brother. And Denzil is not there: he is in his second term at All Souls College, Oxford, where he wears a silk tassel on his " square " to show that he is Sir Denzil Clavenger, eighth Baronet of that ancient name. Sir Augustus has been dead for just two years; he fell at the battle of Vittoria in June, 1813, when Wellington defeated Marshal Soult and drove the French back towards the Pyrenees. There is a monument to him in Winford Church, showing Britannia sitting weeping by a large urn, with a quenched torch at her sandalled feet. The inscription is in Latin, and was composed by the Reverend Septimus from an English draft dictated by Lady Clavenger. No longer does Joe Mackery watch the Westhampton semaphore tower for signals telling of victory or defeat. Next to the monument of Sir Augustus stands that of Great-Uncle John, who survived him only six months. There are anchors carved in Great-Uncle John's memorial and sprays of sea-weed, and at the end of the epitaph relating his services to his country in the Royal Navy are these four brief lines:

> *Near this Place also lies interred Joseph Mackery, for*
> *many years his Attached Servant and Friend, who,*
> *after tending him with Exemplary Fidelity, lived only*
> *long enough to follow his Ashes to the Tomb.*

It was a great satisfaction to Great-Uncle John that Sir Augustus should have chosen Captain Fenworth Clavenger as the guardian of his younger children in the event of his death, not only because the old sailor thought highly of the young one, but also because of the compliment to the Navy.

William fully shares this opinion of his captain, whose praises he is singing to his sister and cousin as they saunter towards the cross-roads. Very proud is William that Mamma allows him to act as convoy, and does not insist that the girls should be accompanied by their governess, Miss Pell, who is a most accomplished lady but a rather alarming one. As the young people draw near the milestone a clip-clop of hooves makes itself heard on the cobbled street, and they turn to greet with much affection the gentleman and lady seated in the neat gig now overtaking them. He is a clerical gentleman, but he looks so cheerful and trim that it is difficult to recognise in him the once gaunt and shabby Septimus. Berenice, too, is much less bony than she used to be; but Mrs. Septimus Smith, formerly Miss Letitia Thimbleton, has altered very little. She is still amiable, eager and attentive, and she still wears dove-colour for choice.

And it is now just upon the hour that the mail-coach is due and a hush falls over the little group. Far off along the road from London the rattle and thud of hooves can faintly be heard: and then, louder, a long flourish on the guard's horn. Does that mean——? Nearer, now—and a cloud of dust can be seen above the hedge at the last bend. Charlotte grasps William's arm, but he gently disengages himself so that he can lift to his eye the spy-glass given to him by Great-Uncle John. When the other watchers see what he is about they look at him for a moment more earnestly than at the road. Then they hear him say in a voice hardly above a whisper: "Laurels—they have laurels on their hats. It is Victory!"

And now the coach is here, in all its glory, its scarlet paint-work half-hidden by branches of oak and laurel and bay. The horses, too, are covered with garlands that stream behind them as they gallop. The coachman and the guard have laid aside their many-caped overcoats, revealing the royal liveries which as servants of the Crown they are entitled to wear. Excited passengers on the top of the coach are waving their hands to those below: one of them lets fall a long streamer on which are printed in huge letters the words—*Victory—Wellington—Waterloo*.

The guard has not waited to open the mail-box and extract the vicar's copy of *The Times*—he has it all ready—not neatly folded but unfurled like a banner, and like a banner he waves it over his head before tossing it down to William, who has tucked his spy-glass into his coat-tail pocket and is holding out his hands. Then, to the sound of swelling cheers and with another gay flourish of the horn, the vision recedes towards Westhampton in a cloud of dust.

"Laurels," says Charlotte, softly, "but no crape. Oh, William—oh, Lydia—that means the Duke is safe."

Nobody else has yet had a thought to spare to the Duke. William has handed the newspaper to the Reverend Septimus, who stands up, as steadily as he can, in the gig and—in a voice full of emotion—reads aloud the first official news of the great battle fought on Sunday, June 18, at Waterloo.

All the Clavengers listen, and most of the villagers, the men uncovered, William with his hand at the salute—in which he is solemnly imitated by Arthur; but the younger lads have already broken away and are racing up the village street, crying to the people who hurry out of the cottages—" Laurels— there were laurels on their hats—it is Victory, *Victory*! "

THE END